Cowboy Dreams

Cowboy Dreams

Patricia L. Powell

COWBOY DREAMS

iUniverse books may be ordered through booksellers or by contacting:

iUniverse
1663 Liberty Drive
Bloomington, IN 47403
www.iuniverse.com
1-800-Authors (1-800-288-4677)

Because of the dynamic nature of the Internet, any web addresses or links contained in this book may have changed since publication and may no longer be valid. The views expressed in this work are solely those of the author and do not necessarily reflect the views of the publisher, and the publisher hereby disclaims any responsibility for them.

Cover Illustrator: Lisa Wallace
Editors: Joanne Jaworski and Maria Pease

ISBN: 978-1-5320-2804-5 (sc)
ISBN: 978-1-5320-2805-2 (hc)
ISBN: 978-1-5320-2806-9 (e)

Library of Congress Control Number: 2017910975

Print information available on the last page.

iUniverse rev. date: 06/15/2018

DEDICATION

I want to dedicate this book to God. Without Him the pages between these covers would be blank. It is only because of Him that I have a story to write. With that being said, it is my hope and prayer that whoever reads the words, that He so graciously gave me to write, will be inspired by my story. May this book help start conversations and motivate people to help others who feel as alone as I did growing up. Jeremiah 29:11,13

ACKNOWLEDGEMENTS

When it comes to the completion of this novel, a lot of people helped me along the way. Among those I would like to thank are my family, specifically my mom and my Aunt Diana, for being guinea pigs when it came to the editing process of my earliest draft. That version is nowhere near as good as this final product, so thank you!

Appreciation goes to my previous landlady, America, and former roommates at the "Arizona House" (simply because of the street name). Thank you for helping shape Cowboy Dreams and giving me the encouragement to keep working on it! I will never forget living with you all!

Without the suggestions and comments of Peter Heyrman of Bear Press Editorial Services I wouldn't have thought to turn it into my testimony. Truly, I thank you for that advice!

Many thanks to my editor Jo for doing such a phenomenal job! Your editing and proofreading shaped this project into exactly what it needed to be!

Maria, your final proofreading and suggestions will always be appreciated. And to all of my friends who have supported me as the cover went through each phase. I hold dear your comments and excitement with each Facebook post!

Great gratitude goes to my personal trainer, Rhandee for your continual support as I've shared with you each stage as it came closer and closer to being the story you are about to read.

My amazing cover illustrator Lisa did a superb job creating the exact image I wanted readers to see. I know it took a long time, but the wait was definitely worth it!

Finally, to Brian and Becca Boone, for just being awesome! Promise fulfilled.

On a side note, I also want to thank everyone who has ever been a part of my life. Had you not been there, I would never have had a purpose for writing this book. Whether your influence was positive or less than, I want to thank you for shaping me into a person who God could use to help inspire others. Without your involvement there would be no point for this book.

CONTENTS

CHAPTER

- ONE -

CLAY GIBSON WINS YET *ANOTHER* RACE IN THE SPRINT CUP SERIES! the headline on *SoCal Times* shouted out in bold letters to Logan Austen as he and Nikki Reids came into his motorhome. Picking up the newspaper off the kitchenette's table and grimacing at the announcement, Logan plopped down on the couch. Wishing he could just relax after a long and miserable day out on the track, the headline's screaming words just wouldn't let him.

"Logan, what the hell happened out there? You were supposed to get in front of Clay and keep him from taking that lap!" Nikki reminded him as she stopped at the fridge for a couple of waters before joining him on the couch.

"I guess Clay's just a better driver than me. But it's definitely not for a lack of trying," he replied with a shrug. He twisted off the cap, anxious for the cool water to hit his lips.

"Well then, you're just going to have to figure out another way to get past him because I didn't leave him for you just to have you only come up second best."

"What the hell do you want me to do, Nikki? The man drives like Earnhardt did. Every damn time I tried to get around him, he had me blocked," Logan replied as his eyes washed over Nikki. Her raven hair was pulled back into a smooth ponytail, and her emerald-green eyes constantly left him craving for more.

1

"Figure it out. Because I sure as hell didn't give up my place next to Clay's side for a man who can't even make it into the winner's circle once!" she said as she slipped the elastic out of her hair and ran her fingers through it.

Damn it, why did Clay have to be the better driver? Logan couldn't help but think to himself. He should've been the one in the winner's circle. Not Clay. Heck, had it not been for him introducing Clay to the sport years ago when both he and Clay had needed an outlet to blow off some steam because of their crappy home lives, he wouldn't be in this mess. Logan sat there, reading what he'd already lived through on the track. He couldn't help but wish he could finally take Clay out of the picture. He imagined himself with Nikki by his side as he took over Clay's reigning spot in the winner's circle and the beaming smile on her face as his name was announced over the loudspeaker.

With that thought now overshadowing the less-than-pleasant headline, he stared down at the picture of Clay's number zero-six car crossing the finish line as the checkered flag waved above him. He wondered how he could somehow turn his wish into reality.

Finally! I'm so happy to be out of that house! Kate Bransin, a petite, five-foot-four, raven-haired, twenty-one-year-old with dark-brown eyes, thought to herself as she reached the entrance to the Perkins's backyard.

She, like the Perkins' daughter, had been dealt the life of an only child. At the age of four, the second her parents had told her about the family of three becoming the newest residents of Newport Bay's Seaside Estates, she couldn't help but want to instantly befriend their five-year-old daughter.

Soon after she had, she and Tricia became inseparable. From the moment their parents had introduced them, their shared loneliness became the basis of their seventeen-year friendship allowing them to feel more like sisters. As they grew up, Kate often found herself using Tricia's house as a refuge when she didn't want to deal with her parents' crumbling marriage.

For the vast majority of her life, Kate had treated the Perkins's house as her second home. From summer sleepovers to hours on end of playing Super Mario Brothers, she kept Tricia company. All the while, her mother, Dr. Emiline Bransin, turned her status as a cardiothoracic surgeon into a means of escape from her failing marriage. Night after night, her well-established surgical career at Newport Bay's most prominent hospital, Newport Bay City, helped her turn the label *workaholic* into her second job title.

Unfortunately, in choosing to focus her energy on one surgery after another, she had pushed her husband into an affair. But as Todd Bransin spent that extra quality time with his real estate firm's college-aged intern, it was Kate who had become the real victim.

She found herself either forced to listen to her mother's endless rants as she stayed in denial about the true reality of her marriage, or watch her father choose to drown his loneliness in a glass of whiskey before passing out on the leather couch in his office.

Wishing she could somehow be rescued from the hell that had become her permanent residence, she waited for the day when either parent would wake up and finally admit the truth, allowing her to no longer be caught in the middle as their failed marriage came to an end with a long overdue divorce. Once that happened, she could finally rid herself of the emotional baggage their non-stop misery had left her with and move out of the hell their selfishness had caused her to live in.

"Hey, Kate," Tricia, a slender, five-foot-five brunette with hazel eyes called out after hearing her unlock the backyard gate.

Despite the added company, Tricia kept her eyes fixed on the page of a romance novel she had momentarily traded reality for. As she did, she welcomed the Southern California sun as its heat left her body with a reminder of its warm presence.

"Hi, Trish," Kate returned, relatching the gate as she entered the Perkins's backyard. As she did, she could smell the after effects from the yard's regular maintenance.

No matter how many times she'd entered their backyard, Kate always enjoyed seeing its beautiful landscaping; it gave her the greatest feeling of serenity. The rock deck that surrounded their marble pool reminded her of a desert oasis while the attached

Jacuzzi and waterfall was reminiscent of a day at the spa. The mini paradise also helped put an end to her internal monologue of her parental woes as she made her way over to the lounge chair Tricia relaxed on.

"So, are you excited for tonight, Trish?" Kate asked her, only to watch Tricia maintain her attention on the book she was reading.

Taking a quick sip of her Diet Coke, Tricia finished up the page she was reading before pausing to redirect her attention to Kate. "I'm not so sure I want to go. I'm not really the club type." She felt uneasy at just the idea of being thrust into a crowded club.

After being diagnosed with Asperger's Syndrome when she was a sophomore in high school, Tricia had become more accustomed to being socially awkward around others. Though after the diagnosis, she was at least happy she now had a reason for her weakness in that area. Unfortunately, it was also a weakness that left her without many friends as she had grown up.

Simply because she just didn't get the social cues that her peers understood, while her innate need to strictly follow right and wrong left her to be seen as a goody-two-shoes, Tricia felt the loneliness of an outsider. It also didn't help that those same peers who had misunderstood her had no problem with making her the victim of their bullying.

"I know you aren't, but think of it as my way of celebrating your leaving for Southwestern Kansas State College in the fall."

"Fine."

"Besides, who knows who you'll end up meeting tonight? For all you know, that tall, dark, and handsome man you're reading about just might show up to give you the chance to live out your own romance," Kate pointed out after glancing at the book.

"Kate, I strongly doubt I'll meet my guy at The Cosmos Club." She grimaced at just the thought of once again hoping to find her prince charming, but this time amidst the club's male patrons.

"Then maybe you need to start rethinking the kind of guy you're looking for because I highly doubt you're ever going to find your southern gentleman anywhere in Newport Bay. Hell, the only types of guys you'll find around here are surfers or preppies, not 'good ole country boys,' as you so often like to call them."

"I know, and that's why I'm hoping I'll finally get my chance to meet him when I start school in the fall. To have my country boy walk into one of my classes and then sit down next to me would be my ultimate dream come true." Tricia desperately wanted to make that desire of hers a reality.

It sucked. She had just received her associate's degree in general education from Newport Bay's community college and was looking forward to obtaining a bachelor's degree in liberal arts with a minor in early childhood education from SKSC, yet she still found herself with the constant reminder that despite her college degrees, she had never had a single boyfriend to speak of.

The sad truth was, she had only ever gone out with three guys in her twenty-two years of living, and none of the dates had ever led to a second one. She'd just never felt the chemistry needed for a second date. All she really wanted was a guy who knew the definition of chivalry and actually acted it out on a regular basis. Unfortunately, she had yet to meet that man who she not only felt a mutual attraction for but also knew how to romance her in the way a well-brought-up country boy would.

Though meeting a man with that southern drawl I find so damn appealing certainly wouldn't hurt either! she thought to herself as she pictured her ideal man giving her a sexy grin from underneath a cowboy hat.

"Dang, Clay, you are doing really well with your fan base, especially the women. It seems like you can never go wrong with that smooth southern charm of yours whenever your female fans are around!" Clay's manager and best friend, Bryan Walker, praised him as they headed back to Clay's motorhome during an all-too-brief intermission in their day's hectic schedule.

Despite being only twenty-five, Bryan Walker had become a successful sports entrepreneur with Clay's help. After learning about Clay's interest in NASCAR, it didn't take Bryan long to learn the sport himself before eventually becoming Clay's manager. Thus, Walker Motorsports was born. With the two best friends, who felt more like brothers, working side by side as Clay's racing took on notoriety, Bryan was able to turn their business venture into a profitable one after securing sponsorship from the popular tool brand Evergreen Tools.

As the success of their flourishing partnership continued, Clay had produced a two-year winning streak, and Evergreen Tools found its name becoming even more popular across the country. So as a thank you, Evergreen Tools had taken on the added advertising benefits of hosting a one-day fan event for Clay and his number zero-six car, allowing him and his fans the chance at an interactive experience that they usually never got. With a catered lunch and a fan-driven Q&A session, Clay answered his fans' questions as they'd learned more about his career and personal life. He then brought an end to the day by signing a plethora of autographs, cementing his NASCAR celebrity status with his adoring fans.

"Yeah, I know, and to think, 'fore all this, I was spendin' all my summers herdin' cattle for Logan's grandfather, Old Man Ryer, then sendin' the money back to my mama so she could continue to live in that godforsaken condemned house my dead-beat father left for us to live in," he returned. He flashed back to the tearful scene of his mama finding his father's goodbye letter and then watching her burst into tears the moment she realized that his leaving her had instantly turned her into a single mother.

He hated Sam Gibson with every fiber of his being. He had no clue why he couldn't stay. All Clay knew was that his father had traded life with him and his mama for a better one that didn't include them. Just thinking about it made him cringe at how he and his mama had been forced to suffer through years of barely making it because of his father's choice.

After he and Bryan had walked from the Q&A tent to Clay's motorhome, Logan stopped them from continuing inside. He was the man who had introduced them to the sport that had allowed them to rise above their poverty-stricken childhoods. Despite Logan easily grabbing Clay's attention with NASCAR's proclivity for speed, he'd just as quickly lost it when he'd gone behind Clay's back to cheat with his now ex-girlfriend, Nikki. In a matter of seconds, the friends from childhood had turned to ex-friends when Clay had found out.

"Clay, aren't you hot in that fire suit?" Logan asked as he took in the day's heat. He could feel the warmth the sun brought to his light-brown hair as he ran a hand through it. "Bryan, you'd better get your driver inside before this heat glues his fire suit to his body."

"What do ya want, Logan?" Clay asked as he stared back into Logan's ash-colored eyes.

"Just wanted to say hi, is all," he answered simply.

Despite his surface-level congeniality, Clay couldn't help but take anything Logan said with a grain of salt. Ever since Logan had copped to cheating with Nikki, hurting Clay in the deepest way possible, Clay felt like anything his former friend ever said to him from now on was like fire spat from the devil's mouth.

"Logan, what do you really want?" Bryan interjected, not in the mood to deal with any of the man's bullshit.

"It's like I said, Bryan, I just wanted to say hi."

"So you didn't come by to remind Clay that Nikki is now your girlfriend?"

As Clay stared back at the man, his anger for Logan's actions flashed through his eyes. He couldn't help but continue to feel the pain as his ex-friend's betrayal stayed fresh in his mind.

"No. Besides, it's not like I forced her to be with me, Bryan. Nikki chose to leave Clay for me."

"Yeah, I know. But you could've at least waited for her to break things off with him first. Instead, you took the underhanded approach and became a spiteful bastard about it."

"Hey, that's not fair, Bryan. Nikki and I never meant to hurt Clay the way we did. It just ended up that way."

"Logan, that's a bunch of bull, and you know it. You knew Nikki was with Clay, yet you couldn't leave her as just eye candy. You took advantage, and consequently, ended your and Clay's friendship."

"Bryan, that's not true. The first time Nikki and I hooked up, it was after some heated argument she'd had with Clay. We realized what a stupid mistake we had made and tried to forget about it. But no matter how much we both wanted to, we couldn't get past it and forget what we had done. Whenever we were alone, we kept feeling that same desire to be together."

"Logan, even if that is the case, Clay was your friend. You

should've manned up and told him the truth, not snuck behind his back like a coward and screwed his girlfriend." Bryan took over Clay's job of opening the door and went inside.

"Clay, you do know that it wasn't like that, right? I didn't intentionally take Nikki from you. She wanted to be with me in the end."

"Logan, when it comes right down to it, I loved Nikki. In fact, I was plannin' on askin' her to marry me. But the day 'fore, she told me 'bout the two of ya hookin' up."

"Clay, I had no idea. But clearly, it's a good thing you didn't because she would've obviously said no."

"Logan, what the hell makes you so sure that you're the right one for her? Had ya given us a chance to work through the problems we were havin' at the time, Nikki and I might still be together."

"I highly doubt that, Clay. Just face it, you couldn't give her what she wanted, and it irritates the hell out of you that she found it with me!"

"Screw you, Logan. We were supposed to be friends. But friends don't sneak 'round with their friend's girlfriend and then not say a damn thing 'bout it till their conscience finally catches up with 'em!"

"Well, maybe our friendship has run its course, then."

"Maybe it has, and your takin' Nikki from me was the nail in its coffin."

"So I'm dead to you now, is that what you're telling me?" Logan asked incredulously.

"Logan, I gotta be able to trust my friends. And right now, I don't trust ya. Hell, I don't even know if I'll ever be able to again. Ya hurt me real bad when ya took Nikki from me, and had ya manned-up and told me 'bout you two like Bryan said, well then, maybe, this might've been a different conversation. As it is, it's not."

"So you're throwing away our whole friendship because of it?"

"Logan, if ya had been a true friend, we wouldn't be havin' this conversation to begin with. Besides, I'm not the one who threw it away."

"Whatever. I was hoping we could both get past this, but clearly, we can't."

"Logan, ya hooked up with my girlfriend and then continued sleepin' with her behind my back. How the hell did ya ever figure we were gonna get past it?"

"I don't know, I guess I was just hoping we would. Damn it, I wish Bryan were out here so he could reason with you."

"Logan, Bryan feels the exact same way I do. Hell, why do ya think he kept takin' my side durin' y'alls conversation 'bout me?"

"Because he feels a sense of loyalty to you after you and your mama helped him escape his life as a drunkard's son," Logan answered with the memory of how Bryan's father, Bill, had become a well-known drunk fixed on picking up hot and horny women at the local bar on a nightly basis.

"Yeah, well, he feels indebted to me and my mama for that and probably always will."

"Clay, can't we just please get past this? I already admitted to screwing up. What else can I do?"

"Break up with her. Stop seein' her and then maybe we'll talk."

"Why? So you can try and rekindle the romance you two had? Clay, Nikki's not into you anymore. Even if I broke up with her, it's not like she would come begging for you to take her back. When are you going to get it through your thick head, Clay? Nikki doesn't want to be with you anymore. Deal with it!" Logan replied. His simple hello turned into a conversation that had lost all its appeal.

"Go to hell, Logan. I'm sure the devil's waitin' to welcome ya in!" he ended, unable to think of anything else that could better express how he felt. With clenched fists and a deep breath, he turned around and headed into his motorhome to join Bryan.

"You know he's right, Clay," Bryan pointed out the second he had walked in.

"Right? Right 'bout what?" he asked, still feeling the anger from the conversation.

"About Nikki. Logan's right about Nikki, Clay," Bryan answered.

"Who the hell's side are ya on, Bryan?"

"Yours. But you've got to admit that Logan was right. Nikki did choose him over you. Even though she screwed him behind your back and then apologized for it, she still did choose to stay with him."

"You too? What the hell is this, gang up on Clay time?"

"Of course not. But the truth is, if Nikki had wanted to work through whatever crap you two were going through at the time and stay with you, she would've. But the fact is, she didn't. She chose to continue cheating with Logan, and then said goodbye to you to be with him."

"What the hell, Bryan, you're supposed to be stickin' up for me, not takin' his side!" He pointed his finger at the door.

"I'm sorry, Clay, but the truth sucks sometimes." Bryan shrugged.

"Damn you, just get the hell out!" He continued pointing when he found he could no longer take his friend's lack of defense for him.

"Are you seriously kicking me out just because I'm telling you the God's honest truth about you and Nikki?" Bryan asked in astonishment.

"You're damn right I am, now get the hell out! You are no longer welcome!" he answered, standing there like a little boy who was angry just because he wasn't getting his way.

"Well, that's too damn bad because I'm not leaving!" Bryan remained seated.

"Fine!" Clay stormed off to the bedroom.

"And don't forget, you still have your fan 'thank you' dinner later tonight!" Bryan yelled back just in time to hear the bedroom door slide shut hard.

CHAPTER
- TWO -

C lay glanced over at the mirror and saw he was still wearing his fire suit. After seeing the unwelcome reminder of it sticking to his skin, he separated the Velcro collar and pulled the zipper down to his waist. With the exhaustion from the hot day and his fire suit retaining the heat, he gladly welcomed the motorhome's air conditioning.

"Dang, it feels so good to be out of this damn thing!" he said to himself as he peeled the suit off the rest of his body. He lay down on his bed, his undershirt and boxers the only remaining clothing continuing to make contact with his skin. As he lay there letting his skin breathe in the coolness, he knew that he would soon have to get dressed again. Though this time, it would be a tux.

Clay thought back to the memories of Nikki on his arm as she showed off her stunning body in her own evening wear. He remembered the day he had gone to the jewelry store to pick out her ring, a glamorous diamond that matched her glamorous personality. All that was left was for him to get down on one knee and ask her to be that stunning woman by his side for the rest of his life.

Nikki Reids had been a childhood friend that had turned into his girlfriend once she started watching him race. From dirt tracks to NASCAR speedways, she'd been there to support him. But it wasn't until a couple of years ago that their relationship had turned serious. Clay had begun imagining his life with her cheering him on at each race, being his number-one adoring fan as she watched him drive around the track with their kids rooting for Daddy as they watched his car pass by.

Unfortunately for him, the serious relationship Clay had thought he was in turned out to be one-sided. Despite his dream of what the future looked like, Nikki was on a whole other track with a different racer. She apparently had begun spending more time with Logan as Clay's appeal decreased, though it probably didn't help that Clay more often chose the track over her. This especially proved true when he would use his off time to learn aggressive driving techniques that would make him more like Dale Earnhardt instead of spending that downtime with her.

Clay just never thought she'd actually cheat on him. Had he realized his passion for his career was putting his relationship in jeopardy, he would've seriously considered putting the brakes on being in NASCAR. But as far as he knew, Nikki and Logan were just two childhood friends hanging out, not hooking up each time they found a chance to be together.

Despite being on completely different tracks in the relationship, Clay's heart still loved her. He wished it would've gone away with the day that ended their relationship, but apparently, his heart had yet to get the message that his brain had received with a big red flag.

Clay closed his eyes and hoped a quick nap would alleviate the emotional tailspin his conversation with Logan had caused. He refocused his thoughts on the reminder of his fan "thank you" dinner as the last driver obligation he owed to Evergreen Tools. Feeling his tiredness subside fifteen minutes later, Clay opened his light blues to the ceiling. His brief nap relieved his exhaustion but left him with a heavy heart. It was going to take more than the six months since their breakup for him to be over Nikki Reids.

Clay heard his cellphone vibrate. Curious to see who it was, he picked it up from the bed stand and looked at the caller ID. After seeing the screen display the text message symbol, he followed the prompt to see who had sent it. Unfortunately, as he neared the end of his curiosity, his interest stayed piqued when the word BLOCKED appeared, keeping the sender's identity a secret for the time being.

"Who would send me a blocked text?" he wondered out loud.

Clay – first you lost your girl, now what do you think might be next? You can bet your ass it'll be something you care a whole hell of a lot about!

"What the? Who the hell would wanna threaten me?" He realized that someone was out to get him.

Clay Gibson had been deemed the most notable rookie driver of 2012, as NASCAR's higher-ups took more notice of his driving skills. With various sports reporters keeping the buzz going by proclaiming him to be a promising talent, he found himself with a new celebrity status. And now, someone was threatening him through a text message.

"I wonder if it's just Logan givin' me a hard time for blowin' up at him earlier. Though he did help me get started in NASCAR, why the hell would he wanna take it from me?" He entertained the idea of his ex-friend being the most plausible suspect.

"Clay, are you talking to yourself?" Bryan asked as he was about to knock on the door.

"Yes, but ya might wanna come in to see why." He waited for Bryan to slide open the door so he could show him the threatening text.

"Okay, I'm coming in, then. Clay, what's wrong?" he asked after seeing the worried look on Clay's face.

"Just read it." Clay handed Bryan his cellphone with the text message ready to read.

"You don't think Logan sent it, do you?" Bryan asked, remembering how Clay had ended their last conversation.

"I don't know. I don't know if he'd actually stoop that low. Cheatin' with my girlfriend is one thing, but threatenin' to ruin my career . . ." The thought of the extent to what his ex-friend might go to boggled his mind.

"Despite that, this does seem a bit extreme."

"Okay, then if it wasn't Logan, who the heck else would wanna send me somethin' like this?"

"No names come to mind, but while you get ready for tonight's dinner, I'll make some calls."

"Bryan, I don't necessarily think that that's a good idea." Clay stopped him.

"And why not? Don't you want to find out who sent it?"

"Yes, but I also don't wanna go sparkin' any fires either."

"And how would my making some calls spark a fire?"

"Bryan, if ya start askin' 'round, then whoever sent this text message is just gonna end up stayin' silent so their identity doesn't 'come known."

"So you'd rather have me do nothing, instead?" Bryan asked, searching his mind for another possible solution.

"No. Why don't we just see how this text message thing plays out? Maybe this was just a one-time thing, and whoever sent it just wanted to see how I would react," he answered, hoping that that would be the case. He didn't want to have to already be protecting his career from whoever had texted him this first threat.

"Fine, if that's how you want to handle this. I won't make any calls just yet. But if you get another one, you can expect that it'll be the first thing I do, got it?"

"Thank you. Now if ya don't mind, I do believe it's time for me to go get ready for my fan 'thank you' dinner."

With that, Bryan moved aside so Clay could head into the bathroom and take a refreshing shower before finally having to slip on the tux he had to wear as the guest of honor.

Irritated that Clay had once and for all ended their friendship, Logan headed back into his motorhome. The day's race had long been over, and all Logan had to show for it was a second-place finish. Sure, that kept him near the top of the points bracket, but it had also kept him brutally aware of how much better Clay was. Logan just couldn't seem to catch up to him. Whenever he would try to find a way around him, Clay would just as easily block his attempt.

The second-place finishes wouldn't have been so bad except for Nikki constantly reminding him of that particular shortcoming. She wanted to be with a winner, not a runner-up. Unfortunately for both, Logan couldn't figure out how to deliver. The winner's circle would always be just out of his reach unless he was in a race that didn't include Clay.

"I'm back!" Logan called out as he once again traded the day's heat for his motorhome's AC.

"And?" Nikki asked while she sat at the dinette, painting her toenails.

"Well, I can tell you that Clay officially no longer wants to be friends. Nikki, he's through with me, and I don't blame him for it."

"That's it? You're going to let him put an end to your friendship just like that?"

"What else can I do? He's still hurt over us going behind his back."

"Like I told you before, figure it out," she flatly replied in between adding more color to her nails. "Though, you can thank me for getting the ball rolling for you," she added with a devilish smile.

"What are you talking about?"

"Logan, since you can't seem to man up and figure out a way to destroy Clay, I took some initiative for you."

"Nikki, I never said I couldn't do it."

"Fine, then just consider it me helping you get started."

"But I don't even know what you did!"

"And you don't need to. Just know that something's been done to hopefully make Clay a little less on his game than normal the next time he's out on that track."

"Whatever, I'm not dealing with this right now." Logan hated Nikki's ability to make him feel like less of a man. It's not that he couldn't screw with Clay's mind, he just hadn't had the time to sit down and figure out how he was going to do it. *Damn it, maybe Reese and Tyler can help me figure this out.* He left Nikki to finish her nails.

Walking over to Tyler Woods' motorhome, Logan wondered if the three of them could even come up with something that could scare Clay enough to affect his driving. Something that only scared him and not get them kicked out of NASCAR, or worse, sent to jail.

Knocking on the door, he could hear two people playing a video game. "Come on in," he heard Reese McKibbon call out.

Opening the door, Logan thanked God for the invention of AC as he took a seat on a couch. Fixing his eyes on the flat screen, he watched as Tyler and Reese concentrated on their game. "Do you both still have an ax to grind with Clay?"

"Why do you want to know?" Reese asked.

"Because Nikki wants me to destroy him and his career."

"And I take it you're looking to us to help you do it?" Tyler jumped in.

"Well, you both are tired of him landing in the winner's circle every race, aren't you?"

"Uh, yeah," they answered in unison.

"Then you've both got a reason to help me."

"I suppose, but what did Nikki say when you'd told her you were coming over here to ask us for help?" Tyler asked, putting the game on pause.

"She doesn't know I'm here."

"So, you left your girlfriend in your motorhome to do her bidding?" Reese teased.

"Can it, Reese. I'm just tired of being seen as a guy who can't measure up. I want to finally beat Clay and once and for all show Nikki that the man she left her ex for is worth it."

"Aw, has your ego been bruised, Logan?" Reese teased once more before receiving a glare that told him to stop.

"So will you guys help me?"

"Sure. Besides, if we can kick his ass out of the winner's circle, that'll mean more money and sponsorships for us," Tyler easily agreed for them both.

CHAPTER
- THREE -

"Are you ready to meet some hot guys, Trish?" Kate asked as they buckled themselves into Kate's black '68 Ford Mustang that sported chrome fenders. Turning on the engine, she listened to its beautiful purr before gearing and gassing the classic car into action by driving them out of their gated community and off to the newly opened Cosmos Club. She had been waiting to go there ever since she'd first seen it advertised on a billboard.

"Yeah, I guess so," Trish answered with a nervous nod, shifting her eyes to her passenger-side window to observe the world around her.

"Good, because I'm hoping to meet someone who'll take my mind off my parents' damn marital issues. I am put in the middle of their stupid crap too damn much!" Kate declared. She then blasted the radio to drown out her parents' lingering voices in her head.

"Your cranking up the music makes me wish I had something to go crazy about!" Tricia yelled so Kate could hear her over the loud lyrics.

"Please, you just need to finally meet your Mr. Right!" Kate returned as she drove them into the club's parking lot a few minutes later. "And tonight, we will both hopefully accomplish that goal." She parked her car in the last spot available and turned off the engine.

With a deep breath, Tricia got out of the car and mentally

17

prepared herself for the packed club and loud music. Heading into the new building to enjoy a night of desperately needed fun, they showed their IDs to a burly man wearing a dark burgundy turtleneck with a black suit and matching shoes. Kate paid their cover and they ventured further inside.

Upon seeing the crowded dance floor, Tricia felt her anxiety well warranted. She spotted a section of adjacent tables and thanked God that there was a guardrail separating her and Kate from the flurry of people dancing. Seeing only one vacant table, Tricia quickly took a seat.

"Trish, I'm going to go get us some drinks. I'll be right back," Kate informed her after a quick glance at the dance floor before focusing her attention on the line at the bar.

Giving her a brief nod, Tricia watched Kate head toward the bar. Turning her attention to the dance floor, Tricia found herself captivated by the various couples' dance styles. It fascinated her how they moved to the beat of the music, and it made her wish that she had her own guy to dance with so intimately.

"Dang, I'm so glad that's over with. This tux irritates the hell out of me!" Clay exclaimed, immediately beginning to undress the second he had stepped back into his motorhome. He couldn't get into his bedroom fast enough to take the rest of it off.

"Well, it sure helped you impress those women. I'm pretty sure the majority of them were undressing you with their eyes," Bryan replied as he followed him back inside.

"Tell me 'bout it. Had they not had dinner there, I would've been their main course."

"Either that or their dessert," Bryan joked as he thought about the women and how many of them looked like dogs salivating over a bone the second they saw Clay walk into the room in his tux.

"Yeah, sometimes it scares me just how damn good lookin' all those women think I am!" He chuckled as he thought about how the women were practically drooling over him.

"Right, uh huh, sure it does. But speaking of dessert, there's a new club called the Cosmos Club that just opened up. You want to go check it out?" Bryan asked as he headed into the bathroom to change out of his suit and tie and into some more comfortable clothes.

"Ah, I don't know. I'm kinda tired," Clay replied as he changed into his regular look of jeans, a white undershirt, and a plaid overshirt. He complimented it with a brown cowboy hat over his black hair, a varnished silver belt buckle, and a pair of brown, well-worn cowboy boots.

"I know, but I thought we could use a little fun tonight. You know, to help you get over seeing Logan today and then receiving that damn text message," Bryan explained as he changed into his usual pullover sweater and khaki look, and then slipped on a pair of black-and-white tennis shoes.

"I suppose a night out at a club might be nice," he agreed as he came out of his bedroom.

"Great, then let's go. By the way, you're driving!" Bryan informed him as he grabbed Clay's keys and tossed them to him.

"I guess this means that you're givin' me the directions, then?" he asked when he realized that he had no idea where the place was.

"Yep," Bryan answered as they headed for Clay's powder-blue 1954 Ford truck.

After Bryan navigated their way to the club, it wasn't long before Clay pulled into its driveway and began looking for a place to park. With no empty spaces to be seen, he was about to head across the street to park when he watched a couple of the club's patrons come out of the entrance and head for their vehicle.

"I guess God's on our side with the timin'," Clay announced as he looked up with a brief thank you before trading places with the vehicle.

"Well, this weekend is the grand opening," Bryan pointed out as they headed for the club's main entrance. After paying the cover, they headed inside to find a table to sit at and a cold beer to drink.

As they walked around the maze of people to find a place to sit down, Bryan was able to spot an open booth. Sliding in to claim it as theirs before anyone else had the chance, he turned his attention to the bar while Clay took in all that the club had to offer. As Bryan kept his eyes on the crowd of people keeping the bartenders busy, his gaze fell upon on a woman with long, wavy black hair. As his eyes scanned her body, he saw she wore a black camisole with a short white skirt covered in outlines of black, pink, and white flowers. Then, to add emphasis to her already well-defined curves, she wore a pair of black heels that showed off her sexy legs and gave her butt a slight lift. Bryan had never seen a more gorgeous woman in his life!

Damn, I've got to go meet her! He watched her patiently wait for service. After taking in each curve of her body, his eyes gradually left her assets to check out the various tables for two. As he scrutinized each one, he noticed a lone brunette occupying one of them, leaving him to wonder if the empty chair belonged to the black-haired woman. Had she come with a date, or was she alone?

"Hey, Clay, you see that brunette sitting all by herself at that table next to the dance floor?" Bryan asked with the realization that, whoever had left her sitting by herself had given Clay the perfect opportunity to go introduce himself.

"Yeah, what 'bout her?" he asked once his eyes had found the woman.

Despite the distance between them, Clay could easily tell that she wasn't as provocatively dressed as many of the other women in the club. Instead of showing off her assets in a blunt way, she wore a nice black-and-white patterned blouse matched with a pair of dark-blue jeans and black boots.

"Well, I'm about to find out if her friend is a certain hot woman at the bar. So why don't you go introduce yourself to the lonely brunette and hopefully score us a couple of seats at their table while I go get us some beers?" Bryan suggested as he continued to watch the woman who had captured his attention wait her turn to order her drinks.

"She does look pretty cute."

"Great, then what do you say we go introduce ourselves to our future wives?" Bryan jokingly foreshadowed before getting up to make his presence known to the dark-haired beauty who had sparked an attraction in him.

"Excuse me, but is that seat taken?" Tricia heard a male voice with a definitely noticeable southern drawl ask her while her eyes remained fixed on the crowded dance floor.

"Huh, what?" she asked once the masculine voice had made its presence known to her brain, telling her to redirect her attention to him. Once she had, her eyes followed the voice to reveal a five-foot-nine man with broad shoulders and a cowboy hat staring back at her.

Tricia couldn't believe her eyes. A man who dressed just the way she liked was asking her if he could sit down at her and Kate's table. As she took in his appearance with utter disbelief, her eyes couldn't help but automatically light up as they scanned everything he wore, which comprised the look of a man she found so incredibly attractive. His belt even had a shiny oval buckle with the imprint of a mustang on it, completing his appearance. She had been so surprised that she had completely forgotten to give him an answer to his question. He continued standing there waiting for her response.

"I asked ya if that seat was taken," he repeated with an added nod toward Kate's currently vacant seat when he'd noticed that she still had yet to answer him.

"Oh, right . . . sorry. But to answer your question, yes. It's actually my best friend's. She just went to get us some drinks. So if you want to sit down, you'll have to grab another chair," she finally answered once her brain had caught her up to his question and then kicked into gear to answer it.

"Sounds good to me," he agreed with a nod, looking around the seating area for another empty table. Seeing a table that he could borrow two chairs from, he easily accomplished Bryan's goal by adding themselves to the girls' table. "The other chair is for my friend Bryan once he and your friend get back from the bar," he added after seeing her questioning look.

"Oh." She glanced over at Kate to see that she was now in conversation with his friend as she waited for their drinks.

"By the way, I'm Clay Gibson. And you are?" he asked after sitting on his chair with its back facing her and then extending his right hand out to her.

"Clay Gibson? Your name sounds familiar, what do you do?" she asked, realizing she'd heard it before.

"I'm a race car driver. I drive the number zero-six car in the

NASCAR Sprint Cup Series." He smiled when he realized that his profession could come in very handy.

"That's right, I've actually watched you race before," she replied with a timid smile as she accepted his gesture. "My dad got me into watching the circuit."

"Oh, and what'd ya think?" he asked as he fixed his eyes on hers.

"That you're good," she answered.

Just the way he looked at her, Tricia felt an unexpected tingling feeling shoot through her. It was so strong, she wondered if he'd felt it too.

"Just good? Not amazin', or the best driver ya've ever watched?" he teased her.

"I . . . um."

"By the way, ya still have yet to tell me your name." Her hazel eyes made him want to keep looking into them. It was like no one else in the club existed as he found his attention glued on her.

"Oh, sorry, it's Tricia Perkins."

"Well, it's nice to meet ya, Tricia Perkins," he returned with another smile as he kept his hand connected to hers.

It was a smile that not only sent butterflies to her stomach but also kept her reminded of the extreme attraction she felt for him. Tricia couldn't deny it; she felt a definite spark between them. The scary part about it was the way he looked back at her with the most gorgeous blue eyes she'd ever seen on a man. It was clear Clay had an interest in her, yet because she had never experienced this kind of mutual attraction before, she was scared to believe it. "You too, Clay."

CHAPTER

- FOUR -

"I'm back, and I brought a friend," Kate announced as she and Bryan arrived at the table with everyone's drinks.

"Great, I was getting thirsty!" Tricia said, finally letting go of Clay's hand. She could barely look away from him.

"And it looks like you've made a friend too," Kate added as she watched Tricia's interaction with Clay.

Giving Kate a timid smile, Tricia quickly accepted her Diet Coke.

"And I suppose that would be my cue," Bryan announced. "Kate, meet my best friend Clay Gibson. Clay, Kate Bransin." Handing Clay his beer, Bryan then took a seat next to Kate.

"Nice to meet you, Clay," Kate said, "and this is my best friend, Tricia Perkins. Tricia, Bryan Walker."

After shaking Bryan's hand, Tricia quickly returned to the security of her soda. But as her security blanket disappeared with each sip, she felt a new discomfort. Sitting next to Clay fueled her nervousness. She stretched out her legs and in doing so, she felt her leg accidentally bump Clay's.

Damn it! she thought to herself when she realized that there was no possible way he hadn't felt it.

Feeling the movement against his leg, Clay took a sip of his beer and glanced over at the only likely culprit. Curious as to how far he should take it, he inwardly smiled then repositioned his legs underneath the table.

"Sorry," she quickly apologized before moving her legs back to their original position. But as she did, she felt her leg slide up his as she brought it back over her left. Feeling the extended contact with his left leg, she felt another spark shoot through her. Just by having her jeans accidentally make contact with his had caused her body to be hit with another reminder of how attracted she was to him.

"Clay, I . . ." Tricia began to apologize, only to find out that the second time around had been no accident when he'd interrupted her apology with a wink.

Feeling her stomach filling with more butterflies, Tricia contemplated her reaction to his subtle flirting with her. With a quick glance at Kate and Bryan, she realized she was too shy to say or do anything with them still sitting at the table. Then as if God Himself was purposely providing her with an opportunity, she watched Bryan get up from his seat and ask Kate if she wanted to dance.

With an eager yes, Kate followed Bryan onto the dance floor where Tricia watched them mix in with everyone else. Glancing over at Clay as he took a sip of his beer, Tricia wondered if he was going to ask her to dance as well. Though the thought excited her, it also made her nervous. Just as she was going to bite the bullet and hint for him to do it, his words stopped her.

"So, do ya think they make a cute couple?" he asked as he watched his best friend sensuously dance with hers.

"I guess," she answered as she watched Kate lose herself to the music while Bryan enjoyed their closeness.

"What 'bout us? Do ya think we might make a cute couple, Tricia?" he asked, looking directly at her and slowly sliding his hand onto hers and intertwining their fingers.

"I uh . . . think you're being a little forward," she answered. But as she looked down at their connected hands, she could feel her heart race at just the feel of his hand against hers.

With every sensation he caused her to feel, Tricia knew that the spark he kept stoking between them he could undoubtedly feel as well. Despite that, her fear of the unknown held her back on wanting to just give in to the obvious attraction she felt for him. Even with his cowboy look making him seem like he was a godsend, she wasn't about to let her emotions take control of the wheel while her head rode shotgun. She was going to do her damnedest to stay level headed while he flirted with her and keep her emotions away from directing her head's decisions when it came to him.

Not wanting to lose the feel of his hand over hers but letting her fear win out, Tricia removed her hand from underneath his. But after she had, she found herself unexpectedly missing the feel of his hand against her skin.

"Yeah, I guess you're right. I am bein' way too forward, aren't I?" he apologized, finding himself wishing that she hadn't removed her hand from his.

Whatever this spark was between the two of them, Clay ached to keep her hand in his. Even with them barely talking, he could feel an intense connection to her. It was one that blatantly told him she had an interest in him, and he couldn't give up on it.

"Just a bit." She turned her attention back to their friends, wondering what it would be like to dance with Clay like that.

As this intense feeling settled in him, and with Bryan and Kate giving him a reminder of how dancing could bring him and Tricia closer, he realized that he needed to ask her to dance. But right as he was about to attempt just that, a group of women interrupted him.

"Excuse me, but you're Clay Gibson, right? *The* Clay Gibson?" one of the women asked as she led the group in their mission to put an end to their celebrity-driven curiosity.

"Yes, that would be me." He nodded, figuring the group was just more fans wanting his autograph.

After listening to the women squeal with delight, Tricia watched him sign his name and car number on whatever object each woman had to give him. Then, once the last item had been autographed and the fawning had come to an end, she watched the women leave their table with squeals and giggles of delight over having just met their favorite race car driver.

"So, do you get a group of women asking you for your autograph all the time?" she asked, realizing the major issue she would end up facing if the spark between them ever led to anything. After playing back the women's reactions to their getting an autograph from him, she immediately recognized her urgent need to keep her heart's defensive line up against him and make sure it stayed up.

"Pretty much." He shrugged. Autograph signing had become more of a routine for him than the novelty it had once been. "So would ya like to dance, Tricia?" he finally asked with the prospect of getting to enjoy her moves like Bryan was continuing to do with her friend.

"No thanks, I barely know you," she replied, giving him an excuse that would help her keep her want of not adding herself to the millions of women who already wanted to date him.

"Right, that makes sense. I wouldn't wanna dance with a stranger right after I'd met 'em, either, no matter how cute I thought she was." He hoped his words would get her to change her mind.

After hearing his compliment, and even though she didn't want to, Tricia couldn't help but smile. She quickly turned her head so he wouldn't be able to see her blushing. But when she had finally turned back to face him, she could see that he was smiling. No, not just any smile, but a sexy "I know you were blushing" sort of smile.

Damn it, that sexy grin of his isn't helping me one bit! she thought to herself as her reaction to his facial expression was a tell-all for how she really felt.

"So, how 'bout that dance, Tricia?" he asked again when he could see that his grin was having the desired effect on her.

Just as she was about to answer his question, another woman came up to their table with a different question in mind. Instead of just wanting an autograph like the first group of women had, she was more interested in being the next woman who got to dance in this hot, NASCAR driver's arms.

"Sorry, ma'am, but I've already got me a dance partner." Before Tricia knew what was happening, he was grabbing her hand and leading her out onto the dance floor.

CHAPTER
- FIVE -

"But, Clay, I never said yes!" Tricia reminded him as he pulled her through the crowded dance floor until he'd found an unclaimed area for them. An area that despite the crowding of all the other sweaty people, allowed each enough room to enjoy the music while the other club patrons continued to dance to the beat.

"I know ya hadn't, but I wanted to dance with ya, anyway," he answered simply although with a hidden anticipation for when the music would allow him to wrap his arms around her once it had taken on a slower beat. "And truthfully, I was gettin' tired of my time with ya bein' interrupted," he continued smoothly.

"Well, I guess since we're out here . . ." she finally agreed despite the reluctance she still felt. Even though she had mentally forced up a defensive wall for her heart, it didn't help that his charm was like a dog slowly digging its way to the other side of a fence that wouldn't stop until it had successfully made it underneath and to the other side.

"Good, 'cause this way, I doubt another woman's gonna try and bother me while I'm with ya." He smiled in triumph as he watched her loosen her body up enough to enjoy dancing with him.

Smiling in return, Tricia let her guard down a little and began showing off her moves as the song's lyrics played out. At first, their dancing together kept intact an innocence she had hoped would remain throughout the song's entirety. But as the music helped loosen up her inhibitions, another club patron accidentally bumped into her, causing her to get pushed into Clay and, consequently, reignite the reminder of the spark between them.

"Oh my gosh, I am so sorry, Clay," she quickly apologized so he wouldn't get the chance to wonder if she'd done it on purpose.

"Don't worry 'bout it. Tricia, I know it was an accident." They continued dancing to the fast-paced music. After feeling her body briefly press up against his, he found that he was happy it had happened and wondered if she secretly felt that way too.

"Good, because I'd hate for you to think that I was trying to make a move on you, especially after I'd called you out on being so forward earlier," she continued over the loud music.

"Don't worry, I wasn't." The music took on a slower beat.

"Honeys and gents, as much as I love that bangin' hip-hop sound, I think it's time I gave those couples out there a chance to express their love for each other. So, guys, if you and your honey ain't on the dance floor yet, get out here, 'cause this one's for you!" The DJ went from spinning a hip-hop record to a slow song that neither knew.

"Okay, Clay, I think that's enough for me." She decided that the change in tempo had given her a good excuse to leave the dance floor, allowing her to escape the awaiting feeling of his arms being wrapped around her waist.

"Are ya sure? 'Cause I'd hate for us to waste a perfectly good song." He watched other couples take their place on the dance floor while those with no dance partner walked off.

"Yeah, I'm sure. I mean, that song really took it out of me." She pretended to be too exhausted to continue dancing with him. She didn't want his arms around her waist, charming her into giving in to her feelings for him.

"If you're sure," he repeated, hoping to God that she would change her mind. Even though a part of him still reeled with a lingering pain over Nikki, he was actually enjoying his time with Tricia and didn't want to see it end so soon.

But before Tricia could continue with her plan of *not* being in his arms, she glanced over at Kate and saw the look she displayed as she slow danced with Bryan. It was one that said, "Come on, Trish . . . give him a try. You never know, he just might be your tall, dark, and handsome!"

"On second thought, I guess we can stay for this song," she reluctantly agreed. She figured that even though she was going to keep her wall up with Clay, she could at least pretend for one night for Kate's sake.

"Glad to hear it, Tricia," he replied happily. He figured that no matter the reason for her change of heart, he was still going to get to wrap his arms around her like he'd been wanting to do ever since he'd pulled her out onto the dance floor.

"Clay, it's just a slow dance. Don't think it means anything more than that," she reminded him when she heard his tone reflect more happiness than it should have.

"Oh, I know. I'm just happy ya changed your mind 'bout it." He drew her into his arms then wrapped them around her waist.

As he did, she could feel the heat resonate from his body. Just the feel of his hands on her waist and his arms by her sides alerted her to his masculinity. It also reminded her of the loneliness she felt, and her longing for a man's touch.

"Good to know, I guess. Let's just get this slow dance over with so Kate can see that I've given her no reason to give me a hard time since I am taking advantage of my time with you." As she wrapped her arms around his neck she was reminded yet again of his feel and her unfulfilled desire.

"And why would your friend wanna do that?" he inquired.

"Damn, I probably shouldn't've said that to you . . . it must've sounded really weird . . . I'm sorry." She mentally smacked herself for unintentionally including him in that part of her life already.

"Apology accepted, but I still wanna know," he persisted.

"Okay fine, Mr. NASCAR driver, not that you really need to know at this point, but I'm a twenty-two-year-old who's never had a boyfriend. So by my saying that, I merely meant that Kate would end up questioning me about it later on if she saw that I hadn't chosen to take advantage of my time with you, given that you are my type and all."

"Huh . . . good to know." He smiled with the knowledge that he might want to "fix" her problem. "So, if I'm your type, then what's with the unwillin'ness to wanna dance with me? Given that it would usually be the other way 'round when a woman is in fact interested in the man she's with," he asked, once again, capturing her eyes with his.

"Simple. You're a NASCAR driver. And by the fact that you've already had several women come up to you tonight, I'm not about to throw out the red carpet to my heart for you," she answered honestly.

"True, but they all only wanted my autograph."

"I highly doubt that, but either way, you've probably got a million other women just waiting to take my place right now. I know that one woman who asked you to dance couldn't've felt more disappointed when you'd told her no." She gestured with her eyes in the direction of their table, remembering the woman's saddened face right after Clay had denied her request in order to pull Tricia onto the dance floor instead.

"So? The majority of 'em just think I'm hot. I bet ya that most of 'em only consider me a fantasy and nothin' else," he countered, trying to convince her of the opposite.

"Clay, it doesn't matter. The point is you've already got plenty of women after you, and I have yet to have my first boyfriend. So, I just don't want to take that chance." But as she looked into his eyes for confirmation of her words, his gorgeous blues brought her back to their intense connection.

"Tricia, ya may think that, but who did I choose to dance with?"

"Clay, I know you forced me out here with you. But that's not the point," she answered with eyes that begged to be understood.

As Clay and Tricia stayed focused on each other, up in a VIP booth, Nikki watched the chemistry they shared. *Damn it, that is supposed to be me!* she thought to herself as she watched the way Clay held Tricia in his arms. He kept her close to his body and his eyes on hers as if she were the only other one in the room. *That bastard, and simply because he wasn't ready to have sex!* She thought about the real reason she'd turned to Logan. She was ready and willing, and Clay wanted to wait for marriage. *If he just wasn't so damn hot, I wouldn't give a damn about who he held in his arms now!* Logan's presence brought an end to her internal rant.

As if the reality of her dancing with him was really just a

dream, Tricia began contemplating the romantic notion of giving him a kiss. Despite having just met the man and it being her first, the idea of already being that affectionate with him became more and more favorable as the lights danced around them. But as her mind played out the different possibilities for her enchanted affection for him, she felt herself get bumped up against him again. Only this time, she heard clanging metal as their belt buckles collided with each another.

"Sorry about that," she apologized again, though this time, with the feeling of his eyes gazing into hers, causing her to feel an even deeper connection with him.

"Don't worry 'bout it. One little clang ain't gonna ding the metal," he assured her, "but if it'll make ya feel better, I can check for damages later."

"I would appreciate that. I'd hate to have accidentally damaged your belt buckle. It looks so nice and expensive."

"No problem, and if there's a scratch or two, I'll make sure to send ya the bill."

"Funny."

"I thought it was."

"Whatever," she replied with an eye roll. She couldn't help but return her gaze back to his.

"Well, Tricia, since the one song's ended, and another's begun, did ya wanna head back to the table, or stay for another one?"

"I suppose one more song won't hurt since I probably won't ever see you again after tonight."

"Ya sure like to analyze things, don't ya?" he asked after watching her really think about the question before answering it.

"Sometimes. It's my decision-making process," she answered. *Thanks to my Asperger's.*

"Then it must take ya a rather long time to make a decision, if that's the case."

"No, I can make a decision without analyzing things. Analyzing just provides me with the logical reasoning for when I do make my decision."

"I see." He watched as a person running across the floor bumped into her, causing her to completely close the gap between them, resulting in her once again being able to feel his body heat resonating through his clothes, though this time, even more so.

"Whoa, I am so sorry, Clay. I just keep getting pushed into you."

"Hey, don't worry 'bout it. I've got no broken bones. However, ya might've dinged my belt buckle again," he teased, happy to once again get to feel her body so close to his.

"Ha, ha. So why aren't you all dressed up for going out to a club, anyway?" She subconsciously adjusted her arms around his neck and began playing with the hair at his nape.

"Who says I'm not, darlin'?" he asked the moment he felt her fingers take on a more personal role with him.

"Just answer the question, Clay." She replayed the way the reference sounded with his southern drawl.

"I take it ya like my callin' ya that?" He grinned and raised his eyebrows after watching her smile form the instant she'd heard the term of endearment come out of his mouth.

"What makes you think that?" she asked as his facial reaction to her response kept them both sidetracked.

"Your smile kinda gave it away."

Darn. She couldn't help but think to herself, despite her expression giving away that thought as well.

"Ya know, ya really need to work on your poker face . . . darlin'." He watched her disappointment spread across her face.

"You're going to keep calling me that whether I deny my liking it or not, aren't you?" she asked as she replayed its use with his southern drawl for a second time.

"Yep."

"So, do you call every woman you dance with, darlin'?"

"Nope, just the ones who call me out when I'm bein' too forward."

"I guess that means I'm not the only one, then." She continued to stare into his bright, baby blues.

"Touché, darlin'."

"You still haven't answered my question about your chosen attire, Clay," she reminded him, indirectly putting their conversation back on track.

"I wear what makes me comfortable, and this outfit makes me comfortable."

"Well, what about for fancy events? Like dinner parties or weddings?"

"For those, I'll trade in my comfortability. But for the most part, this outfit I've got on right now is the one people usually see." He thought about the tuxedos he had to wear for his NASCAR black-tie events and the one he had on earlier that evening for his sponsored fan "thank you" dinner.

Hmm, I wonder what he looks like in a tux? she thought to herself as her brain tried to picture him in one.

"And you had said no to dancin' with me," he reminded her with a questioning look.

"What makes you think that I don't regret my changed decision?"

"Well, considerin' the fact that we've been out here for more than a couple of songs . . ."

"Maybe I just got lost in listening to the lyrics," she replied with the first excuse she could think of.

"Darlin', if that were true, then ya wouldn't've been starin' into my eyes non-stop durin' each song, and ya wouldn't be playin' with my hair like ya are now." He realized that even though her conscious was putting up a wall for him, her subconscious wasn't.

Damn! she thought to herself and accidentally made a face as she quickly removed her fingers from his hair.

"Maybe we should quit this dancin' and ya let me help ya with your poker face, instead?" he teased the second he saw her face clearly display the emotion she felt.

With that, all Tricia could think to do was rest her head on his shoulder. Since she was probably never going to see him again after tonight, what'd it really matter if she danced with him like they'd been together forever? All she really wanted was to finally have her chance at a romance with a guy. And if her brief time with Clay Gibson was all her life was going to give her for that experience, then damn it, she was just going to forget about reality for the time being and let herself enjoy every second his arms kept her so close to him.

CHAPTER

- SIX -

C lay readjusted his arms around Tricia's waist the moment she leaned her head against his shoulder. *Dang, she feels so good like this!*

Her slender body felt absolutely perfect in his arms as he held her against him, and even though he knew that she was only acting this way because she thought that their dancing like this was just a one-time thing, deep down, he could feel a want for her that made him want to prove her otherwise.

Now all he had to do was try his damnedest to convince her that being with him was a good idea. Though, as he thought more about it, he wondered if he was even emotionally ready for her, considering his post-breakup mindset. Yes, it was Nikki who had broken it off, not him. So it wasn't like he'd already known that the end of their relationship was coming. But what had hurt him the most about it all was that, in the end, he really had loved her. He had opened himself up to her and given her his heart only to be told he wasn't the one she wanted after all. Nikki wasn't just a girl he'd grown up with but a woman who he'd seriously thought about marrying.

"Thank you for the dancing, Clay. I really enjoyed it," Tricia dreamily whispered to him, bringing him out of his thoughts.

She couldn't help but want to stay in her dreamy state of mind as she danced so closely with her momentary Prince Charming.

"You're welcome, darlin'." They heard the song's last line of lyrics come to an end, informing them that their time in each other's arms would soon be over.

With a serene nod for her finally getting her fairytale night, Tricia released her arms from Clay's neck and headed back to their table with the knowledge of what returning to reality would mean for her; she was still single.

As she walked away from him, Clay couldn't help but check out her body. He was impressed by the natural swing of her hips and greatly wished that he'd been able to see more of what her curves had to offer him.

"So how was your night with tall, dark, and handsome, Trish?" Kate asked her after getting up to meet her while Bryan worked on finishing his beer.

"It was nice. As Clay held me in his arms for those few dances, I really felt like I had gotten to live out a little bit of my romance novel."

"Sounds like he really made an impression on you," Kate pointed out as she watched Clay head their way.

"I suppose, but just for tonight. I strongly doubt that anything will ever come from my dancing with him."

"And why not, Trish? He seems exactly your type."

"Oh, I know. But he's also a NASCAR driver."

"So? That sounds like a bonus given your enjoyment of the sport."

"Normally, I would think so too. But Kate, I just think that he's got way too many women after him, and I really don't want to be put in the position where I have to prove myself better than all of them," she declared.

"Well then, I don't know how you're going to handle this, but I asked Bryan if he and Clay would walk us out to my car. You may not want anything more with his friend, but I am definitely interested in pursuing something with Bryan," Kate informed her.

"I guess I can deal with that, though I hope Clay doesn't feel like he's getting mixed messages, especially with the way I ended our dancing out there," she replied with a sigh.

"Why, what did you do?"

"I rested my head on his shoulder and then whispered my thanks for the dancing."

"Oh, well . . . was that it?"

"I also told him that I enjoyed it." She wondered whether she should now regret having told him that or not.

"Trish, you probably have nothing to worry about," Kate answered after thinking about the different ways Clay could've possibly taken Tricia's words.

"Good, because I only acted that way after figuring I'd never see him again," she reasoned right before he joined them.

"Are you girls ready to go?" Bryan interjected. "Clay, Kate's asked us to walk them out to her car."

"Sounds good to me," he agreed and shot Tricia a wink.

"Aw, damn it!" she exclaimed when she realized that their dancing hadn't been the end of it.

"Sorry, Trish. I guess your night with tall, dark, and handsome isn't over after all," Kate quietly apologized.

"Whatever, let's just go," she replied when she realized that Clay was going to keep using his charm to try and win her over. As much as she didn't want to admit it, their dancing together had brought out her deep craving for the passionate romance she wished to have with a man.

"This '68 Mustang's yours?" Bryan asked Kate after she had led them to her car.

"Yeah, my parents gave it to me for my sixteenth birthday. Muscle cars are sort of my thing," she answered. She thought about how she'd used it as a momentary escape from her parents whenever their problems became too much for her to deal with.

"Nice. Clay and I came in his '54 Ford truck."

Tricia couldn't help but light up again. Despite her adamant not wanting to date the man, everything about him seemed like it matched what she looked for in a guy so perfectly. The only attribute he had yet to claim was if he liked to cook. If he said yes to that, she knew she'd be in real trouble.

"Ya impressed by that, darlin'?" Clay asked her with a grin.

"Well, I do like the classics too," she answered. She hated not having a poker face.

"Then why don't ya come with me and I'll give ya a first-hand experience of it?" he offered, and before she had the chance to accept or reject his offer, he began walking back to his truck.

Damn it, the dancing was supposed to be it! Why does he have to keep encouraging my interest in him? She realized that she had no choice but to follow him; she really did want to see his truck.

"Hey Kate, while they're checking out his truck, did you want to give me your number?" Bryan asked her the second they were alone.

"Sure," she answered, watching him pull out his cellphone to program it in.

"So why's it have all that dried-up dirt on it?" Tricia asked, not even considering any of the possibilities.

"Darlin', I'm from the country. I use it for transportin' hay . . . and sometimes muddin'."

Clay thought about how he had modified it for mudding by installing seatbelts.

"I knew that." She was curious as to what it would be like to go mudding with the man.

"Sure ya did, but if ya'd like to take a peek at it, go right 'head," he returned. "Ya like what ya see?" He watched her examine every inch of its metal body. He couldn't help but wonder what it would be like to take her out there with him. *Damn, she'd look so dang hot sittin' in my passenger seat!* he thought to himself.

"Yeah, it's really cool . . . and I can see what you mean about the dirt. You said you used it for mudding too?" She zeroed in on the word.

"Yep, when I have time off from racin', I like to hit the backcountry and go muddin'."

"Cool, I've never been, but I've always wanted to go," she stated, although not meaning to insinuate that he ask her out.

"And here I thought ya were against havin' a relationship with me." He gave her a look after picking up on the meaning behind her words.

"No Clay, I merely meant it as just a fun thing I've always wanted to do. I have no intention of wanting to start something with you," she denied, though deep down, knew her heart was telling her head that that was a lie.

"Right," he returned with folded arms.

"Clay, I'm telling you the truth, and I'm sticking to my decision of not wanting to date you."

"And ya don't think my smooth southern charm can convince ya to change your mind 'bout me?" he asked, closing the gap between them after she'd paused her scrutinizing.

"No, I don't." She could feel her heart racing for him while he stood so close to her.

"I see. Then would ya at least like to climb on in and get a real feel for what sittin' in one of these oldie machines is really like?" he asked as he looked into her eyes.

"Um, yeah . . . sure," she answered, unable to escape his eyes as they drew hers back in.

"Then, there ya go, darlin'." He reached out and unlocked the driver's door for her, all the while keeping his eyes on hers.

"Thank you, I appreciate it," she returned with a shy smile. She turned her focus to getting in the truck. Sitting inside a classic was something she'd always wanted to do after seeing them at the many car shows her dad had taken her to growing up.

"No problem, just watch out for the . . . mud." he began, as he watched her start to climb up into his truck.

Unfortunately, by the time he'd finished his warning, it was too late. She'd already stepped on some fresh mud that partially covered the step, causing her foot to slip. As she felt her shoe lose traction, she felt his hands against her sides as he braced her.

"Ya okay there, darlin'?" He couldn't help but breathe in her hair's sweet fragrance.

"Yeah. I only slipped, Clay." Her new position against him made it so that she'd need his help to rebalance.

"I know ya did, I watched it happen," he replied, wishing he could take advantage and kiss her neck.

"Then you should also know that I'm fine. I just need you to let go of me so I can regain my balance."

"Okay, then . . . there ya go." Their closeness disappeared.

As Tricia regained her balance, a breeze informed her of his body's scent. It was an aroma that reminded her of her dad's Old Spice aftershave, and one that made Clay smell so damn good that she just wished it would continue to linger on long after their night had come to an end.

CHAPTER

- SEVEN -

"You don't think Kate and Bryan saw what happened, do you?" she asked as his intoxicating scent left its imprint on her brain.

"Nah, they're too busy flirtin' with each other to have noticed," he answered after looking in their direction. "Why, were ya hopin' Kate would rescue ya from me?"

"Ha, and no, I just didn't want her concern for my fall to interrupt my chance at getting to sit in your truck." She turned back to it so she could make a second, but hopefully much more successful, attempt at getting inside.

"Just make sure to watch out for that mud," he reminded her.

"Don't worry, I will," she replied, carefully climbing into his truck, this time, without slipping.

"Congratulations, darlin', ya did it!" he joked as he climbed in after her and shut the door. "So how do ya like it? Is it everythin' ya'd ever imagined it to be?" He intentionally gave her a hard time while enjoying their time alone.

"You sure know how to warm a girl's heart, Clay. Yes, it's awesome. In fact, it's always been my dream to own one someday. I just love these kinds of classics."

"Who says I was even tryin' to warm your heart, darlin'? I was merely makin' conversation," he smirked.

"Oh."

"Unless of course, ya were hopin' I would charm ya into datin'

39

me?" he asked, figuring that that was exactly what she had been expecting from him.

"And why would you think that?"

"'Cause deep down, ya know ya wanna start somethin' with me, regardless of how many women ya think are clamorin' for my attention." He rested his arm on the cushion behind her.

"Whatever, Clay. I'm just enjoying tonight for what it is, that's all." She sat back against the cushion and closed her eyes. "What I would give for some good country music and a two-lane road surrounded by fall foliage right now."

"Ya sound like my kinda girl, darlin'." He smiled while holding back his desire to lean over and kiss her while her eyes remained closed.

"Of course I do."

"Then I just have one question for ya," he began, going about charming her in another way.

"Yes?" she asked, opening her eyes.

"Who's drivin'? I figured that since this is my truck, I would be. But it's your scene, so ya may have somebody else in mind?"

"You sure are persistent, aren't you?"

"You're damn right 'bout that, darlin'."

"Well, to answer your question, I don't actually know at the moment. But when I do, I'll be sure to let you know, okay?"

"That'll be fine. That way, I can also make sure to get their information, ya know, for insurance purposes."

"Very funny," she replied dryly, shaking her head and rolling her eyes at his poor comedic skills.

"Hey, I thought it was . . . unless of course, ya'd rather just skip this mystery driver, and let me be the man in your scene instead?" he offered with a grin he hoped she'd not only find very sexy but too irresistible to refuse.

"Please, you're not going to charm me into giving you a yes, Clay."

"I don't know, I've often been told that my charm can be pretty persuasive."

"And for some women, I'm sure it can, Clay, but for me, I think I'll just take that as my cue to tell you goodnight." She pulled on the passenger door's handle to get out.

She found its jammed mechanism preventing her from leaving his truck. *What the, why won't it work?* she wondered to herself when she realized that the door was now trapping her in his truck with him.

"Uh, here, let me help ya with that. That door can get pretty stuck sometimes. I've been meanin' to fix it but just haven't gotten 'round to it yet," he explained when he saw the worried look on her face.

"Um, okay," she responded, worried about her current dilemma.

"Tricia, I can tell ya right now that I'm definitely not someone ya need to feel 'fraid of, and I would certainly never take advantage of a woman like that," he informed her of his built-in moral compass when he continued to see the fear in her eyes.

"And I appreciate that, Clay. But being that I've got a stuck door on one side of me and a man who I barely know on the other, I think my concern is perfectly valid. So if I were to feel like I was in any sort of danger while I sat here with you, I'd have to pray to God that either my door would suddenly open the instant I needed it to or that I would somehow be able to get past you . . . and the likelihood of my succeeding with either isn't very good."

"Well, ya can trust me, Tricia. I promise I won't do anythin' to hurt ya or take advantage of ya in any way." Then as proof of his word, gave her as much distance as the truck's cab would allow.

"Still, I think I should call it a night, so if you would please open my door for me?" she decided.

She watched him reach across her and force the handle's mechanism to work so she could finally get out of his truck. Just as he finished opening her door, she felt a sudden vibration against her side, causing her to jump a little, and consequently, brush her chest up against his arm.

"Are you okay?" he asked with surprise.

"Yeah, sorry. Kate just sent me a text message, and the alert scared me," she answered after taking her cellphone out and looking at it.

"Do ya mind if I ask ya what she said?"

"You can ask, but I won't tell," she answered after reading it.

"It's too bad that I'm faster than ya, then," he replied, and before she could stop him, he took the cellphone out of her hand and looked at it.

"Clay, that's my cellphone!" she exclaimed as she watched him keep it temporarily hostage.

"I know, and it looks like Kate has my interest in mind," he returned with a smile after reading the text.

"Clay, that text is none of your business!" she continued but this time with an attempt at getting her cellphone back.

"Uh uh, and based on what it says, I think it is," he begged to differ after reading Kate's text urging Tricia to either get his number or give him hers before she left his truck.

"Well, you already know that I'm not doing either of those two things, so you might as well just give me back my cellphone," she reminded him then held out her hand.

"Ya do realize that I could just as easily program my number into it right now, right?"

"Yes, and if you do, I'll just delete it the second I get the chance."

"Ooh, you're gonna make me really work for a date, aren't ya?" he asked with a grin as he kept her cellphone away from her.

"Clay, you might as well just forget about it because you won't ever be able to get me to say yes to you. You may be persistent when it comes to asking me the question, but I'm just as hardheaded when it comes to my answer," she informed him, grabbing her cellphone.

"That may be true for now, darlin', but you'll come to find that I'm one stubborn country boy," he returned with a smile that would make it hard for her to easily forget him.

Tricia found herself with her hand partially over his and his lips within inches from hers. She could hear her heart beating louder and faster. Clay Gibson was becoming a very dangerous man for her, and if she didn't escape now, her heart would be in serious trouble.

CHAPTER
- EIGHT -

Waking up hours later to the sun shining through her bedroom window, Tricia gazed out onto Newport Bay's coast. Her view of the glistening water helped keep her mind settled as she thought about her night with Clay Gibson. Sure, her time with him had been short-lived, but as she'd danced in his arms, he'd made her feel like she had finally found her very own Prince Charming, or at least, her temporary one.

"It just sucks that he's exactly the kind of man I've been longing for, but probably has more women than I can count just waiting for the chance to be with him," she complained aloud as she continued to stare out at the beautiful view.

As she watched beachgoers occupy the sand with their towels, umbrellas, and volleyball games while others took advantage of the salty waves with their boards and body surfing, she could definitely see how living in the hills had its perks. She had a view that most of the city's residents didn't have.

As she thought more about the scenery her parents' wealth had provided her with, she remembered Clay's job and how if she'd actually said yes to going out with him, she would finally have a chance at becoming a NASCAR driver's girlfriend. A label she'd often thought about after her dad had introduced her to the sport and she'd seen how hot some of the drivers were. The only problem with it was the fact that she wasn't the type to compete for a man's attention when she already knew how highly desired he was by other women. Though, if he kept at her like he had in his truck, then maybe her perception of just being another woman added to the list of the many already competing for him was wrong.

"God, why does he have to be the guy I desire when I already know that a relationship with him would be dangerous territory?" she asked with an unfazed look out at the ocean.

She just hated the fact that even though she was so against dating him, the way his blue eyes looked into hers told her that they knew how to capture her and keep her captured. She couldn't help but want to stare back at them as they played their own part in his mission to date her. Man, the way she'd felt while she danced in his arms, and then how he'd caught her after her unsuccessful first attempt at getting into his truck. His arms had given her such a sense of security as she felt the strength he possessed that she now had a taste for more.

"Damn it, why did everything about him have to make me end up wanting him so badly, despite the reality I know I'd face? I just hate the fact that he knew he could charm me whether I'd let him see me fall for it or not!" she continued with an annoyed shake of her head. "Well, at least I don't have to ever worry about seeing him again!" She looked at her alarm clock, telling her that it was time to get up and get ready for a day of shopping with her mom.

Feeling nothing but displeasure for that particular activity, she got out of bed and began to get ready. It wasn't until after she'd slipped on a new pair of underwear and fastened her bra that she found herself pausing when she passed by her full-length mirror. As she looked at herself, she fantasized about Clay standing right behind her and whispering into her ear with his sexy southern drawl. Then, as if to reenact his physical presence being so close to her, she placed her hands on the part of her body where his hands had caught her.

With her thoughts of him deepening, and her fantasies of them taking complete control of her mind, her actions of getting dressed ceased. She was now letting her imagination run wild as her fantasies of what he could do to her caused her to become stuck in a dreamlike state of mind where anything she pictured felt so real.

"Tricia, are you going to be ready to go soon?" her mother

asked with a knock on her door. The interruption brought her back to reality.

"Yeah, Mom, just give me a minute." She finished getting dressed by hurriedly putting on a pair of jeans, a graphic tee, and a pair of faded, navy-blue Converse.

Now ready to shop for her upcoming school year, she and her mom headed for her mother's silver Mercedes Benz SLK.

"Now, don't go having too much fun, you two!" her father called out as they passed by the family room where he was spending his Saturday morning watching a football game.

"Don't worry, Dad . . . at least I won't!" she called back as she followed her mother to her car.

As Tricia and her mom headed for the mall, she couldn't help but wonder what the odds were of seeing Clay again.

Kate laid on her bed thinking about her brief time with Bryan. She remembered looking into his brown eyes and couldn't believe she'd met a man who was not only crazy gorgeous but knew how to dress. If she'd been given the chance to pick her ideal man out of a catalog, Bryan Walker would've been it. His southern sophistication fit perfectly with her city-girl lifestyle. Sure, she'd lived in a beach town all her life, but she'd always imagined living somewhere with a faster pace. She continued with her delicious thoughts on the man and heard the familiar sound of her cellphone's ringtone. After looking at the display screen and seeing the unfamiliar number, she pressed the talk button to answer it. "Hello?" she asked, wondering if she should've just let it go to voicemail instead.

"Yeah . . . hi, is this Kate, Kate Bransin?" a male voice asked her.

"Yes, why? Who's calling?" she asked.

"It's Bryan, Bryan Walker . . . from The Cosmos Club," he finally announced.

"Oh, hey . . . I was hoping you'd call," she finally greeted with a much more relaxed tone.

"Well, I couldn't just let your number go to waste, now could

I?" he flirted as he stretched out on his bed to have what would hopefully be a very enjoyable conversation with her.

"No. I just wasn't expecting you to call me so soon."

"What can I say, Kate . . . you made an impression on me."

"Glad to hear it."

"I hoped you would be, but as you probably already know, there's another reason why I called you."

"Oh?" she asked as she continued to play along.

"Yes. In fact, I think it's one you'll be quite happy about," he continued, purposely dancing around the question.

"Bryan, just ask me out already!"

"Someone's a bit eager to be asked out," he teased, enjoying her take-charge attitude.

"Well, my night with you was very enjoyable. So, it only makes sense that I'd want to see you again," she explained after realizing that her comment had made her seem way too pushy toward him.

"And I'm definitely glad to hear you say that, Kate. So, with that being said, Kate Bransin, will you please go out on a date with me?" he finally asked.

"Yes, Mr. Walker, I would be glad to," she answered with a smile.

"So, when would you like this date of ours to be, Miss Bransin?"

"How does tomorrow night sound?" she asked with an overwhelming anxiousness to see him again.

"Sounds like it's not soon enough," he answered with his own natural charm.

"I think your charm is going to get me in trouble, Bryan."

"I hope it does, Kate." *I hope it does.* She gave him her address and the access code to the gate.

After he had written it all down, he hung up his cellphone, happy at the thought of getting to see her again.

"Now the only question left is . . . what should I wear?" Kate got off her bed to view her options.

Even though her date with Bryan wasn't until the next night, she wanted to get a head start in figuring out the perfect outfit to wear.

CHAPTER

- NINE -

"So you're seein' Kate tomorrow night, huh?" Clay asked Bryan as he swiftly worked the video game's controller while relaxing at Bryan's house.

"Yeah, I figured that after I pick her up from her place, we'd grab some Chinese takeout and then head back here for a romantic candlelit dinner and maybe a movie."

"Sounds like a nice evenin'."

"I thought it would be. Though, you do know that you're going to need to be gone when we get back here, right?"

"Don't tell me you're already gonna try and sleep with her on your first date unless, of course, ya only saw her as a one-night stand and nothin' else?" Clay asked with a glance in his direction.

"No, give me a little credit. I just want to be alone with her, that's all."

"Right. Well, I figured I'd just head back to my motorhome and make a midnight run 'round California Speedway's track anyway."

"Clay, why don't you just go out on a date with her friend instead? You and Tricia looked pretty good together out on that dance floor."

"She never gave me her number, and she made it clear that she wasn't going to ask me for mine," he answered with the memory of Kate's text message in his mind.

"Huh, I could've sworn she was into you."

"Oh, she is, but she's already made it abundantly clear that nothin's ever gonna happen 'tween us," Clay informed him while remembering the way she'd looked into his eyes and the hardheadedness she showed by not giving into her obvious attraction to him.

"Then what's the problem?"

"She thinks I've got way too many women after me, so she doesn't even wanna try and 'come a part of the competition," Clay answered with a shrug.

"Well, she does have a point, Clay. You do have a trail of ladies waiting for you. Heck, last night's sponsored dinner is proof enough of that."

"Yeah, so . . . I can't help it if all those women find me attractive. Besides, they're only in it for the perks my job'll give 'em. I bet ya that the majority of 'em could care less 'bout me and just wanna be spoiled by the money I make from it," Clay answered with annoyance.

"And I know you can't, Clay. I'm just telling you that your reality makes it understandable as to why Tricia's not going to just open her heart to you the second you ask her to."

"Bryan, while we were slow dancin', she told me that she's never had a boyfriend 'fore."

"Well, damn. Then you are definitely going to have a hard time in convincing her to date you."

"I know," Clay replied with a grin, anxiously anticipating the challenge.

"Clay, why are you so intent on getting her to date you when you've already got countless women who you don't even have to persuade?"

"Sometimes the challenge makes the chase worth it."

"Do you even have an actual interest in the girl, or are you just doing this because she told you no and you want to prove to Nikki that she made a bad choice?" he asked him flat out.

"Bryan, I'm only gonna tell ya this once, so don't ya dare bring up the subject again. My desire to convince Tricia to date me doesn't have a damn thing to do with Nikki, okay? I am not a petty man and would certainly never do that to a woman just to spite my ex!"

"Clay, now, you know that if *that* were true, you wouldn't be getting so damn emotional about it."

"Bryan . . ."

"Just wait. I know that you loved Nikki and had thought you were going to marry her, but that's over with. You need to get on with your life, Clay."

"And that's exactly what I plan on doin' with Tricia. Bryan, I'm gonna make her fall for me," Clay stated confidently.

"Damn it, Clay. Tricia's right to be cautious about you!" he exclaimed the moment he heard Clay's self-proclaimed mission for her heart.

"What the hell is that supposed to mean?"

"Clay, you can't just make the girl fall for you because you've got a bruised ego from your ex."

"Bryan, that's not why I would do it!"

"Sure it isn't. You're just so damn pissed off that Nikki didn't pick you over Logan that you can't help but want to prove her wrong. And you're going to do it by playing with an innocent girl's heart. Damn it, Clay . . . you ought to be ashamed of yourself!"

"Bryan, it ain't like that at all!"

"So you're telling me that you don't want to make Tricia yours just to spite Nikki?" he asked, giving Clay a skeptical look.

"Yes, well . . . damn it, I don't know!" Clay realized that the line separating his mission to make Tricia his and wanting to make Nikki regret her decision to leave him had become blurred.

"Then maybe that's something you need to figure out first, especially if you still plan on pursuing Tricia despite her already telling you no."

"Yeah, you're probably right." Clay sighed. He was all too aware of the mental torture his recent breakup was causing him.

"Clay, are you even attracted to Tricia, or do you just want her because she told you no?"

"Of course I am, Bryan. I wouldn't be goin' after her if I didn't find her so damn appealin'. Hell, just the way her hazel eyes looked into mine and how she felt in my arms is reason enough for me to wanna change her mind 'bout us so damn badly. And that part of it has nothin' at all to do with Nikki," Clay answered after thinking deeply about the real truth behind his feelings.

"Good, and I guess since she is so against dating you, you are going to have to pursue the hell out of her in order to get her to change her mind about you," he said after hearing the sincerity in his friend's voice.

"Tell me 'bout it. So do ya got any ideas as to how I can see her again, given that she wouldn't give me her number?" Clay asked when he realized that without Bryan's help, he wouldn't have a chance in hell of seeing her again unless God Himself made it a part of His plan for him.

"Yeah, I think I may know of a way," he answered with a smile and hoped that Kate wouldn't have a problem with him wanting to help Clay try and win her best friend over.

As the night became the backdrop for scheming, Logan met up with Reese and Tyler in his motorhome, hoping to avoid any late-night eavesdroppers. Now that the three were working together to kill Clay's racing career, they needed to come up with a foolproof plan that would make him question himself each time he got behind the wheel. The more they could screw with his mind, the better.

"So . . . Reese, Tyler . . . have either of you come up with anything?" Logan asked, desperately needing to hear them say yes.

"Besides messing with his head with some anonymous threats, we can tail him for a while," Reese offered.

"And you don't think he'd be smart enough to catch on?" Logan asked skeptically.

"Not if we do it for a brief period of time. I'm thinking just one or two weeks, and then match that with a threatening text, and voilà, Clay's questioning what the hell is going on and, ultimately, can't think straight during his next race," Reese explained.

"And you think that'll really work with him? Reese, this isn't some kind of crime drama on TV," Logan reminded him.

"I know that, and yes. Hell, just imagine if it was you. If you had someone tailing you every so often and then combined that with threats, wouldn't that mess with your head?" Reese replied.

"Yeah, I see your point," Logan replied.

"And honestly, he doesn't even have to be tailed for a whole week. Just two or three times and we'll have him watching his back even after we've stopped screwing with his head," Reese added.

"That sounds like it'll work," Logan agreed.

"Trust me, Reese and I'll have it covered," Tyler reassured Logan.

"Okay, so who will do what, then?"

"How about Reese and I figure that part out just in case someone finds out and rats on us?" Tyler suggested, leaving only him and Reese to know who would be responsible for which scare tactic.

"That sounds even better!" Logan easily agreed, happy to know that if the three of them did get caught, he wouldn't be able to say who did what when asked.

Later that night, as Logan crawled into bed as Nikki lay asleep, he gave her a quick kiss before lying on his back. With a deep sigh, he thanked God that with the help of Reese and Tyler, he would soon be able to prove his worth to Nikki and that she hadn't been wrong in choosing him over Clay.

CHAPTER

- TEN -

"Did you get Clay's number, or give him yours . . . like I texted you to do?" Kate asked Tricia as Kate pulled possible outfits from her closet to wear on her date with Bryan.

"No."

"And why not when we both know that he's your type?"

"Because I don't want to have to deal with the mess of women who already want him."

"Seriously, Trish? That's your reason for saying no to anything with him?"

"Hey, it doesn't have to be good enough for you, just me. Besides, it's the truth. I don't want to put myself out there for him when I know that I'm only one of many."

"But he's everything you've ever wanted in a guy . . . and you're willing to say no to that just because you're afraid of a little competition?"

"Kate, I'm not afraid. I'm just not willing to compete for his attention. I'd rather just meet a guy who doesn't already have a lot of women wanting to be with him."

"Are you sure that's not just your Asperger's giving you an excuse? I know you were always worried about how it would affect your relationship with a guy if you met someone you were really interested in."

"No, Kate, I really just don't want to be added to the list of women who already want to be with him."

"Even though, by the way he acted around you at the club, you'd be at the top?"

"Even though."

"Well, I suppose that's your choice. I just hope you don't regret it in the end." Kate began comparing the outfits in her full-length, three-way mirror.

"And I won't," Tricia replied with a façade of confidence. *Or at least, I hope I won't!* She glanced at Kate in the mirror and remembered her fantasies of her and Clay in her bedroom.

"Good, now what do you think about this dress?" Kate asked as she held up a short, black-and-white floral print dress with pink spaghetti straps that had a pink sash around the waist that tied in the back.

"I think it'll look very cute on you."

"Good. I figured I'd match it with my black pumps and the black headband with the flower on it."

"Sounds very flowery."

"I just hope Bryan likes it."

"I'm sure he will, Kate."

"Well, he's picking me up at seven, so you'd better go. I don't want to still be getting ready by the time he gets here."

"Okay. Well, have fun on your date, then," she said, taking her cue to head back home.

"Hi Clay. Tuning up your race car?" Nikki asked him as she approached him torquing something under the hood.

"Shouldn't ya be cheerin' on your boyfriend somewhere?" Clay answered as he kept to his work.

"Come on, Clay . . . we were friends for a long time before I was your ex," she reminded him.

As Nikki took in another hot day, she couldn't help but find herself attracted to the sight of Clay wearing his white T-shirt without his usual plaid overshirt. The man was hot, and the way she watched his biceps move with each turn of the wrench made him even hotter.

"Ya mean 'fore ya cheated on me?"

"Clay, you know I already told you how sorry I was for that."

Lessening the distance between them, Nikki couldn't help but feel regret for ruining what she'd had with him. If she had just held back her desire for sex, she could've still been the woman on Clay's arm, enjoying the spotlight with him.

"Honestly, Nikki, it doesn't even matter anymore." He stopped his tune-up when he realized that their conversation was making it hard for him to concentrate. "Ya chose to be with Logan, so that's the end of it."

"But does it honestly have to be? Clay, you and I had a great thing. We complimented each other so well."

"Nikki, what the hell are ya doin'?" he asked as he watched her seductively walk over to his side of the car.

"You know, I could break up with Logan, and we could try and make it work again." She slid her arms around his waist, giving him a hug.

"And why would I wanna do that when ya already know I'm not gonna sleep with ya if we did?"

"Because I miss you, and I miss what we had, Clay. You know me so much better than Logan does. Hell, you know me better than any man could."

"Nikki, what's this really 'bout?" he finally asked, removing her arms from his body.

"Last night, after I'd made Logan take me to The Cosmos Club, I saw you dancing with some brunette, and it made me nostalgic."

"Ah, so you're jealous now?"

"No, you can dance with whomever you want," she lied. "I just remember how it was with us. How just the feel of your body pressed up against mine was an instant turn on."

"But that's over now. Ya've moved on, and I need to too." He stayed rigid as he watched her maneuver around him to block him from going back to working on his car.

"Are you telling me that you don't miss that too? That you don't miss the feel of my body in your arms or the way my lips felt against yours each time you kissed me?" She hoped her words would stir enough desire in him that he'd lose his concentration the next time he was on the track.

"No, but ya hurt me, Nikki. The day ya left me was the day

ya broke my heart, and that's not somethin' I'm 'bout to forget anytime soon."

"Even if I remind you of what we had?" She pulled him into an unexpected kiss.

Taken aback, Clay pushed her away. He couldn't believe that she would do something like that. The Nikki he'd known would've never forced herself on a guy. She didn't have to because she had a sweet disposition about her that made them come crawling to her. Unfortunately, that was the Nikki he'd known before he'd become a racer.

"Damn it, Clay, you're supposed to be mine!" she exclaimed when she realized that her kiss hadn't done what she'd intended.

"Nikki, you chose to cheat on me. You're the one who decided to end our relationship, not me!"

"I know, and I was a complete idiot for that . . . I'm well aware."

"Then ya should also know that it means we're done. No second chance."

"But why, Clay?"

"It's the same reason I'm no longer friends with Logan. I don't trust ya."

With a huff of defeat, Nikki pushed Clay out of her way and headed back to Logan's motorhome. Shaking his head at the woman he no longer knew, Clay finished up with his car before returning to his motorhome.

As Tricia got ready to spend an evening at home, she changed into pajama pants and added the comfort of slippers to her sock-covered feet. She then headed downstairs for a much-desired cold snack. Once in the kitchen, she grabbed a pint of her favorite ice cream—cookies and cream—and a spoon. She then parked herself in front of the TV, where she planned to spend the rest of the night devouring the cold deliciousness and watching a Saturday night movie.

With her legs stretched out on the coffee table, her ice cream on her lap, and her spoon ready to bring the ice cream's tastiness to her mouth, she turned on the TV and began flipping through the channels. As she continued to look for a decent, not yet seen flick, she heard the doorbell ring. Curious to see who it was, she set the remote on the couch and the ice cream container with her spoon inside on the coffee table.

"Be right there!" she called out as she made her way to the front door. She got closer to the door to see who it was through its leaded glass. *What the? No way . . . it can't be . . . he doesn't even know where I live!* she thought to herself when she saw a man dressed similarly to Clay.

The man stood on her front porch waiting for her to open the door. All she could see was the top of his cowboy hat as he kept his head tilted toward the ground. *Could it really be him?* she wondered at the possibility. *Though, honestly, how many other guys in Newport Bay dress like Clay?* She realized that the chances of it being someone else were way too remote to even consider. "Hi, Clay," she greeted the second she'd opened the door and he'd lifted his head to look at her.

"Well, hello there, darlin'," he returned with a big smile. He looked down at her clothes to see that she was dressed for a night in.

Aw crap, I forgot, I have my pajama pants on! His scan of her body reminded her of her recent wardrobe change. Despite her being vehemently against dating the man, she definitely didn't want him seeing her in her pajama pants.

"Uh, what are you doing here, and how did you find out where I live?" She could feel her heart beating out of control and wished she'd had time to change into something more appealing.

"Simple, darlin', Bryan gave me Kate's code for the gate, and then he asked her for your address." He smirked.

"Oh, which means the security for that information is greatly lacking." She replied, immediately trying to cover her nervousness.

"Or that it was meant to be given out to just the right person," he countered, leaning an arm up against the doorframe.

Tricia was just glad she hadn't decided to take off her bra, as well, because that would've been even more embarrassing. "Clay, I hope you know that your being here is completely pointless. I already said no to a relationship with you, so you might as well just turn around and go back home," she reminded him, doing her best to keep her guard up despite the feelings his presence stirred up.

"And miss seein' ya in your T-shirt and pajama pants? Not a chance, darlin'." He shook his head with a grin, then scanned her body a second time.

CHAPTER

- ELEVEN -

U nable to stop from blushing, Tricia did her best to come up with a response. "You're lucky I'm not just shutting this door in your face."

"Aw, darlin,' ya know I'm just teasin' ya. Besides, I already told ya that I'm one stubborn country boy . . . so this is just me provin' my word," he reminded her with a sexy grin that only a country boy could pull off.

Imagining herself in one of her novels, Tricia briefly pictured herself pulling him into her house by his shirt as his sexy grin made her want to taste his lips. Realizing that that could only be a fantasy, she pulled herself out of it and gave in. "Fine. Come on in, then."

"Glad to hear it, darlin,' otherwise, I was 'fraid ya were gonna end up keepin' me out here till the sun came up." He thanked her with an appreciative tilt of his hat before removing it as she stepped aside.

Seeing his full head of black hair, enough for her to run her fingers through, kept her nerves on end. Tricia could just imagine messing it up as her lips got to know his. But it wasn't until after she had closed the door behind him and turned around that she was given an unexpected view of his butt. *Damn it, he's even got a nice round ass to look at!* she thought as his qualities continued to stack up on the pros.

"Ya've got a nice home, Tricia."

"Thanks, so now that you've accomplished your goal in getting into my house, Clay, what was your next objective?"

"Didn't really have one. I was just wantin' to spend more time with ya," he answered honestly.

"Wow, you must be a regular charmer with your female fans, based on that response," she replied as she felt his answer hit its intended target, her heart.

"Maybe, but my charm is always the truth."

"I think I'm going to regret inviting you in," she sighed. She knew he wasn't going to give up on fighting for her heart.

"Darlin', ya can definitely trust that I won't let that happen!" He headed for the source of the background noise he'd heard the moment she'd opened her door.

Feeling like her heart was about to pound out of her chest, Tricia followed him into the TV room. She couldn't believe that he was actually here. He wasn't just an illusion she was seeing from reading one too many romance novels.

"So what were ya watchin'?" He took a seat on the couch and placed his hat on the coffee table.

"I hadn't actually found anything yet. But you're welcome to it if you'd like." She offered the remote to him.

Not caring to watch TV, Clay said, "If ya'd like, I can wait for ya to change into somethin', and we can go out like I'd originally planned."

"Clay, I already told you that I'm not going to date you."

"Fine, then we can just order a pizza and see 'bout that movie."

"A pizza sounds good, I guess."

With a smile, Clay pulled out his cellphone. "Any place, in particular, ya want me to order from?"

"Pizza Hut and my favorite is a Hawaiian pan pizza."

"One Hawaiian pan pizza from Pizza Hut comin' up, then." He pulled up the website and put in the order. "And I'll even splurge on somethin' for dessert."

Smiling back at him, Tricia wondered if she could let her guard down just this once, and then after they'd finally said goodnight, she could be okay with never seeing him again.

"So now that I've got dinner and dessert ordered, did ya wanna find some candles to go with it?"

"I see you want to make this night as romantic as possible for us."

"Well, the candles would bring a glow to your face . . . not that ya need it since I think you're quite beautiful already."

Deciding to enjoy the night for what it was, Tricia leaned in and gave him a kiss on the cheek. She then followed it up by curling her legs against his.

"And here I thought ya were hellbent on resistin' me." Clay smiled as he returned the gesture with his hand on her leg.

"I'm having fun, Clay."

"Glad to hear it, though mind ya, we got forty-five minutes 'til that pizza guy gets here."

"Forty-five minutes is a long time."

"Then let me make it well worth it." He maneuvered her legs across his before returning his hand to her leg.

"Clay, we're sitting this close and we barely know each other."

"Then tell me 'bout yourself, darlin', and ya can start by tellin' me if ya were plannin' on havin' that ice cream as your sole dinner," he observed after glancing over at the partially melted ice cream.

"My mom, Sarah, just got back from a business trip, and she has yet to go grocery shopping, so I improvised," she shrugged.

"Where from?"

"Cleveland, Ohio. Her company's corporate office is based there."

"Ah, and what does she do?"

"She's the Learning and Development Manager for Sadlers. It's a top Fortune 500 consulting firm."

"Sounds impressive."

"It is, I guess. I'm just used to her being off on a business trip somewhere. It was a regular occurrence for me growing up, so I've learned to deal with her being gone every so often."

"And your dad?"

"My dad, James, is one of the top lawyers of Newport Bay."

"Ya sound like that was hard for you."

"Well, he spent a lot of my childhood focused so much on his career that I just felt like I wasn't as important sometimes."

I understand that all too well, darlin'. Thoughts of his dad's leaving flashed through his mind.

"But at least he got ya payin' attention to me," he smiled, briefly caressing her leg.

"True, he did," she returned. "But then when his caseload doubled, our father-daughter time decreased."

"I'm sorry to hear that. That must've been hard for ya to deal with."

"Ah, I got used to it. Growing up, I've had a housekeeper, a babysitter, and two au pairs, though the first stayed for only a day because she got too homesick."

"Wow, I guess it really does take a village to raise a kid."

"Honestly, Clay, I would've loved to have had it been just my parents the whole time. But with my dad so busy with his law firm and my mom on a business trip for a week or two at a time, that's how my life was."

"Still, it couldn't've been all that bad."

"And it wasn't, because of my mom's racked-up frequent flier miles, we got to go on a lot of family vacations that we otherwise wouldn't have."

Just as he was about to lean in and kiss her, the doorbell rang.

"I guess that means our forty-five minutes is up," Tricia smiled.

"Yep, as well as my cue to get out my wallet," Clay replied, removing his hand from her leg.

"While you do that, I'm going to go change out of my pajama pants," she informed him when she realized that even though she didn't want to pursue anything with him, she also didn't want to continue his view of her current loungewear.

"Sounds good to me. Though, just remember darlin', somethin' hot!" He winked as he watched her head up the stairs and out of his sight.

Returning to the TV room now wearing jeans, Tricia found Clay setting their food and a two-liter bottle of Diet Pepsi on the coffee table beside the ice cream.

"Ya sure know how to disappoint a man," Clay teased when he saw that she didn't even put in the effort to at least show off her legs.

"Sorry, jeans make me comfortable."

Whatever helps, I guess. He wondered if there was another reason why she hadn't chosen to accentuate her body more for him.

"Well, I'd say bon appétit, darlin', but considerin' we don't have any dishware or napkins, that may make it a little hard."

"Oh, no problem, I'll get them."

Tricia grabbed the needed items from the kitchen before rejoining him at the table.

"Did ya also wanna find those candles?"

"Nah, I think keeping the lights on will be better," she answered, not sure how much romance she was okay with, especially if she wasn't taking any of it seriously.

Realizing the pizza and the movie were the best he was going to get right now, Clay decided he'd just have to accept it.

They settled into their dinner and Clay returned to finding their entertainment. He came across a celebrity news channel that was talking about him.

"NASCAR Weekly's hottest bachelor, huh?" Tricia repeated what the host had said as the TV showed a picture of Clay from his fan "thank you" dinner.

"That was taken the day we met," he explained, thanking God it was just that picture and not one of the many ones he'd taken with Nikki. "Those were just some of the fans at the dinner."

"Clay, it's okay. I know it comes with the territory," she assured him as she watched him finish off a slice of pizza. *And that's also exactly why I don't want to date you,* she thought to herself.

"I appreciate that."

"You know, I think I'm glad you got the dessert too. These dunkers are good!"

"I can tell. Ya have a little of the chocolate still on your mouth."

Tricia ran a napkin over her mouth and looked at Clay for confirmation of her success. Unfortunately, she didn't receive it.

"Here, let me get that for ya," he offered, then closed the distance between them so he could easily wipe the chocolate off her mouth.

"Um, okay," she nervously agreed.

With a nod, Clay reached his hand up to her mouth and wiped off the remaining chocolate with his thumb. As if his first action hadn't been enough to elicit a response from Tricia, he brought his thumb up to his mouth and licked it off.

"Damn!"

"Mm, you're right . . . they are good," he agreed with a mischievous smile, licking his lips to hopefully push her over the edge.

"Thanks." Tricia couldn't help but feel dumbstruck as she stared back at him. As her eyes went from his to his lips, all she could think about was kissing him.

"And that, darlin', is the beginnin' of me seducin' ya," he informed her. Then, with a wink, he returned to picking out something to watch on TV.

CHAPTER
- TWELVE -

With dinner now finished and the desire for privacy just in case her parents came home unexpectedly early from their own date night, Tricia realized that the den would be her and Clay's best option.

"Since I couldn't find anythin' worthwhile for us to watch, did ya have a DVD we could watch instead?" Clay asked as he finished off his last dunker.

"Actually, my parents have a den," she informed him, gathering their trash and dirty dishes while he carried the uneaten food and soda into the kitchen.

"That sounds even better."

As Clay was about to follow, a package of bikini-style underwear caught his attention as he walked by the kitchen island. "Um, Tricia, is this yours?"

Turning around to see what he was talking about, she saw him holding the remaining package of underwear she had forgotten to put away after she and her mom had returned from shopping.

"Is this package of underwear yours?" he asked again, this time looking at her with raised eyebrows.

"I, um . . . must've forgotten them." She backtracked to take it from him.

"So this underwear is yours." He grinned, glancing at her jeans.

"Clay, just give me the damn package."

"Damn, and I was so hopin' I'd get to find out ya wore a thong," he teased with mock disappointment, snapping his fingers.

"Who says I don't? For all you know, that package could be just one kind I wear," she countered.

"I wouldn't mind findin' out," he challenged, calling her bluff.

"Clay, you know that's not going to happen. So please just give me back my underwear." She grabbed the package and tried to take it from him.

"Why, am I embarrasin' ya by doin' this?" he asked, looking into her eyes for a straight answer.

"No, but since I can't even the field by seeing what kind you wear, I'd rather just have you give it back to me so I can put it upstairs. Unless you're willing to let me guess?" she asked, slipping her free hand around the waistband of his underwear.

"Tryin' to make me loosen my hold, darlin'?" He grinned.

"Nope, just curious to see if I could figure out what kind you wear."

"Care to take a guess? Not that I'd actually tell ya if ya were right. I'd have to get to know ya better first for that." He was enjoying the competition.

"In that case . . . no."

"Damn, and I was so hopin' I would get to watch ya try and figure it out."

"Clay, just let me have them back so I can go put them away, and we can go watch that movie in the den."

"Aw, ya give up too easily, darlin'."

"You want me to fight for them, Clay? Fine, I'll give you a fight!" With one quick movement, she swiftly pulled her arm back and brought the package and his hand behind her back. "Clay, you were supposed to let go," she informed him now that the distance between them had vanished and her other hand was hooked around his neck.

"And miss this chance of my bein' close enough to kiss ya, I don't think so." He stood with his lips within inches of hers.

"Clay, I . . ." she began, unsure of what to say next.

"Now, Tricia, it's one thing for me to seduce ya with my charm, but when it comes to my kissin' ya, I've gotta ask ya first . . . so

65

are ya gonna say yes to my kissin' ya, or would ya rather me just let ya go, instead?"

With her heart racing at just the thought, she finally gave him her answer with a contented smile.

Smiling back, he closed the distance between them and kissed her lips. Feeling his hand cup her face, Tricia felt their chemistry ignite as his lips brought butterflies to her stomach.

"Now, aren't ya glad ya let me into your house?" he teased after slowly releasing his lips from hers.

"Yeah, I am." She forgot how she'd wound up in his arms in the first place.

As her racing heart steadied, she thought about returning her lips to his but then remembered their reason for going to the den. "You still want to go watch that movie?"

"Sure," he answered with a happy smile.

After showing Clay to the den, Tricia left him to pick out a movie from her family's extensive collection while she added the forgotten underwear to the rest she had already put away. When she had rejoined him, she found him staring at her dad's state-of-the-art sound system.

"So did you find a good movie for us to watch?" She was a little nervous now that they had kissed.

"Yeah, I haven't seen this one in a while." He handed her *The Little Rascals.*

"Nice choice. It's very funny and really cute." She took it from him and put it in the DVD player. "Did you want a snack, too, or did the dessert fill you up?" she teased with the remembrance of wanting to kiss him.

"A snack sounds good. What do ya have?" he answered with a knowing smile.

"Take your pick." She turned on a light that exposed a metal rack full of candy options and a personal popcorn machine to its right.

"Wow, your parents don't spare any expense, do they? First, the theater-sized screen, then the high-tech stereo system, and now, your own mini-concession stand. Man, your parents must want everythin' to seem like the real deal."

"Yeah, they liked the atmosphere of a movie theater so much

that they wanted to bring it home," she replied with a shrug, feeling used to it all by now.

"Well, ya've definitely given Bryan somethin' to be jealous 'bout." He wondered what Bryan's reaction to her parents' den would be.

"Good to know. Now, what snack did you want?"

"I'll just have whatever you're havin'."

Great, and what I want is at the very top. She looked up at the box of Musketeers, realizing that she would need something to stand on in order to get it. "Okay, no problem." She grabbed a nearby stool.

The next thing Clay knew, he was watching her take off her slippers and step onto the stool. "Do ya need any help with that?" he asked as he watched her shirt rise up a little as she stretched her arm up to get the two bars of chocolate. He couldn't help but stare at her gorgeous body as she showed off a little more skin than usual. It also didn't help that her jeans perfectly showed off the curve of her butt as she leaned her body toward the rack in order to get their last chocolate treat of the night.

"No, I'm good," she answered as she reached up a little higher.

"Okay, just let me know if ya need my help, then," he offered. He was enjoying seeing her body like this more than actually wanting to help her. Hell, if he had his way, they'd skip the movie, and she'd let him put his hands all over her instead.

"It's okay, I've . . . got it!" she assured him when she was finally able to grab the bars. But just as she did, she slipped, causing her to scream as she felt him catch her.

"Ya okay there, darlin'?" He watched her scared reaction slowly turn to a look of relief.

"Yeah, I think so." She took in what had just happened to her and thanked God that Clay had been there to catch her.

"Good, though ya seem to be fallin' into my arms quite a bit lately," he teased.

"It has only been twice, thank you very much," she replied, feeling the need to defend herself with the facts. "Once, with my first attempt in getting into your truck, and second, this time."

"Well, either way, you're makin' yourself out to be the world's clumsiest woman, or at least, the clumsiest woman I've ever met," he continued teasing as he kept his eyes focused on hers.

"Clay, I'm not clumsy!" she argued back.

"Does vertically challenged suit ya better, then?"

"I'm not that either!" she replied with a shove to his chest.

"Ooh, so now ya wanna try and hurt the guy who caught ya? Aren't *you* a well-mannered damsel in distress?"

"Please!"

"Well, you are hittin' me instead of thankin' me . . . which, by the way, are ya okay for me to set ya down now?"

"Oh, right, I had completely forgotten." She realized that her free hand was still holding onto him, while her other held their candy bars.

"Sure ya did."

"Clay, I did."

"Then why am I still holdin' ya, darlin'? Why do I still have yet to hear ya tell me to set ya down?" he challenged with another grin.

"Fine, you can set me down, then." She displayed an eagerness for getting out of his arms even though, deep down, she enjoyed it just as much as he did.

"So now that ya've gotten our candy bars, which, by the way, ya still have yet to give me mine . . . are we ready to watch this movie?" He sat back down on the couch.

"Yes, and here's your damn candy bar, Clay!" She tossed it at him.

"Ooh, feisty too," he returned with a grin that almost made her insides melt.

"You bet your ass I am, now scoot over so we can finally watch this movie." She took a seat next to him.

"Thank ya for the candy bar, darlin'." He moved his left arm to the cushion behind her.

"You're welcome, Clay." She offered an appreciative smile, snuggling up to his side as the movie's previews took their turn.

With his charm finally easing her into wanting him, Clay took in the nice feel of her body against his. He'd never had a woman feel so perfect against him as she did, and he couldn't help but think it a damn shame she was going to have to leave his side once the movie had ended. With the way her head rested against the crook of his shoulder and how her left hand played with a button on his overshirt, he felt like she was just the right fit for him. *Damn, she just feels so natural for me!* he thought as he moved his arm from the cushion to around her body.

Cuddling up to Clay's side felt so surreal to Tricia. She had never felt such peace as she sat curled up against him. Sitting with him in such an intimate way just felt so innate, and so right, that she hated knowing that once their movie was over, she would have to remove herself from the comfort of his side in order to put it away.

God, this feels so good! she thought as she kept her hand busy with a shirt button. As she did, she would glance up at him every so often to see his reaction to the movie or if he was trying to sneak glances at her too.

Tired of fidgeting with it, Tricia moved her hand to his undershirt. When she did she could feel his tight skin underneath. Clay's body felt so fit that she began to wonder what he looked like with his shirt off. Did he sport a very chiseled six-pack, or just slightly toned abs? Either way, her curiosity for the answer kept her mind busy with thoughts of him shirtless. But as she brought him and his hot body back into her fantasies, she watched him move his right hand from his side and intertwine it with hers.

Holy crap, what is going on here? she immediately thought to herself as his hand took on a whole new approach to his being intimate with her.

Just the way Clay's hand played with hers showed her that he wasn't taking any of this as lightheartedly as she was. He was serious about his intentions. Realizing that, Tricia had no idea what she was going to do. It was easy letting the romance happen when she thought it was all just for tonight, but with the way he caressed her side and how his fingers were now intertwined with hers, she was clearly wrong about that.

God, what am I going to do? Am I even ready for this, ready for this man? She continued sitting intimately with Clay in a way she had only ever imagined sitting with a guy. *And to actually feel a mutual attraction for him?* It all just scared the hell out of her. She couldn't help but think that reality had taken a vacation for the time being, and right now, before it returned, she needed to just enjoy being in his arms.

"Ya enjoyin' the movie, darlin'?" he asked, glancing at her.

"Yeah, Clay, I am." Her momentary thoughts switched gears to the scene being played out on the screen.

"Good, 'cause I am too." His caressing her side made him want to do so much more with her.

God had definitely blessed him when he saw her show up at her door in her T-shirt and pajama pants. Just the way the cotton material hung off her butt made him want to stick his hand inside and feel around. And now that she was wearing fitted jeans, well, damn!

With his attention now turned to her body, Clay ended up missing the rest of the movie. Not that it mattered, since the feel of her against him had already overridden his interest in the movie anyway. *I wonder if she'll let me kiss her again once this movie's over? It would certainly be a great way to end this spur-of-the-moment date.* He pictured pressing his lips against hers a second time.

After the last scene had ended and the credits had begun rolling, he got his answer. He wanted to kiss her again. Removing his hand from hers, he brought it up to her chin and gently brought their lips together for the second time that night.

His lips make me feel like I'm in a fairytale. Tricia felt Clay's lips on hers. This was a night she hadn't been expecting yet had turned into her dream come true.

Happy that he had followed Bryan's advice in pursuing Tricia, Clay felt a peace wash over him as their kiss ended. Tricia wasn't at all what he'd expected, but he was slowly finding out that she was everything he wanted in a woman.

Looking back at him, Tricia felt mesmerized by each kiss he gave her. As they waited in the moment for whatever was to come next, she once again let her reality fade from her mind when she realized she had a brief opportunity to break out of her shell. Defying her need to continue resisting him, she quickly straddled him.

Surprised, Clay watched her take control.

With a brief smile and an overwhelming desire for more

affection, Tricia brought her hands up to his face and began releasing some of her pent-up passion onto him with full force. But as her lips took in the unquenchable thirst that years of loneliness had left her with, she couldn't help but question what the hell she was doing. Yet, despite the alarm going off in her head, she kept her lips against his, taking in the feel of his facial hair underneath her fingers and the way his lips gladly accepted hers. She had never planned on making out with the guy, but that was exactly what she was doing, her hands free to mess up his hair in the process. It wasn't until she felt his hands on her sides that she was suddenly reminded of reality, instantly bringing their kiss to an end.

"Clay, I'm sorry . . . I just . . . I can't do this!" She stopped after practically attacking his lips with hers. "Even though I finally gave in to you by letting you give me my first kiss earlier tonight, me making out with you like I haven't seen you in forever . . . it's just not right, and it just isn't me. I don't know what the heck I was thinking!" She got off his lap and took a seat on the cushion next to him. Tucking her legs into her chest and resting her arms on her knees, she couldn't have felt more embarrassed.

"I gave ya your first kiss, huh?" Tricia was unlike any woman he had ever met before.

"Yeah, in fact, that was what I was about to tell you right before you asked me if it was okay," she answered with a shy smile.

"Had ya told me that 'fore I kissed ya, I would've had ya find me those candles so that I could make the moment more romantic for ya."

"Clay, it was plenty romantic with the way you held me in your arms and how it was so spontaneous. I'm just embarrassed that I returned it with such an aggressive kiss."

"Don't be, Tricia, 'cause your kiss showed me just how much ya long for the kinda relationship I wanna give ya. Everythin' 'bout it told me what your heart really wants despite your stubbornness to keep arguin' against it."

"I don't know. I guess I just wanted to take advantage of the opportunity. I just shouldn't've pushed it like I did," she replied, shaking her head at herself and still feeling ashamed for her actions.

"Tricia, we can definitely take it slow if that's what ya need. I have absolutely no problem with that." He realized that her desire to kiss him with such aggressiveness was because of her lack of experience with men. "Since this is obviously a new thing for ya, we don't have to make out like crazy, if you're not ready to." He placed a comforting hand on hers before returning his arm to the top of the cushion.

"Glad to hear it," she replied, despite still feeling extremely self-conscious for her sudden, and very forceful, actions.

"Though, I gotta admit, I definitely did enjoy it."

"I'm sure you did, even though it was a side of me that came out unexpectedly."

"Regardless, it definitely keeps me wantin' ya more and more." He caressed her arm. "Besides, your kiss just admitted to me what we both feel for each other since the moment we shook hands, and ya better believe that I'm not givin' up on that!"

"Clay, can't we just make this thing between us a one-time occurrence and go back to our regular lives tomorrow?" She hoped that this fairytale would end so her heart could get off its ride on the roller coaster of love.

"No darlin', your kiss just lit a fire inside me that can't be extinguished by just a one-time occurrence."

"Damn it!" she replied with the realization that this ride with him was far from over.

CHAPTER

- THIRTEEN -

"Kate, how could you let Bryan give Clay my address?" Tricia asked her the second Kate answered her cellphone.

"Trish, he simply asked me what it was. I can't control who he gives it to, though I'm glad he did."

"How can you say that?"

"Because you now have a chance at a real romance."

"But why does it have to be with him, Kate? Why can't my first boyfriend be someone whose career isn't majorly supported by a female fan base and who I don't have to worry about missing so damn much when he's out on the road racing?" she asked defeatedly.

"Trish, you should be thrilled that you met someone like him. A man who possesses all of the qualities you want in a guy."

"And normally, I would."

"Then what's the problem?"

"He's a celebrity, Kate."

"So . . . they want love too."

"I know that . . . but him with me?" she pressed. She still couldn't wrap her mind around a guy of Clay's status wanting to pay attention to her.

"Trish, I think that's something you need to tell him."

"Damn it, I can't believe this is happening to me!"

"What, that you like a guy who's a famous NASCAR driver?"

"No, that I made out with him last night, and now he probably thinks that our kissing solidified my want for a relationship with him."

"You made out with him?"

"Yep. The man gave me my first kiss, and then at the end of the night, I returned the favor by making out with him."

"Wow, Trish. When you get in the game, you certainly don't take much time to warm up."

"I didn't mean to, Kate. It just sort of happened, and now, Clay probably thinks that I'm all gung-ho for us having a relationship."

"So does that mean you don't want to be with him, then?"

"Damn it, I don't know."

"Great, now I'm confused."

"Tell me about it."

"And you know what that means, right?"

"Yeah, now I've got to talk to him about it."

"Good, now at least that part is all cleared up," Kate joked.

"Very funny. Now the only problem I have is how to get in touch with him."

"Don't tell me that after you had rushed your lips to his mouth, you forgot to ask him for his number?" Kate shook her head.

"Yeah, I guess by the time he had left my house, neither of us were thinking about that."

"Then I guess you're in luck," Kate replied, knowing that he and Bryan were currently downstairs in her family's TV room checking out her father's new, high-tech stereo system he just had installed.

"Why do you say that?" Tricia asked, suddenly feeling her heart begin to speed up.

"Because he's here, Trish."

"Wait, what?"

"Bryan wanted to check out my CD collection, as well as bring over some of his. We both liked the soundtrack to the movie we watched last night, so he wanted to compare tastes. As for Clay, once I had told Bryan about my father's top-of-the-line stereo equipment, he told Clay, and I guess Clay was so impressed by your dad's setup that he wanted to check out my father's too."

"Oh."

"Trish, you haven't told him about your Asperger's yet, have you?"

"No, why?"

"Because that might help him better understand your hesitation."

"Kate, it's not just about that."

"Then you can tell him what it's about when you bring your butt over here."

"But, Kate."

"Tricia, the second I get off this cellphone with you and let him know it was you I was talking to, don't you think he'd be hurt if I didn't tell him you were coming over? That alone would give him a mixed message about your time together last night."

"Yeah, I suppose it would."

"Good, see you in five, then." Kate immediately hung up so Tricia wouldn't have the chance to change her mind.

Mentally preparing herself for admitting her real hesitation for the relationship Clay kept pressing her for, Tricia thought back to how she'd felt each time he'd kissed her. Despite her fear of the unknown, her feelings told her that she wouldn't stop desiring another kiss from him. Clay was offering her a chance at a real relationship, something she'd wanted all her life. Now the only question was: could she put her fears aside to let herself finally experience the kind of romance she'd only been a third wheel to, or would she give in to the unknown and, consequently, let herself lose out on what could potentially be one of the greatest gifts God had ever given her?

"Are you guys enjoying my father's sound system?"

"Yeah, your father definitely gives Bryan somethin' to work up to," Clay answered.

"Hey, my system's pretty good," Bryan retorted.

"True, but it ain't the best," Clay returned.

"Glad to see my father gives you something to shoot for, Bryan, and it'll certainly give me another reason to want to come over to your house."

"Uh, should I give you two some time alone?" Clay asked.

"No, but what you should do is prepare yourself for Tricia, because she's on her way over."

"She is?" Clay asked.

"Yes, and she needs to talk to you."

"'Bout what, is everythin' okay?"

"Clay, that's something she has to tell you . . . it's not my place." They heard the doorbell. "And that must be her."

I could've sworn things were good 'tween us when I'd left her house last night. Clay watched Kate leave the room. Her words had been so cryptic that all he could do was wait until Tricia told him what was going on.

But after hearing Tricia's voice the second Kate had opened her front door, he knew that her heart was worth fighting for.

"Hey, Trish, come on in," Kate greeted.

"Hi. Where is he?" she asked nervously. All Tricia wanted to do right now was cry from the stress.

"He's in the TV room with Bryan. They're like kids in a candy store looking over my father's new sound system."

"He's probably comparing it to my dad's."

"Yeah, I got the distinct impression he wants Bryan to upgrade his," Kate agreed, stepping aside for her to come in.

"Maybe I should just have you get his number for me, and then I can talk to him about it later."

"Tricia, that wouldn't be fair to him, and you know that. Now go!" Kate replied.

With a deep breath, Tricia followed Kate's command as she headed for the man whose sole objective was to get her to date him. Following Bryan and Clay's voices as they continued scrutinizing the stereo equipment, Tricia braced herself for seeing Clay again. But the closer she got, and the more she heard his southern drawl, Tricia realized that this conversation was going to be hard on both of them.

"Clay, can I talk to you?" she asked as she entered the room.

Clay nodded. "Sure thing, darlin'. Is everythin' okay?" Both he and Bryan had turned to look at her.

Leaving Bryan to continue checking out the sound system, Clay slipped a hand into hers. "Where would ya like to talk, darlin'?"

"Outside's fine, I guess."

"Outside it is." He slipped his hat back onto his head. He

then led her out to the Bransin's backyard, where the romantic ambiance of a porch swing right in the midst of a reddish-orange and yellow sunset and the glow of the pool's light awaited them.

Letting go of her hand to offer her a seat on the porch swing, Clay sat down next to her. Automatically, he stretched out his arm on top of the cushion as they got comfortable.

"Comfortable enough?" she teased as she watched him rest his foot on his opposite knee.

"Pretty much," he answered with a simple smile. "The question is, are you comfortable?"

As comfortable as I can be for what I'm about to tell you, she thought to herself.

"Enough," she answered, drawing her legs up to her body before turning to face him.

"So what was it ya wanted to talk to me 'bout?" Clay couldn't help but wonder if she was about to give their relationship the green light or put an immediate stop to it with an unwelcome red one.

"I'm scared, Clay."

"You're scared? Scared 'bout what, darlin'?"

"This."

"But why?"

"Because, as I told you before, you would be my first boyfriend. That is, if we even get to that point."

"I remember."

"Right. Well, there's more to it than that."

Slightly adjusting his body to look at her head on, Clay waited for the rest.

"You've heard of Autism, right?" Clay nodded. "Well, have you ever heard of something called Asperger's Syndrome?"

"No, not really."

"Well, that's what I was diagnosed with when I was a sophomore in high school. It's also called High Functioning Autism. Basically, it's a learning disorder that also affects a person's understanding of social cues."

"Ah." Clay now understood. *It was the reason why she didn't change into somethin' sexier for me last night. She didn't realize that that was what I was expectin' her to do.*

"Yep. So, what most people get when it comes to what's socially appropriate, I don't."

"It's okay, Tricia, I get it."

"But do you really, Clay? This is something I've had to deal with my whole life, and I don't even always get it. I feel like I'm always having to learn what everyone else already knows."

"Yeah, Tricia, I do. Your Asperger's is what makes ya unique."

"You can definitely say I'm that," she responded with a smile.

"Darlin', I hope ya realize that your syndrome doesn't deter me from wantin' to date ya."

"And I appreciate that, but there's a part two to this conversation."

"Oh?"

"Yep, it's the other reason why this, you and me, is so hard for me to really accept as reality." Finally, she was ready to tell him about her childhood.

CHAPTER

- FOURTEEN -

As Tricia took a moment to figure out the right words, she couldn't help but think about how surreal it was that she was actually going to be having this conversation. She'd only ever imagined how the guy would respond as the dialogue played out in her head.

"Clay, growing up, I was bullied," she bluntly started. "From elementary school to high school, my classmates treated me like I was their emotional punching bag."

"Wow, Tricia, I'm so sorry." He wanted to take her into his arms and apologize for every person who had treated her less than her worth.

"Thanks," she replied with a faint smile. "I would've loved to have had a guy like you around to have stood up for me."

"And ya can bet that pretty ass of yours I would've."

"In fact, that was something I had constantly prayed to God for. I don't think there was ever a day that went by that I didn't wish that my Prince Charming would come rescue me from my life." Her tears began to fall.

"Aw, darlin'." Clay removed the distance between them and held her.

"Unfortunately, that's not all I have to tell you," she continued.

"Go on then."

"After all of those years of emotional abuse where I would literally cry myself to sleep at night, I wanted to kill myself."

Hearing Tricia talk about suicide left Clay speechless. As poor as he had been growing up, taking his own life had never been a thought he'd ever contemplated. But to hear Tricia admit to hating life so much that it had been a serious desire at one point broke his heart.

"Clay, Kate doesn't know about this part of my life."

"I understand."

With a deep breath, she went on. "The reason why you scare me so much is because I've never had my feelings for a guy returned. When I told my first crush about my feelings for him, his friends made fun of me for it."

It felt like it was just yesterday as Tricia relived the moment in her mind. Despite Clay's effort in ridding her of her tears, more came.

"Clay, that first crush was just the start. That pain was followed up with two other guys asking me out as a joke."

"Wow, I'm truly sorry ya had to deal with that kinda stupidity."

"Those are just two examples. From my childhood until I graduated high school, that's how I was treated. I had few friends, especially at school, and going to sleep at night became a blessing and a curse."

Seeing the odd look on Clay's face, she realized that she needed to explain.

"Bedtime meant I could use my dreams to escape my life, but then I realized that I would eventually have to wake up to face another day."

"Ah."

"Yep, and the really sad part about it all was that I think I was treated so cruelly because of my Asperger's. Because my peers didn't understand me, and I didn't understand me, I grew up thinking I wasn't worth it and that there was something wrong with me."

"All I can say is that I'm sorry, Tricia. No kid should ever be made to feel that way. Ya were robbed of your childhood."

"Yeah, I was . . . but all of that is why dating you terrifies me."

"And I get it, ya were put through hell and never got to experience a guy actually carin' 'bout ya."

"When you grow up with the message that you're not good

enough, only to be told you're beautiful once you get to college-age, the damage has already been done."

"I completely understand that, Tricia. But the thing is, I still wanna be with ya. Neither your syndrome nor this other fear of the unknown makes me wanna give up on pursuin' somethin' with ya."

"Clay, maybe we can just have fun while you're in town?" she offered. Her fear wouldn't release its hold on her that easily.

"No, I wanna date ya. I wanna get to know ya."

"But why can't we just enjoy the physical with each other? Why does this need to become a full-blown relationship for you?"

"'Cause my emotions are already there. That, and I'm not the friends-with-benefits type."

"I just don't know if I can do this."

"Tricia, we'll take this relationship as slow as ya need. As I told ya 'fore, I have no problem with that."

"I just . . . I just don't know, Clay."

"Well, how 'bout this, then? We go out on just one date. That's all I'm askin' from ya right now. Just one date. Then when that date's over, ya can decide."

Hearing Clay plead for her to go out with him was a new experience for her. As she considered his request, it dawned on her that his words were telling her just how different he was from the guys she'd grown up with. "Okay, I'll give you one date."

"Thank ya, darlin', and I'll definitely make it one date where you'll feel nothin' but romanced."

"You sound as if you're well versed in that department." She figured he probably had plenty of relationship experience.

"My mama taught me how to romance a woman."

"Did she now?"

"Yep, and one thing that would definitely help me is if ya would give me your number," he grinned.

"I suppose I can do that," she replied with a smile.

Taking out his cellphone, Clay added her name and number to his contacts. As he put his cellphone back into his pocket, he briefly wondered if he should give her his number. But right as he was about to mention it, Tricia maneuvered herself in his arms so that she could comfortably go back to watching the sunset paint the sky with its array of colors before it turned dark.

"Kinda feels perfect right now, doesn't it?"

"Yeah, it does."

Taking a moment for another kiss, Clay gently connected their lips again. Despite the tears that had been fueled by Tricia's life story, Clay had been given an unexpected romantic end to his evening.

"By the way, what is that flavor that tastes so good?" he asked after licking his lips.

"My watermelon chapstick." She took the tube out of her pocket and showed it to him.

"Hm, ya must've wiped it off with your napkin 'fore we kissed last night."

"Probably."

"Well, I'm sure glad I got to taste it now, 'cause it certainly does add to the already sweet taste of your lips."

"Being a charmer must be your M.O., Clay."

"It is second nature to me, darlin'."

"I can tell; it just slips off your tongue so easily."

"Good thing I have your number, then."

"Why's that?"

"'Cause now I'll be able to charm ya even when I'm out on the road."

"Please don't make me think about that right now. I just want to enjoy this sunset with you."

"Sounds good to me."

Clay couldn't have been happier. He had Tricia back in his arms and a green flag for their first date.

CHAPTER

- FIFTEEN -

As the sunset faded into darkness, Clay noticed that Tricia had fallen asleep. Seeing her serene face as she rested in his arms made him hate the fact that he was going to have to wake her up. But right as he was about to whisper for her to wake up, Bryan knocked, causing her eyelids to open.

"I've been told it's time for me to go, darlin'," he whispered as he watched her break free from her sleepiness.

With an understanding sigh, Tricia was freed from his arms as they headed back inside. Walking to the front door, Clay followed Tricia out, leaving Bryan the time to say goodbye to Kate.

"Bryan, I'm gonna walk Tricia back to her house. I'll be right back." Clay slipped his hand back into Tricia's.

Feeling the warmth of his skin against hers, Tricia couldn't help but enjoy the feelings Clay gave her. He was so smooth with his actions, yet so gentlemanly at the same time.

As they reached her front door and she put her hand on the doorknob, Clay paused. "Tricia, did ya want my number too?" He felt nervous with her for some reason.

"Um, I can just get it from you when you call me."

"Yeah, I suppose that'll work too."

"Well, goodnight, Clay." She prepared to go inside.

"Hold on a minute, I'm not finished." He stopped her, pulling her to him.

"Did you forget something?"

"Yeah," he answered, keeping her close to him. "A kiss."

With a smile, she removed his hat as she wrapped her arms around his neck. Within seconds, his lips pressed against hers. He took his time with a sensuous kiss.

"Mm, the only thing you were missing with that one was your tongue," she pointed out with a smile once he had slowed their kiss down before ending it.

"Eventually, darlin'."

"Goodbye, Clay." She put his hat back on his head.

Watching her go back inside, Clay felt like he was already falling in love. Despite the fact that he and Tricia had only known each other for such a short time, he couldn't help but feel like he was already hooked on her.

"I see that whatever Tricia needed to talk to you about resulted in a good ending for you both," Bryan said as he watched Clay get into his truck.

"Yeah, I finally got her to agree to go out with me," he replied as Bryan drove them back to his house.

"Glad to hear it. Now what about Nikki?"

"What 'bout her?"

"Are you over her to the point of being able to start something with Tricia?"

"Yeah. The Nikki we grew up with is long gone, Bryan. When I'm with Tricia, she stirs a want inside me like no other woman has."

"What do you mean 'the Nikki we knew is long gone,' Clay?"

"I mean that she's done a whole one-hundred-eighty-degree turn with her personality. Bryan, she forced herself on me right 'fore I got ready to go over to Tricia's last night."

"Wow, that does sound like a whole other person."

"Exactly. Hell, she tried to convince me to give us another shot. She acted like she still held a flame for me."

"Huh, I wonder what this sudden interest in you is all about?"

"Honestly, I have no idea, and I don't wanna know."

"You don't think she changed her mind about leaving you for Logan, do you?"

"Don't know, but I wouldn't be spendin' all this time tryin' to win Tricia's heart if there was even the slightest chance I'd wanna take her back."

"And here I thought you'd be more heartbroken over Nikki."

"And for a while, I was, till I saw how much she'd changed. I don't know what happened to the Nikki I dated, but apparently, whatever it was made her a much better fit for Logan."

"And yet you were the one she had chosen to date first."

"That's 'cause she didn't know I was wantin' to wait 'til marriage, unlike Logan."

"So she tried to seduce you into you taking her back? That doesn't make any sense at all."

"No, it doesn't, especially since I won't change my mind on waitin'."

"I feel bad for Logan, then."

"Yeah, well maybe that's what he oughta expect from her if she's willin' to cheat on me with him."

"Maybe, or maybe there's something else going on."

"Like what, Bryan?"

"I don't know. The whole Nikki coming onto you thing just sounds suspicious."

"Maybe she actually does regret cheatin'?"

"I highly doubt it. Clay, you two were together for four years. Hell, I went with you to pick out the ring. Why would she keep screwing Logan for the last two of it, if deep down she regretted it?"

"Good point. I'm just glad I never actually got down on one knee and asked her."

"She would've probably just told you no, and then that would've been the end of your relationship."

Imagining that being the case, Clay thanked God that he hadn't gone that far with his proposal. He'd barely thought out what he was going to do the day she'd dropped the news on him. Fortunately, the jewelry store was all too happy to refund the purchase when he'd told them the reason for the return. He was also immensely happy that he was able to keep it out of the public's knowledge. That would've been all he needed, a headline that read "Rookie NASCAR Driver Clay Gibson Gets Cheated On and Dumped by Girlfriend for Another Driver *After* Proposing."

Happy that he could still save that moment for when the girl, and the time, was right, Clay's thoughts were brought back to Tricia and the last kiss they'd shared. Now that she knew he wanted to date her, he found himself nervous just thinking about going on their first date. Tricia was a surprise for him. Even though she was a beginner at being in a relationship, Clay felt refreshed by her natural intimacy.

Damn, I can't wait to taste that watermelon chapstick on her lips again! He remembered the way her soft lips felt against his and heard his cellphone vibrate. It was another blocked text.

Clay – that kiss you gave that brunette looked hot. Too bad she didn't pull you inside for more!

"Uh, Bryan, we got a problem!" Clay stated after realizing he and Tricia had been watched.

"What's wrong, Clay?"

"I got another text from a blocked number. But this time, the person's not threatenin' me, they're stalkin' me!"

"Damn it! Do you at least have an idea as to who it might be?"

"Maybe Logan, but since I made it clear to Nikki that the interest is gone, there would be no point for that."

"And I have absolutely no idea who else it might be. So, we're back to square one."

"Bryan, ya don't think that maybe Nikki's lied to Logan and told him that I want her back, do you?"

"Would there even be a point for her to do that?"

"Not that I know of, but then again, the girl is full of surprises these days, so who knows if she's playin' us against each other."

"Does Logan even know where Tricia lives?"

"How could he when he doesn't even know 'bout her?"

"Then obviously there's someone else who's got it out for you."

"Crap, what the hell am I supposed to do? If I mention this text to Tricia, it's gonna damn sure scare her off. But if I don't, it's gonna make me have to start bein' more cautious 'round her, and that's gonna make her start askin' questions."

"It sounds like you're in a hell of a no-win situation, Clay."

"You're damn right 'bout that!"

CHAPTER
- SIXTEEN -

After pulling his truck into his driveway, Bryan turned off the engine. Clay got out of the passenger seat, leaving barely enough time for Bryan to pull the key out of the ignition.

Clay couldn't believe it. No one had ever tried to mess with his life like this before. As far as he was concerned, no one had a reason to. He'd never cheated in a race, and he'd never bashed anyone for their driving. He simply drove the best way he knew how—aggressively. Though maybe that was the problem right there. Maybe he was too aggressive. But it was NASCAR. If you wanted to win, you had to prove yourself worthy. You couldn't just expect other drivers to give you the win, so how the heck else was he supposed to drive?

Feeling tortured by his dilemma, Clay waited for Bryan to get out of his truck and unlock the door. Clay immediately headed for the fridge with the intent of using a cold beer and the TV to distract his mind from this second blocked text.

Pausing by the answering machine to check his messages, Bryan dropped his keys in a bluish-green clay bowl he had made as a kid in art class. As he listened to the requests to be called back, the last message got his attention.

"Welcome home, Bryan. I sure hope you enjoyed helping Clay get his hands on that hot brunette." Bryan froze, his eyes widening in alarm as he listened to the camouflaged voice.

"Oh, you didn't know I knew anything about her, did you?

Well, I do. So, you'd better make damn sure that your driver starts watching his back from now on. It'd be a shame if his new girl had to watch his career go up in flames. Well, have a good night, Mr. Walker, and please, don't forget to share my message with Clay."

"Shit!"

Whoever was stalking Clay also knew Bryan's personal number. Not only that, they knew how to stay anonymous.

"Damn it!" was all Bryan could think to say as he found himself becoming personally involved. "Clay, you're going to want to listen to this message."

Clay listened as Bryan played back the message. Mentally using the wall to destroy Bryan's answering machine, Clay headed back to the couch in defeat.

"Who the hell hates me so much that they've resorted to threatenin' me and someone I care 'bout?"

"Sorry to sound like a broken record, but I don't know."

"Then can ya at least tell me how to deal with all of this so that I don't have my sponsor backin' off of me?"

"Clay, as long as you keep this mess to yourself, that won't be an issue. But as for Tricia . . ."

"Don't tell me you're gonna tell me how to handle datin' her as well."

"Yep, and you're not going to like my answer."

"Why not?"

"Because it means not dating her."

"Bryan, I can't do that. We just agreed to go out on a first date. Ya can't expect me to slam on the brakes now, especially after I got her to agree."

"Clay, I know all of that, but I also know that if you deal with the threats first, then you don't have to worry about Tricia possibly being collateral damage if whoever's messing with you decides to use her to do it."

"So ya want me to tell Tricia that a first date just won't fit into my schedule right now?"

"If that's the best excuse you can give her that'll still leave the door open a crack, then yes."

"Bryan, I know you're just lookin' out for me, but as I told ya 'fore, I just can't. I can't kill any chance we might have together by postponin' our first date for a future date that may never come."

"Fine, then you'd just better be damn careful."

"I will."

$$\sim$$

With the headlights off on her dark green, Jaguar F-TYPE, Nikki disappeared from Tricia's gated neighborhood, speeding away the second she passed the gate. After following Bryan's truck to the gated community, she had stayed behind until someone else had allowed her access. She couldn't believe it; Clay already had his arms around another girl. Instead of remaining the lonely victim of her cheating, he'd actually replaced her.

"How could he do this to me? What the hell is he thinking?" she asked, hitting the steering wheel with her fist.

Clay wasn't supposed to move on. He was supposed to stay pining for her until she got tired of Logan and wanted Clay back. After all, why wouldn't Clay want her back when she was Nikki Reids, the best he was ever going to have?

At least, that was what her mom had always told her. As Nikki contemplated how she could prevent Clay from moving on with his life, it dawned on her how much her mom's statement had impacted her.

Growing up, she had been the tomboy of the group. Despite being the only girl amongst Clay's friends, she had always been the one to prove she could hang with the boys. Secretly, Clay had also been her first crush. Though she'd never told anyone, especially when he'd grown into his looks, she still wanted him to be hers.

But then she had gone through puberty, and life changed. Her body took on the looks that got every guy's attention. Her black hair, emerald eyes, slender hourglass figure, and long legs made her a beauty all the guys wanted.

She was the most popular girl in school and learned she could use the attention to her advantage. Unfortunately, her popularity never translated into her and Clay dating. Instead, she found him more focused on his new interest in racing. That was until her mom saw his natural talent on the track displayed in a newspaper headline.

"Nikki, have you seen how well your friend Clay Gibson is doing now?"

"Yeah, Mom, I've even gone to watch him race a few times."

"Do you know if he has a girlfriend?"

"Nah, I think he's too concentrated on racing to be dating anyone right now."

"That's too bad. You know, with your good looks and Clay's success, you could become very well off."

"Mom!"

"What? You still like him, don't you?"

"Yes."

"So then, take advantage. Besides, your stepfather and I could use the help. Just think of what you being in the spotlight could do for us."

It was like her mom had used the words that had opened the door to her future. From that point on, Nikki began dressing in a way that would no doubt get Clay's attention. With her figure-flattering outfits, she became overly interested in his racing and easily went from just childhood friend to girlfriend. Nikki watched as his social symbol elevated her status just like her mom had said.

Being on Clay's arm was now a regular event for her. His celebrity gave her an unquenchable thirst for the spotlight. She reveled in being his arm candy but realized it wasn't enough. She wanted Clay to take her to bed. She wanted to feel him work her body in a way that left her breathless. Unfortunately, as their relationship turned serious, she found that his insistence on waiting for marriage wasn't going to change.

Despite countless attempts at trying to seduce him, she couldn't get him to give in. Clay believed that sex only came with marriage, and she was definitely not ready to be tied down. At least, not without the reminder of a ring.

With that understanding now made crystal clear to her, she remembered Logan. Even though he wasn't as hot as Clay or as skilled behind the wheel, he was still an option. She could keep dating Clay while she slept with Logan on the side, allowing her to stay in the spotlight with the added satisfaction of being sexually pleasured on a regular basis.

Had it not been for Logan growing a conscience, she could've kept both relationships going. Unfortunately for her, he lacked the balls to keep lying to Clay, bringing her cheating to a stop.

Driving back to Logan's motorhome, Nikki found herself with another mission. Not only was she going to boost Logan's career by destroying Clay's, but she was also going to put a serious dent in Clay's love life if he thought he could actually have a relationship with this new girl.

CHAPTER
- SEVENTEEN -

"Ladies and gentlemen, boys and girls, welcome to the Dannon 500 qualifiers at the California Motor Speedway. We at the California Motor Speedway would like to welcome everyone to today's qualifiers and remind you all to stop by the raceway's concession stands for a nice cold beverage or tasty treat while you watch your favorite driver do what he does best on this beautiful, Southern California day," welcomed the announcer.

"Clay, are you ready to be the pole leader?" Bryan asked as he came into Clay's motorhome.

"Do ya mean have I let this threatenin' text message mess get to my head?"

"Actually, I was just wondering if you were ready to go. I wasn't meaning mentally. Though, I guess you do bring up a good question. Do you think you can still race with all that's going on?"

"Bryan, I'm gonna have to. Till the person behind all this decides to either show me their identity or quit harassin' me, I'm gonna have to figure out a way to block it all out."

"That's only if you want to maintain the best advantage at the start of the race. But knowing your skill, you could still win even if you were put in as the last car," Bryan chuckled.

"Thanks for the confidence, but I honestly hope we figure out how to solve this mystery soon."

"Unfortunately, without any suspects, the answer to that equation looks very dim."

With a sigh, Clay prayed to God he could mentally focus on his task ahead. Otherwise, without success on the track, he'd start to lose his sponsors. If that happened, the end of his career in NASCAR wouldn't be too far down the road.

"Clay, maybe you should put your desire to be with Tricia on hold for now or at least wait until this whole mess has blown over."

"I can't do that, Bryan."

"Why not, when it could possibly be the key to keeping her safe?"

"I want her too much."

"But you don't want to put her life in danger, do you?"

"No."

"Then maybe you should just cool your heels for the time being and let this game of threats play out before you try to stir up a romance with her."

"Not gonna happen. I'm not gonna let this person control my life. I've finally convinced Tricia to give us a chance, and I'm not gonna ruin that by lettin' this person win."

"Even if that means ending it to keep her safe?"

"Even if. Hell, all else fails, I'll 'come her personal bodyguard," he declared. He knew that he had something with Tricia he didn't want to let burn out.

"Then whatever happens to her is on you."

"It sure is, and I'll be damned if I let whoever this bastard is harm her in any way."

"Clay, you really care about Tricia, don't you?" Bryan asked as he watched Clay get all fired up about protecting her.

Clay realized that he had never come close to being that passionate for Nikki during their entire relationship.

"Yeah, I do. There's just somethin' 'bout the way I get lost in her eyes . . . and her hardheadedness is so sexy it creates a cravin' in me for more."

"Sounds like she's really gotten your attention."

"Yep, and that's exactly why I can't give up on us for the sake of this bastard."

"Okay, then, you just maintain the pole position for Sunday's race, and I'll make some calls to see if I can finally end this."

Watching Clay head out of his motorhome dressed for racing,

Bryan grabbed his cellphone to see if he knew anyone who could help them. He felt like he'd suddenly transformed into Sherlock Holmes with his own mystery to solve.

After getting out of his race car, Clay took off his helmet and saw that he was once again the unofficial pole leader. Seconds later, he was bombarded by sports reporters.

"Clay, how's it feel to once again have pole position?" a reporter from ESPN 2 asked.

"It feels great. My pit crew at Walker Motorsports is doin' an awesome job."

"Your car seems to be doing much better this qualifier. Did your crew do something different to it this time?" asked a reporter from the NBC Sports.

"My crew just tweaked the car a little so it would perform at optimum level, nothin' too extravagant. Just a few new mechanical fixes here and there, that's all."

"Sounds good. So do you think having pole position will put you in even better shape for winning the Dannon 500 on Sunday?"

"Yeah, I definitely think that it'll help my chances. But then again, I feel my drivin' will also be a key factor in whatever happens Sunday."

"Clay, do you think your driving is frustrating the other drivers? I know you tend to drive more on the aggressive side," a Fox Sports reporter asked.

"I'm sure some drivers don't like the way I drive simply 'cause it's how I end up winnin' most of the time. But for them, I just have to say that it's too bad. I don't do anythin' illegal. I drive aggressively, and I believe that if other drivers began drivin' that way, too, then they'd have a better chance at winnin' more races as well."

"But don't you . . ." the reporter continued until Bryan cut him off.

"Thanks so much for all your questions and concerns, but that'll be all for today," Bryan said as he guided Clay away from the crowd of reporters and cameramen and back to his motorhome.

Making their way back through the pits, they ran into Logan and Nikki. Wishing he could just bypass the pleasantries, Clay stopped to give each what he hoped would be a very brief hello.

"Hi, Clay, I saw that you got the pole position again. Congrats," Logan greeted.

"Thank ya, I appreciate it."

A brief glance into his ex's eyes reminded him of the many times he'd slipped a hand through her silky-soft black hair. Fortunately for him, the flashback went away just as fast.

"I'm really sorry how things ended between us. I never meant to hurt you like I did." She still hoped she could find a way to get to him even if her words were only a front.

"Nikki, it's over and done with."

"I know, but . . ." She let go of Logan's hand and pulled Clay aside so she could talk to him privately.

"Nikki, I got nothin' else to say to ya."

"Clay, if I were okay with us *not* having sex, would that make things different?"

"No, and I highly doubt ya'd be okay with it in the long run."

"Why not? Can't a girl realize she's made a mistake and want to go back and fix it?"

"Yeah, but the problem is as I told ya 'fore, I don't trust ya anymore."

"But, Clay, we could get back to that."

"How, Nikki? How would ya changin' your mind again make me wanna take ya back?"

"Because I'm sure that what was between us before is still there. We just have to give it time to be rekindled."

"Nikki, no. We ain't gonna happen again. I'm done. We're done."

"Clay, it doesn't have to be that way. We can go back to us."

"Nikki, Logan's standin' right over there. What makes ya think I'd even wanna rekindle us when you're so willin' to try to get back with me when your current boyfriend's only standin' feet away?"

"Because I miss you that much."

"Well then, I guess you're just gonna have to find a way to deal with it 'cause we ain't happenin'. Bryan, let's go."

"Sounds good to me, buddy. Bryan nodded to Nikki and Logan as he and Clay headed towards the motorhome.

CHAPTER
- EIGHTEEN -

"Have ya been able to find anyone who can help us figure out who's behind the threats?" Clay asked. He headed to his bedroom to change out of his fire suit. He needed to call Tricia after what would hopefully be his last conversation with Nikki.

"Unfortunately not with the blocked texts, but as far as my answering machine tape is concerned, I know a guy who used to contract for the FBI and may still have the equipment that'll figure out whose voice it is."

"Sounds hopeful."

"Well, assuming I'm right, we'll get at least one question answered."

"Then let's hope you are."

"Yeah, let's hope," Bryan agreed as he turned back to the door. "I'll let you know what I come up with."

"See ya later, then."

Clay took out his cellphone and scrolled down to Tricia's number. He couldn't wait to hear her voice as he called her for their first date. It had been something he'd meant to do much sooner, but the mess he was in had gotten him sidetracked.

"Are you all packed and ready for school?" Kate asked Tricia as they hung out on Tricia's bed.

"Pretty much. I feel like I just need my boarding pass and I'm good to go."

"Have you told Clay yet?"

"No, we haven't even gone out on a first date yet."

"So if you're interested in the guy, you should let him know that you won't be in Newport Bay for much longer."

"Kate, neither will he, so what does it matter? He'll be on the road to each race, and I'll be at school in Kansas."

"It only matters if you actually want to date him, Trish, and I know you do."

With a telltale smile at just the thought, Tricia knew she couldn't deny Kate's statement.

"So how about this: your parents are throwing you a going away party, so why not invite him to it?"

"Yeah, I guess I can do that."

"There you go. When you invite him, you can fill him in on your temporary move to Kansas."

Tricia knew that Kate was right. Even if distance was already presenting itself as an obstacle in their potential relationship, she still needed to let Clay know about her plans for the fall.

With her mind set, Tricia was about to excuse herself to make the call when she heard her cellphone ring. Taking her flip-phone out to look at the caller ID, she didn't recognize the number. Instead of just letting it go to voicemail, her curiosity compelled her to answer it. "Hello?"

"Hi darlin', it's me." She was surprised to hear Clay's voice. It caused her heart to thud faster.

"Kate, it's Clay," she whispered with her hand over the receiver. Kate motioned that she was going downstairs.

"Hi, Clay," Tricia answered. She couldn't help feeling very shy and girlie all of a sudden. It was like the strong, confident side of her had decided to take a vacation and left her with the unsure-of-herself version. "Are you calling about our date?"

"That'd be a yes."

Stretching out on her bed, Tricia wondered how flirtatious their conversation was going to get. She also wondered how he was going to take her going away for school in the fall. It was funny, just thinking about telling him made her realize just how much she was actually going to miss him.

"Glad to hear it, so when were you thinking?"

"I'd wanna say as soon as possible, but since my schedule's pretty full right now, it may not be for a while."

"Clay, speaking of . . ."

"Speakin' of what, darlin'?"

"You should know that I'm going out of state for school in the fall. Kansas, to be exact."

"Oh. Well, that's definitely good to know."

"Which means that dating might be harder to do than you originally thought."

"Tricia, I don't care. I will make the time even if it means me flyin' ya out to wherever I am."

"Clay, I'll be in the middle of school. I can't just fly out to meet you somewhere."

"Why not if it's durin' a weekend? Ya fly out after your last class on Friday and then fly back 'fore your first class on Monday. It's as simple as that."

"But Clay, what if I have an exam I need to study for? That's not realistic."

"Fine, then I'd fly out to you. Ya can give me all the excuses in the world, and I'll just figure out a solution for each one."

"Damn it, why can't you just let us fizzle out?"

"One reminder for ya, our unplanned date."

Thinking back to it, Tricia was flooded with the feelings from his kiss and the way her heart beat faster at just being around him. "That was a pretty amazing night."

"And that's precisely why I'm not lettin' us go that easily."

"But, Clay, is it really enough?"

"It is for me. Besides, are ya really ever gonna forget how I made ya wanna kiss me with that chocolate?"

"Damn, you are making me so wish you were right here in my bedroom with me."

"Can I ask what you're wearin' then?" he teased.

"Clay, I am *not* going there with you."

"Why not when ya've already got my kiss on your mind?"

"Because Kate's downstairs, and I don't know you nearly well enough for that."

"Darn, so makin' out with a guy twice doesn't earn him some stimulation over the phone?"

"No!"

"Darlin', I'm only teasin' ya. But in all honesty, the feelings ya gave me that night let me know we need to make this work."

"And that's sweet, Clay, it really is."

"Tricia, I ain't goin' for sweet. I'm goin' for the truth."

"Clay, I just think that maybe the timing for us is off. Once I'm finished with school and you're on a break from racing, then we could try to make something work." After Tricia had given him yet another excuse she found herself with a sadness she hadn't expected.

"No."

"Then I don't know what to tell you, Clay."

"How 'bout that you'll stop bein' so fearful and give us a real chance."

With a sigh, Tricia realized he was right. She wasn't letting her wall down for him and was using her going to school in the fall as another excuse. It also dawned on her that she'd completely forgotten to mention the party to him.

"Fine. My parents are throwing me a going away party this Sunday since they won't be able to help me move in to my dorm room."

"Unfortunately, I got a race that day, but I'll do my best to swing by afterward. If I can't, then I'll give ya a call 'fore I head to bed."

"I understand."

"Tricia, I ain't givin' up on us. Ya have my word on that."

"Okay, Clay. Goodbye."

"Damn it, I won't!" he yelled into his cellphone even though he could hear the dial tone. Clay was infuriated that their flirtatious phone conversation had ended with Tricia once again trying to back out of starting a relationship with him. "I wish I wasn't so damn attracted to her, 'cause I would've been long gone by now!" In his heart, Clay knew he had no choice but to keep pursuing a relationship with Tricia.

CHAPTER
- NINETEEN -

"Tricia, are you sure your decision to not keep in touch with Clay when he went on the road was a good idea after all?" Kate asked her.

After being dropped off at John Wayne Airport by Tricia's parents, Kate couldn't help thinking that Tricia had made the wrong decision. Instead of giving in to what could be, she'd let her fear overrule her.

Despite Clay not being able to make the party, he had been able to find some alone time with Tricia afterward. With just the two of them in the den, they'd returned to the comfort of each other's arms and enjoyed the time they still had before she had to leave for school.

As their time together shortened and cellphone calls or Skype became their means of communication, Tricia realized that it wasn't enough. She wanted Clay physically with her. Sadly, she had left Clay heartbroken during their last Skype date when she'd told him that their summer romance had to come to an end.

"I'd answer you but, my head would just deny it," she answered as she and Kate headed into the airport. *I just hate the fact that after he gave me my first kiss, he caused me to get so emotionally wrapped up in him . . . and it's not even like we'd known each other for all that long before any of this happened.* She hoped she could use her fall semester to get over him.

"Maybe if you just let the fear go and take a chance on him, you'll find that he's who you've been waiting for all this time."

"You sound like Clay."

"Hmm, two people giving you the same advice. Imagine that."

"Whatever, though speaking of, how are you and Bryan doing?"

"Great, I've never met someone who gets me like he does."

"Glad to hear. Just let me know when the wedding bells start ringing."

"Funny, but I don't know that marrying Bryan would be such an off-the-wall idea. I mean, after all, he is a great guy, and our chemistry is more than I would've ever imagined."

"Sounds like you two really hit it off at the club."

"Oh, we definitely did, Trish! After meeting him, it's like none of the other guys I've dated meant nearly as much. Now let's hurry up to the gate so we can find you an incredibly hotter college guy who'll take your mind off that country boy."

With a smile, Tricia wondered if that would even be possible considering how in over her head she was when it came to Clay Gibson.

As their long flight from Orange County, California, came to an end, Tricia took notice of how the autumn season had taken full effect as their plane descended from the sky. Each tree was so beautiful with its myriad of colors ranging from reds to browns to yellows that she wished she could just frame the scene in her mind so it would stay with her even after the season had changed. As the plane's wheels made contact with the runway, it left her with a happy feeling of finally being back on the ground, even if it was in a different state. But wow, her first view of Kansas was gorgeous!

The Sunflower State proved to be an even more beautiful state in the fall than the pictures on the school's website had depicted. She couldn't help but love the season, her favorite time of year. Seeing the multicolored leaves everywhere made her think of her ideal day that she had described to Clay.

Clay. Damn it, why do all my thoughts have to keep reverting back to him? She wished she could enjoy the season with him by her side.

Not allowing herself one more second to dwell on his missing presence, Tricia pushed her thoughts of him aside as she and Kate headed for baggage claim. Climbing into a cab minutes later, they headed to the hotel Tricia's parents had booked for them. After picking up her car at a local storage facility and then arriving at the school the next day, Tricia finished the process of becoming an official SKSC student while Kate stayed in her dorm and talked to Bryan.

Checking her watch to see how long she'd been gone from her dorm, Tricia realized that she should probably get back. Coming out of the building she saw a professor and a man who way too closely resembled Clay come out of a classroom and begin talking. Tricia's heartbeat quickened at the mere possibility. Upon closer look, she realized that it wasn't just an uncanny resemblance to Clay. He *was* Clay!

What the . . .? What is he doing here? she thought as her heart began to pound.

Tricia couldn't believe it. She had thought she was going to have her whole fall semester to get over Clay Gibson, but look who turned up at her school to prove her wrong. Talk about not taking the word no for an answer. Now he was stalking her!

Maybe if I just walk by them really fast, he won't have the chance to notice me. Tricia's goal was to elude him. Just as she was about to make her escape, Clay turned his head in her direction and saw her. *Aw crap. Now I definitely have no chance!* She smiled cordially the second his eyes met hers. *Damn it, I don't think I'll ever be able to get over that man!* She watched him give the professor a handshake before making his way over to her.

"Um, hi, Clay. How are you?" As she looked into his gorgeous blue eyes, she instantly felt all of the feelings she had for him come rushing back, practically drowning her heart with the reminder of how much she had truly missed him.

"I'm good. I take it ya just started here?" he asked after glancing down at the laptop's carrying case she wore across her body.

"Yep. So what are you doing here, since I don't believe your career will allow you the time for any on-campus classes?"

"To be honest, Kate called me," he answered. "She told me what day ya'd be gettin' here, so I found a way to be here myself."

Clay enjoyed how the hallway's light caused her hazel eyes

to shimmer a little. He couldn't believe how much his heart had missed looking into them.

"I can't believe that she would do that, and for you to purposely follow me here. I . . . I honestly don't know what to say."

Tricia couldn't decide whether she should be flattered at the effort he was making or pissed that he was actually following her.

"I'd be flattered if it were me," he teased. "Stalkin' doesn't paint me in a good light."

"Clay, you're not doing this because you're mad at me for my decision this summer, are you?"

"No. I'm not mad anymore. Tricia, I understand your reasonin' behind it, but that doesn't mean I'm gonna quit tryin'." His only thought was to bring her into his arms and kiss her lips.

"I know it hurt you hearing me kill any chance we might've had together."

"Yeah, it did, but honestly, this hallway isn't really the place I wanna be talkin' 'bout that with ya, anyhow." He slipped his hand into hers.

"Clay, I told Kate that I would meet her for lunch after I'd completed all my errands," she informed him as he led her out of the hallway and into the nearest stairwell.

"And ya still can, but not 'fore we talk 'bout us."

"You needed to bring me to this exact spot in order for us to have that conversation?"

"I want the utmost privacy with ya, darlin'."

"Okay, but the only problem you have now is if someone comes through those double doors or the stairs above in order to get down to the basement." She watched him remove her laptop bag. "Unless you can find something to jam all the doors with," she teased.

"I'll take my chances," he returned with a brief smile.

Before Tricia knew what was happening, Clay pushed her up against the wall and pinned her, bringing his hand to her side while his arm rested against the wall above her head.

"Wow, Clay, I definitely wasn't expecting you to do that." His forcefulness turned her on a little.

"Darlin', that's just 'cause I've missed ya so damn much." His face moved closer to hers.

"I can tell," she replied with a hand on his chest. Feeling his tight skin underneath, she remembered the night he had come over to her house and how it had eventually led to her wondering what he looked like without his shirt on.

"So how 'bout we not talk 'bout us and ya let me kiss ya instead?" He pressed his lips to hers before she even had the chance to answer him.

She answered by wrapping her arms around his neck. Despite her fear continuously fighting her urge to give in to him, she couldn't do anything else but kiss him back. She let the taste of his lips remind her of why she had missed him so much since she had made the decision to end things between them so abruptly. They continued to make up for their missed time by showing affection to each other. Clay let his passion for her explode onto her lips. This sensuous experience became the motivation for her to continue it.

"Damn, I knew I was right 'bout us!" he exclaimed the moment his lips had left the pleasure of hers.

"So what if you are, Clay? That doesn't change the fact that your racing wouldn't provide us with much stability." She came up with another excuse even though she was immensely happy to be back in his arms and feeling his lips against hers.

"Tricia, no matter what ya say, that kiss just told me how damn much we both missed each other."

"I know it did, Clay. I could feel your passion for me just as much as you could feel mine for you."

"Then finally give in to havin' a relationship with me already. Tricia, we can make this work," he pleaded. "Besides, I definitely wouldn't mind givin' ya more kisses like that when I've come back from bein' on the road for so long," he replied with a sexy grin that he knew would trigger her heart.

"You're too dangerous for me, Clay," she replied with her arms still wrapped around his neck.

"And why's that, darlin'?" he responded with another sexy grin as he wrapped his arms around her waist.

"Because even though your southern charm has already won my heart over, my mindset is to play it safe."

"Ah, so your mindset is what I still need to work on convincin'." He kissed her again.

"Clay, don't you think that's enough kissing for now? You do realize we still have to go out on a first date, right?"

"Yeah, I know, but my desire to kiss ya has absolutely nothin' to do with when we go out on our first date. Tricia, I wanna keep kissin' ya 'cause I've missed those sweet lips of yours so damn much."

"It's just my watermelon chapstick you like."

"Well, keep wearin' it 'cause it keeps me cravin' your kiss every time I get a taste of your lips. Hell, I think it's even made me addicted to 'em."

"Addicted, huh?"

"Yep. Each time I kiss ya, the taste of your lips just makes me wanna keep kissin' ya more and more."

"Glad to hear it."

"Good, 'cause it reminds me of when I was a little kid and the watermelon my mama used to bring with us whenever we'd go on a picnic. The watermelon was always my favorite part." His grin caused her to look down with a very shy smile. "Ya know, ya should really stop doin' that. Ya look so damn cute when ya blush." He lifted her chin and kissed her lips again.

"Clay, Kate's probably wondering where I am."

"Then let her wonder. I'd rather keep kissin' ya," he replied before pressing his lips to hers one last time.

CHAPTER
- TWENTY -

"You sure like to be affectionate, don't you?" she pointed out after he'd let her loose from his grip.

"Tricia, right now, I'm just makin' up for lost time. After ya put a stop to any chance we might've had, I found myself thinkin' 'bout ya constantly. Not a single day went by that your name or beautiful face wasn't on my mind." His look was sobering.

"Oh, Clay, I'm so sorry," Tricia began as she realized just how much he actually cared about her.

"Tricia, you'll never know how much it killed me to hear Bryan on the cellphone with Kate, knowin' that I could never share that same experience with you. I swear, it seemed like every time she called and I'd hear Bryan laughin' from somethin' she'd said, I had to go make myself busy with somethin' just to sidetrack my brain from ya."

Tricia couldn't help but feel her own heart break from knowing that it was her decision that had caused him to feel so much pain. "Clay, I am so sorry. I absolutely hate that I ended up putting you through all of that!"

"I'm just glad that Bryan never flew Kate in to be with him and that he always went over to her house to see her. 'Cause I honestly don't think I could've handled seein' her with him, knowin' that ya'd never come along with the intention of seein' me." He watched her eyes fill with tears. "Aw, darlin', I'm sorry, I didn't mean to make ya cry. I just thought ya should know how much I missed ya. After our last Skype date, I found myself feelin' more empty than I knew was possible without you in my arms and your lips not pressed to mine." He cupped her face with his hands and used his thumbs to wipe away the tears that couldn't be held back.

"Clay, I'm just so sorry . . . and you'll never know how much!"

"Darlin', now that I've got ya back in my arms, it doesn't matter." He kissed her with a smile. "Man, ya've got such tasty lips."

Despite the compliment, Tricia continued to feel responsible for Clay's pain. As much as she wanted to give in right then and there, she was scared of the unknown.

Acting as if they were already a couple, they held hands as they walked to the bookstore to finish her errands.

"Oh my God, you're Clay Gibson! *The* Clay Gibson!" the clerk screamed the second she saw him enter.

Tricia watched the girl run out from behind the counter and hug him. Surprised by her overjoyed response to his presence in the store, Clay let go of Tricia's hand and stood there while the clerk continued to cling to his body.

"Oh my God, I can't believe it's you! Holy crap, I can't believe you're here! I think you are the best NASCAR driver ever!" she exclaimed.

"Thanks, thanks so much . . . I really appreciate it," Clay returned.

After getting over being startled, he gave her a proper thank you hug for being a fan and showing her support.

"Oh my God, you are just the *best* driver! Oh my God, this is just so awesome. I can't wait to tell my dad about this. He just loves NASCAR!"

"Thanks a lot. I really appreciate it," Clay returned with a tip of his hat once she'd finally let him go.

"Hey, do you think I could possibly get a couple of pictures with you on my cellphone, that is, if your girlfriend doesn't mind?" asked the clerk.

"Oh, I'm not his . . ." Tricia corrected but was cut off before she could finish.

"Yeah, of course. Ya don't mind, do ya, darlin'?"

"No, I guess not," Tricia replied as she took the cellphone.

Once she had taken a couple of pictures, the clerk grabbed a black marker from the counter and had Clay sign the bottom of her shirt.

"Since she thinks you're the best driver in NASCAR, Clay, do you think she might let me get my stuff for free?" Tricia joked.

"No darlin'. And even if she did, I would still insist we pay for it," he answered, shaking his head at her.

"Ah, you're no fun."

"Oh, I can be fun . . . under the right circumstances." He winked.

"Ooh, the country boy's got a frisky side to him."

"Ya have no idea, Tricia." He came up behind her and wrapped his arms around her waist. "Ya find everythin' ya need, darlin'?" he asked with his chin on her shoulder.

"Yes. In fact, that was the last item I needed, so I'm good to go." Tricia couldn't help but enjoy the feel of his raw maleness pressed up against her and wished it didn't have to go away. Just feeling his heat resonating through his clothes reminded her of one of the many things she had missed about him.

Disappointed at having to let her go, Clay released her from his arms and waited for her to pay for her items. They headed back to her dorm room to see if Kate was still on her cellphone with Bryan.

"It's too bad, Clay. I could've at least gotten a discount on account of that cashier thinking you're the best and all."

"Don't tell me you're already jealous, Tricia?" he asked, taking her hand in his.

"No, Clay, I'm not jealous. I just thought it was adorable how she couldn't stop staring at you the whole time we were in there."

"Ya sure that's not just the jealousy talkin', darlin'?" he asked, caressing her thumb with his.

"Please, Clay, like I have anything to be jealous about. I'm not even dating you, so why should I care what another girl thinks of you?"

"Maybe 'cause ya wanna?"

"Clay, until you can convince my head to join my heart . . . we ain't happening!"

"Then what do ya call the way I was holdin' ya in my arms in that bookstore?"

"Flirtatious fun."

"Tricia, I don't hold a woman like that just for some 'flirtatious fun.' Besides, after what I told ya in the stairwell earlier, you should already know that this ain't just 'flirtatious fun' for me."

"Well, maybe that's how I see it with you!" she stated with the best excuse she could come up with. She remained obstinate at the possibility of them finally being in a relationship.

You may believe that, darlin', but I certainly don't. Clay decided to give her a reminder that his fight for her heart wasn't over. He spun her around to face him and rested an arm against her dorm room's door and his other hand on her side to make sure he had her complete attention. "Tricia, your head may need a lot more work in convincin', but I'm gonna prove it to ya that this isn't just 'flirtatious fun,' got it?" He tipped her chin up and gave her a much shorter but equally significant kiss to prove his point.

"Yeah, I got it." She nodded with a lick of her lips.

Even though Clay's kiss had been meant to be taken seriously, Tricia couldn't help but return to her fairytale each time he kissed her. It was like his lips had some kind of magical power over her that made her think of their relationship as only a playful game of flirting and being affectionate. For some reason, whenever his lips met hers, she just couldn't take it seriously.

"Good, now how 'bout ya open that door 'cause I'm startin' to get really hungry."

Tricia nodded and unlocked the door to her temporary home.

"Finally! Trish, I was wondering what was taking you so long!" Kate exclaimed as they entered.

"Sorry, Kate, I sort of ran into somebody," she replied, as Clay appeared.

"Oh, well then, never mind."

"Hey, so I hear you're comin' to lunch with us?" Clay greeted her.

"Actually, I think that's the other way around," Kate corrected. "You're coming with us."

"Either way, ya've certainly got a nice set up here, Tricia," he said, checking out the newly decorated room. He stretched out on the bed.

"Thanks," Tricia replied, wishing she and Clay were alone so she could join him.

After watching Kate head into the bathroom, Clay gave Tricia a wink and a sexy grin. "No problem, darlin'."

"I, um, Kate, are you ready to go yet?"

"Yeah, just a second," Kate called from behind the bathroom door.

"Well, hurry it up," Tricia demanded, as his arms wrapped around her. "Clay and I are really hungry." She felt his kisses on her neck.

"Don't worry, I'm almost finished," Kate replied, making the finishing touches to her lips.

"Uh, Clay, what are you doing? Kate's going to come out of the bathroom any second now."

"Just revvin' up your engine for me, darlin'."

"Damn, you have such bad timing!"

"Actually, Tricia, my timin's . . . absolutely . . . perfect." He stopped being affectionate the second Kate came out of the bathroom.

Damn you! she thought as the heat he had caused rapidly disappeared.

"So which one of you is driving?" Kate asked, oblivious to the sexual tension Clay had purposely caused Tricia.

"I can if ya'd like," he offered eagerly, wanting to sit next to Tricia in his truck.

"Sounds good to me," Kate agreed, putting her lip gloss back in her purse as the three headed out to lunch.

With each door he held open for them, Clay watched Kate and Tricia pass by, unable to resist taking a glance at Tricia's butt. The rhythmic sway of her hips kept calling out to him. *Damn, what would it be like to have full access to that part of her?* he wondered as they headed for his truck. *And just the feel of my hand on it.* He smiled internally as he opened the passenger door.

"Trish, are you going to be okay sitting next to him?" Kate asked before climbing in.

"Yeah, since it would be kind of weird if you sat next to him instead."

"I suppose you do have a point there."

"Hey, you girls ever gonna get in?"

"Yeah . . . sorry," Tricia replied, hurriedly climbing in.

Tricia slid to the middle seat and found herself making contact with Clay. Curious to how he would react to their being so close again, she slowly looked up at him. Then as if no words needed to be spoken, they made eye contact only, gesturing for another kiss.

"So where are we going to eat?" Kate chimed in, interrupting their moment.

"There's a restaurant called Jack's Place that's supposed to be good," Clay replied, starting his truck.

With the truck in gear and the three of them now on their way to lunch, Tricia leaned back in her seat and relaxed for the ride to the restaurant. Clay placed his right arm on top of the cushion behind her.

"Do ya mind if I put my arm there, darlin'?"

"No. It's your truck. You can do whatever you want in it."

"Good, 'cause I happen to find the ride more comfortable this way."

"Glad to know," she responded playfully.

Her head felt relief from his words while her heart took a turn onto Confusion Street. She began to overthink the situation. She knew he'd wanted to kiss her a few seconds ago, so why would he now just want to put his arm behind her? Did he still want to be in a relationship with her like he'd been trying to convince her, or had he now decided to quit attempting to persuade her and joined her in playing her flirtation game, instead? What was really going on between them? Why would he mess with her head by showing her his desire for her one second, only to not continue with it the next? Maybe he just wanted to be discreetly affectionate with her by placing his arm behind her. Despite whatever was going on between them, she knew one thing was for sure: She was confused, and her Asperger's need to analyze the situation wasn't helping her one bit!

As Tricia decided to forego the confusion his words had caused her, Clay made a sharp right turn, causing her to be pulled into the crook of his shoulder. She put her hand out to counteract the motion but accidentally grabbed his right leg instead of the seat cushion.

"Wow, Trish, maybe my worry about you was wrong!" Kate observed.

"I, um, I'm so sorry, Clay. It's just, your turn. It was just . . . so sharp."

"It ain't no problem for me, darlin'. In fact, I'm quite comfortable with it, to tell ya the truth." He winked.

CHAPTER
- TWENTY-ONE -

"So, Trish, besides reconnecting with Clay, did you happen to meet your roommate while you were out?" Kate asked her.

"No, but apparently she's a huge fan of yours, Clay." Tricia looked in his direction.

"Oh?" he asked, resting his arm on top of the cushion behind her.

"Yep, she thinks you're the hottest driver in NASCAR, bar none."

"Does she now?"

"Uh huh. I guess she's all about Clay Gibson."

As Clay listened, he couldn't help but wish to be the straw her soda went through as it made its way to her mouth. "Ah, and do ya care 'bout that, Tricia?"

"Nope, just thought you'd like to know."

"So ya don't care that she's another woman who thinks I'm hot?"

"Why, do you want me to?" she pushed.

"Darlin', I just want ya to know . . ." he began.

Leaning over, Clay whispered the rest into her ear and followed it up with a gentle kiss right below it. It was a strategic approach that would no doubt shoot right through her defensive wall and win the battle completely.

"Wow, Trish. He must've said something really X-rated since you can't stop blushing," noted Kate.

"Oh, I am . . . well . . . hey, wasn't there a raffle drawing for tickets to the next NASCAR race posted somewhere?"

Just the feel of his warm breath on her skin and the sound of his sexy, low southern drawl in her ear had caused her hair to stand on end and her senses to be put on full alert. The kiss emphasizing his comment certainly didn't help her either.

"Tricia, ya do know that ya can just ask me for 'em if ya really wanna go to one, right? Ya don't need to enter a raffle drawin' for 'em," he informed her with a smile.

"Yes," she replied. *I was just trying to change the subject so I could stop blushing.*

Despite feeling embarrassed, Tricia couldn't help but want to replay his racy whisper in her head.

"Besides, with me givin' ya the tickets, ya can be guaranteed a backstage pass for the pits." He hoped that the incentive of a private pit tour from him might sweet talk her into having some more alone time together.

"That does sound really cool considering I've never actually been behind the scenes of a speedway before."

"And I have absolutely no problem with givin' ya a private tour of it all."

"I'm sure you don't, Clay."

"Darlin', I honestly don't. I see it as just another chance for me to get to spend more time with ya," he explained charmingly.

"Oh, Clay, that was really sweet." Tricia kissed him on his cheek.

"Damn, that really was," Kate agreed, wishing that Bryan could've been there.

"Ah, it's just the truth," he replied.

"In any case, I think it would be really cool to go," mused Tricia. "I have missed experiencing the rumbling of the cars' engines when the drivers flip their ignition switches the second the announcer says, 'Drivers, start your engines.' It's just such an incredible feeling to have as the drivers gear their cars into action once the green flag has been waved. And, of course, you've got the excitement throughout the race of the possibility of the cars spinning out or crashing into another one. Although, it's the end laps that really get me. The race to see who'll actually finish first. Man, now that part definitely gets my heart racing and adrenaline pumping."

As Tricia described in detail why she liked and missed the sport, Clay was reminded of the passion he felt for it. For him, it wasn't just about the money but the added rush he got out of going that fast. Speeding around the track at over two hundred miles per hour, hoping to win the checkered flag, and then standing in the winner's circle, was an adrenaline high like no other. But after hearing Tricia's perception of it, he was better able to understand why the fans enjoyed the sport so much. No matter how a person participated in it, whether behind the wheel or as a spectator, NASCAR could definitely give each participant a rush.

"Will that be all for you?" their server asked, bringing Clay out of his thoughts.

"Yes, sir," Clay answered.

"Here's your check, then. You can bring it up to the front when you're ready."

As Clay picked up the check, a woman in a pink halter top and a white bejeweled miniskirt came up to their booth. She wore big, silver hoop earrings and overly applied makeup.

"Hi. You're that hot NASCAR driver, Clay Gibson, right?" She leaned over the table to purposely give Clay a direct view of her cleavage.

"Yes, I am," he answered.

The combination of her calling him hot and the way she leaned over their table yelled *trouble*. It especially didn't help that he couldn't see Tricia's reaction without turning his head.

"Glad to hear it, because my name's Roxanna and my friends and I were wondering if you wanted to come party with us later tonight since we all think you're so damn hot and all." She leaned over more and waved to a table of equally trashy looking women with her fake nails.

"So . . . what do you think, hot stuff?"

"I, um, thanks for the invitation, Roxanna, but as ya can see, I'm already busy."

"Aw, are you sure, baby? Because my friends and I can guarantee you one hell of a good time . . . if you know what I mean," she said, winking at him.

"Yes, he's sure. But thanks for the invitation anyway." As

Tricia spoke, she placed her hand on Clay's thigh. It was a move both Clay and Kate immediately noticed.

"Oh, I'm sorry honey, but I'm going to have to hear that from him. You know, since you weren't the one invited."

"That's too bad, now please go back to your table because he's not interested," Tricia continued with a tight squeeze on his thigh.

As Clay sat there, he wondered if their conversation was going to get him in trouble. Knowing that the more heated their words became, the more Tricia was going to squeeze his leg and move her hand closer to the danger zone gave him plenty of reason to worry.

"What are you, his girlfriend?" Roxanna asked.

"No, just someone who thinks his time is better spent with people who don't show off what they've got in a very slutty way." She moved her hand up his thigh, adding more pressure to his anxiety with another squeeze. Clay forced himself to mentally control the pressure that was already beginning to build up, especially since it was Tricia's hand on his leg.

"Excuse me, but who are you calling slutty? I'll have you know that many guys actually like how revealing I am," Roxanna informed her.

"That may be, but this guy's not one of them. This guy likes his woman classy . . . and tastefully dressed, not showing everything she's got to the whole world without a concern for what others may think." Tricia took a moment to size up her cheap-looking competition.

Clay watched the two women fight over him while Tricia maintained her tight hold on his leg. He thanked God that the woman flaunting herself in front of him couldn't see where Tricia's hand was on his thigh or the danger she was about to get him into if they didn't stop their conversation, *and soon*.

"Oh really, so you don't think my assets will turn him on?" Roxanna asked.

"Um, Tricia?" Kate interrupted in an attempt to warn her.

"Not now, Kate." Tricia's Asperger's kept her one-track mind on the conversation. "Nope, so you can just turn right around, head back to your table, and tell all your friends thanks but no thanks because this man's staying right here!" She spoke confidently as she unknowingly came closer and closer to putting Clay in a very awkward situation.

"Please! One night with me and your man will see what he's been missing!" Roxanna proclaimed.

This conversation may end up gettin' me in trouble, but I like the fact that she called me Tricia's man! Clay thought as he continued to resist the pressure of Tricia's hand. *Damn, if we were only alone!* However, he realized the implication of that thought and quickly tried to think of whatever else he could to sidetrack his brain.

"Yeah, well . . . I don't think so!" retorted Tricia. Oblivious to her hand on Clay's inner thigh, she swiftly moved her other hand up to his face and brought him into one of the most passionate kisses she had only ever dreamt about giving him.

Oh crap, this is so not helpin' me either! But what the hell, at least the woman got her to give me another kiss! Clay was overcome by Tricia's intense lip embrace as he struggled to maintain his composure concerning the placement of her hand on his leg.

Kate was even surprised at the extent to which Tricia would go to defend Clay to some woman who'd hit on him in front of her. As she watched Tricia publicly make out with a man she refused to be in a relationship with, she knew her refusal wouldn't last much longer.

"Fine, suit yourself!" Roxanna watched the man they'd fought over place his hand on Tricia's face and finally decided to walk back to her table with the knowledge that she'd been beaten at her own game.

Tricia felt Clay's hand on her skin, and she realized she'd gone too far. At first, it had only been meant to prove a point, but now she was in dangerous territory. With that understanding in mind, and the knowledge that Roxanna was no longer a front row audience, she removed Clay's hand from her face and brought her kiss to an end and exclaimed, "Geez, some women!"

"Damn, darlin', I think I like ya bein' territorial over me!" Clay stated after putting his fingers to his lips. He felt like he had to realign his jaw from all of her passion.

"What are you talking about, Clay? I was just defending you to that slutty looking woman!" she asked.

"Darlin', that kiss was way more than that, and ya know it. Tricia, ya were bein' territorial over me."

"No, it was not, Clay, and no, I was not being territorial over you. I was just defending your taste in women," she tried to explain, even if it was only an excuse.

"Sure ya were."

"Clay, I was!"

"Tricia, ya've been hurtin' me more than helpin' me this entire time," he informed her.

"What are you talking about, Clay? I just helped you get that woman to leave you alone."

"Tricia, look at where your hand is on my leg."

"What?" she asked with confusion then looked down at his legs to see that her hand was very close to being in dangerous territory for him.

"Uh huh."

"Oh, I'm so sorry. I didn't start anything for you, did I?" she asked, immediately taking her hand off his leg.

"No. Fortunately, I was able to control myself. But ya were pretty damn close."

Had she moved her hand up any further, he would've either had to quickly think of something to forget that her hand was there or slide it off in a very discreet way.

Tricia felt bad about the awkwardness she had almost caused him. She was about to continue with her apology for being so unaware of it when she realized that she now had the perfect opportunity to pay him back for purposely getting her turned on earlier. "You know, Clay, it's actually too bad that I stopped my hand right there because I could've easily . . ." She slid her hand back onto his leg, but this time, put it even closer to his danger zone. She then added a racy whisper in his ear and emphasized it with a slighter, but more intentional, squeeze of his inner thigh.

"Now, darlin', that just ain't fair!" He immediately removed her hand from his leg.

"Hey, you started it in my room. I'm just returning the favor."

"Fine. But it still doesn't discount the fact that ya were bein' territorial over me. Not that I minded it, or anythin'. In fact, I actually liked it. I liked seein' ya defend me to her." He brought their conversation back to the real issue at hand while feeling pleasantly surprised that she would turn his own tactic against him.

"But I'm not being territorial over you, Clay! I have no reason to be since we're not together! I was only defending you to her like you just said!"

"Darlin', when a woman kisses a man like that, it usually means that she's got somethin' to prove . . . be it to herself or others," he concluded before picking up the check.

"Whatever. Hey, did you want my help with that considering I did order the most food?" she asked as she watched him take out his wallet.

"Nope. I've got it covered."

"Are you sure, Clay? Because it's not like you have to pay for all of us," Tricia took out her wallet to share the damage.

"I know, but as I said 'fore, I got it covered." He placed a hand over her wallet to stop her.

"But Clay . . ." she began, even though normally she loved getting a free meal.

"Trish, just let the man pay the check if he wants to," Kate advised.

"Darlin', it's okay. I got this," he repeated while looking her dead straight in the eyes. He could tell that even though her head kept wanting to trump her heart in being with him, her eyes were desperate for the opposite. No matter how many times her words denied him, her eyes and kiss told him the truth every time.

"Fine, if you want to, but just know that you don't actually have to. Since we're not dating, it's not your responsibility to pick up the check." Their eyes remained locked.

"I know that, Tricia. But considerin' the fact that I was raised to pay for the meal whenever I go out with a woman, or women," he paused to gesture in Kate's direction, "I automatically feel that it is my responsibility to cover the check. So why don't ya just put your wallet back in your pocket and let me pay for lunch, okay?"

"Okay."

"Thank you," he accepted with an appreciative nod in return. "Now, I do remember the server tellin' us that we gotta go pay the check up at the front. So, why don't you girls go wait for me in my truck while I finish takin' care of this? Sound good?" Taking his keys out of his shirt pocket, Clay handed them to Tricia in a way that would make her feel sparks.

"Yeah, okay," Tricia agreed with a nod as their brief touch made her heart race, pleading for her to just give in to him already.

CHAPTER

- TWENTY-TWO -

"Are y'all ready to head back to the school?" Clay asked, climbing back into the driver's seat.

"Yes, and thanks for paying for lunch, Clay. I really appreciate it," Kate acknowledged as she reapplied her lip gloss.

"It was no problem," he accepted with a nod before bringing his truck back to life.

Driving back to Tricia's dorm, Clay realized that he needed Tricia to finally make a decision. It was crystal clear to him how resistant she was to dating him, but he also knew that he couldn't keep his heart on the line for her if she was going to remain that way.

He parked his truck. "Hey, Tricia, could ya wait a minute, there's somethin' I need to talk to ya 'bout." He placed a hand over hers.

"Um, sure."

Handing her keys to Kate, Tricia made herself comfortable against the passenger side door. "I see you fixed the passenger door."

"Yeah, I figured I'd better so I didn't have another person worryin' 'bout their exit strategy," he teased. Tricia put her legs across his lap.

"Good to know. So what's up? What did you want to talk to me about?"

Tricia watched Clay rest his left arm over her legs while his other stayed on top of the seat cushion. She wondered if her attitude about them being a couple was about to be drastically changed.

"Us."

"What about us?"

"Tricia, I've already made it abundantly clear how I feel 'bout ya."

"I know that, Clay."

"Then ya should also know that I can't do this anymore."

"You can't do what, Clay?"

"Put my feelin's out there for ya when all you're gonna do is keep it just a game."

"Clay, that's because this absolutely terrifies me."

"But why, when I've shown ya time and time again how I feel 'bout ya?"

"Because I'm not used to that as my reality."

"Then I can help ya get used to it. Tricia, I wanna be with ya. When I'm not, I miss ya like crazy."

"And that's the problem, Clay. You're going to be out on the road and I am going to be here. That's too damn hard for me to deal with."

"Tricia, even though we'll both miss each other like crazy, just the thought of me never bein' able to wrap my arms around ya again or kiss ya with more passion than I hold for racin' would be damn harder. Hell, it would be worse!"

Feeling tears at just the thought of his words, Tricia didn't know what to do.

Closing the gap between them, Clay brought her into his arms. "Tricia, I know you're scared, but I can also see how much ya want this. I could see your desire for us in your eyes at the restaurant, and I know ya felt it each time we kissed."

Wrapping her arms around his neck, all Tricia could do was cry out her fear. She hated that it was this hard for her to say yes to him, but the grip of the unknown held her captive.

"Darlin', I hate to do this to ya, but for my own heart, I need to know if you'll finally be willin' to take a chance with me, or if I just need to give ya a final goodbye right here. 'Cause even though I flew out here to be with ya, I can't keep puttin' my heart out there for ya if ya won't ever let yourself take it."

Slowly lifting her head to look at him with her tear-stained face, she grabbed a hold of his white shirt with both hands and kissed him with a passion that told him she was all in.

Smiling at her response, Clay happily took her back into his arms as they enjoyed this defining moment.

"Clay, ever since I can remember, this has been all I've ever really wanted in life. To meet a man who could sweep me off my feet with all of the qualities that matter to me and then live out that fairytale life in the country where we're sitting on our front porch swing and watching our children play. But it's always been just a dream for me. I never thought I'd actually meet a man like that, like you. So, it scares the hell out of me that this dream of mine could actually become a reality."

"So does that mean ya also want the 2.5 kids, a dog, and the white picket fence surroundin' the front yard?" he teased.

"No, and I never understood the half."

"Thank ya for not makin' me have to say goodbye to ya. I really think it would've done me in."

"I'm sorry, Clay, that I put up such a fight for this. For us."

"Darlin', ya have no need to apologize. I completely get your hesitation. Just know that ya drive me crazy like no other woman ever has. I find myself missin' the hell out of ya every day, and even though our flirtin' has been just a game to ya, I can honestly never get enough of your sexiness."

"Turning your charm on full blast, I see."

"Nope, just tellin' ya the honest truth."

"Speaking of honesty, Clay . . . had I kept my hand on your leg, would I have pushed you to your limit?"

"Ya would've if I hadn't immediately brushed it off after your racy comment," he answered with a grin.

"What would you have done had I pushed you to that point?"

"Taken off my hat and shown ya my hair."

"Sounds sexy."

"Yep," he answered with a smile, "and it makes me damn glad I wear one!"

Me too, but for another reason.

"By the way, don't forget your swimsuit."

"Wait . . . what?"

"Well, you're gonna need it for when I pick ya up at five o'clock for our date this Saturday," he explained with a big smile.

"Oh . . . okay, I'll make sure to bring one, then."

"Ya do that, and remember, the more skin, the better," he teased, giving her body the once over.

"Goodbye, Clay. See you Saturday at five." Giving him a quick kiss, Tricia got out of his truck and headed back into her dorm.

CHAPTER
- TWENTY-THREE -

"Kate, how could you tell Clay where I'd be today?"
"Because Bryan told me how miserable Clay has been since you broke things off with him. Tricia, you never even gave the man a chance before you ended things to stay safe."

I already know that! She was a little pissed that Kate had gone behind her back but, at the same time, was grateful that she had.

"So are you done being fearful, or was lunch the last time I'll get to see you and Clay together like that?"

"Yes, and no. You will be happy to know that before I left his truck, he told me that he'll be picking me up at five o' clock for our date this Saturday."

"Finally! It took you long enough to put your guard down and let him in."

"Kate, that's not fair."

"Sure it is. Clay's done nothing but prove himself interested in you, and yet it took you this long to finally take advantage."

"Kate, there are just some things you don't know about me."

"Oh? Like what?"

"It's nothing I'm ready to tell you. But just know, I have my reasons for waiting as long as I did."

"Fine. I'm just glad you two will be going out on a first date. That is, if you don't count the night he came over unexpectedly, as one."

"That was our unofficial first date, and no, I don't."

"Either way, I'm glad you're letting him officially romance you."

"Speaking of, since the date is while you're still here, that'll mean you'll end up being here all by yourself."

"No, I won't. Bryan's in town."

"He is?"

Tricia remembered Kate's cellphone call with Bryan and realized that seeing Clay should've told her that Bryan was probably in town as well.

"Yeah, after I told Clay where he could find you, he told me that Bryan had a meeting with potential sponsors."

"Oh. Well, that's great to hear."

"Yep, and since Clay's also got a race on Sunday, maybe tonight I could get Bryan to give me a personal tour of Kansas Speedway."

"Kate."

"Relax, Trish. We'll probably end up just going out to dinner."

"Are you sure you're okay with this, Kate? Because I really don't want to be the girl who ditches her best friend for a guy."

"Yes, I'm fine with it. Besides, you two need this date."

"I think Clay would definitely agree with you on that one," Tricia laughed.

"Well, he's right. You've been hot and cold with him since you two first met."

"Honestly, that's because I've been so afraid of our chemistry. Kate, Clay is the first guy I've ever felt that spark with the second we touched. Hell, just the way his blue eyes held mine told me that there was something deeper there."

"And I'm glad he's made such a huge impression on you, Tricia. It's been your whole life in the making."

❧

"Man, I am so happy she finally agreed to *us* and that we're finally goin' out on our first date!" Clay exclaimed, driving back to his motorhome.

Even though his battle for Tricia's heart had caused him more frustration than he would've normally put up with, he was happy to finally be taking her out on Saturday. *And just the thought of gettin' to see her hot body in a swimsuit . . . damn!* Clay couldn't have been more anxious to see her hot curves in a swimsuit. But as he imagined her in one, dripping wet from the water, he glanced over at his cellphone, bringing him out of his thoughts of Tricia. He wondered who was behind the blocked texts and disguised voicemail on Bryan's answering machine. He shook his head at all the frustration it had caused him. The cellphone's ringing startled him.

"Clay, I've got some news on who left the voicemail," Bryan informed him, bypassing the hellos.

"Ya do? That's great. So, who's the damn bastard who's been threatenin' to wreak havoc on my life?" he asked.

"Not exactly. It's Nikki."

"Who did ya just say?"

"Clay, it's your ex-girlfriend."

"But why? What would Nikki have to gain from any of this?"

"I don't know, honestly. But what worries me most is that she knows about Tricia."

"But how could she? Unless . . ." Clay swallowed a big gulp of air. His ex-girlfriend was now stalking him and threatening Tricia in the process.

"Damn! I wish I could've told you it was someone different. Like another racer who had a grudge against you."

"We only know that she's behind the voicemail, right? We still don't know who's behind the texts? Or if she's responsible for both?"

"That would be correct."

"Damn it, Bryan. How do I tell Tricia that my ex is stalkin' me and possibly threatenin' me with texts?"

"You don't. You leave her out of this until we figure out how to confront Nikki without her being the least bit suspicious."

"Damn it. I just told Tricia that I'm gonna be pickin' her up on Saturday for our first date."

"Glad to hear it! I know it's been a damn long time in coming."

"It sure has. But Tricia and I've talked, and she's finally ready to start somethin' with me."

"Well, congrats, buddy, and I hope your date goes well."

"Me too. Now that ya know, I'm gonna need ya to take Kate out so she won't be left alone in Tricia's dorm room the whole night."

"No problem. We'd already made plans for tonight, anyhow."

"Kate really orchestrated me seein' Tricia again, didn't she?"

"To the last detail."

"Wow, Tricia's got one carin' best friend."

"You do, too, Clay." Bryan ended the call.

With one piece of the puzzle figured out, Clay set his cellphone back on the cushion. But after he had, he watched it vibrate. Hoping it was a text from someone he knew, he waited until he came to a red light.

Clay – I hope you take heed to the warning left on Bryan's answering machine. Because I would really hate for your new girlfriend to end up watching your career go up in flames.

CHAPTER
- TWENTY-FOUR -

"Dang, Kate, ya look good!" Clay exclaimed when he saw the black dress she wore. "Bryan won't be able to keep his hands off ya."

"That's the point, Clay."

"Oh, well . . . have a good time, then. I suppose Bryan's got a car pickin' ya up?"

"Yeah. I'd better get going so I don't keep his driver waiting."

"'Bye, then."

"Clay, I know that you finally convinced Tricia to have a relationship with you, but that doesn't mean you won the battle because you've still got to convince me. So you'd better stay good to her and not break her heart or mistreat her in any way, got it? You and I both know she deserves better than that."

"Ya have nothin' to worry 'bout, Kate. I would never do those things to her. I have only the purest intentions for her heart."

"Good, because otherwise, you'll have me to deal with, and you definitely don't want that."

"No, Kate, I definitely don't."

"Good. Well, bye, then," she said with a friendly wave.

After watching Kate disappear from his sight, Clay entered Tricia's room and finally closed the door to the hallway. "Damn, darlin', you're gonna make this date hard on me, aren't ya?" Clay couldn't help but check her out while she stood bent over her laptop, reading her last few e-mails.

"What are you talking about, Clay? I agreed to go out with you, didn't I?"

"That's not what I'm referrin' to, Tricia," he answered as he kept his eyes on her long legs. Legs that were only being covered by a pair of jean shorts.

"Then what's wrong, Clay?" she asked, still not paying attention to his gaze.

"Nothin's wrong, darlin', ya just look so damn good." He was happy that they were going swimming later.

"Thanks. I thought you'd like it," she answered with a smile.

"Oh, I definitely do." *I think ya look hot in anythin' ya wear.* He was eager to see her in her swimsuit.

"Well, I did pick it out especially with you in mind."

"Ya did, huh?"

She'd chosen a light-blue cami under a white overshirt allowing him a view of her cleavage that her regular T-shirts didn't give. She wore a pair of jean shorts that could've only looked sexier if they were cutoffs, and her hair was pulled back into a ponytail with a black elastic. A pair of Converse completed the look of a laid-back Saturday evening date.

"Uh huh, so what do you think?" she asked, slowly spinning around.

"I think ya look hot, darlin'."

"I was hoping you would."

"So ya ready to go, Tricia?"

"I think so."

"Did ya remember your swimsuit like I'd said?"

"Yeah, it's right here." She moved her overshirt out of the way to expose the bikini's blue strings.

"Great, then let's go."

"Do I need to bring a towel?"

"Nope, I've got everythin' we need in the back of my truck. Now let's get goin' 'fore it gets dark." Clay couldn't help but laugh as he watched Tricia scurry around her dorm room like a mouse looking for food, checking to make sure she was leaving the room just the way she wanted it.

"Okay then, I guess we can go."

"Finally."

Her lack of readiness reminded him of why the term 'waiting on a woman' was all too true.

"Hey, I was just making sure that I have everything I need while we're gone."

"Darlin', the only thing ya need to worry 'bout bringin' is yourself. I've got everythin' else covered," he assured her as he placed his hands on her sides. "Now, are we ready to go?"

"Hey, now that I'm taking us seriously, don't think it'll be that easy for you," she replied, slipping her hands into his. But as she returned her hands to the familiarity of his, the fact that they were actually going on a date hit her and made her feel nervous.

"I don't. But a guy can try, can't he?"

"Try all you want, Clay, just know that it won't be that easy."

"Darlin', I wouldn't want it any other way with ya. Besides, the chase is half the fun."

"Then I hope you have some good running shoes on."

"If that's the case, then I do believe these boots of mine will serve me quite well."

"You'd better hope so, Clay."

"Darlin', I don't hope, I *know*."

"So, where are we going and what are we doing, anyway?"

"It's a surprise location. We're havin' a picnic and goin' swimmin'."

"Oh, okay. Hence the need for the swimsuit."

"Tricia, you're nervous 'bout this date, aren't ya?" His grin didn't help her.

"Just a little."

"Glad to hear it." He closed the gap between them and gave her a kiss. "I've been wantin' to do that since I first came into your room."

"But we haven't even started the date yet."

"Don't care. After our first kiss, that's what I'm lookin' forward to each time I see ya."

"Wow!"

"Yep, so now let's go." He ushered her out.

They walked hand in hand to his truck. Now that Tricia was on an actual date with him, Clay's chivalry meant more to her than when she just saw them as a game.

131

As they got in his truck, Tricia couldn't help but feel self-conscious about everything she did. Since she was now putting meaning behind their relationship, she saw Clay differently.

"Ya ready to get this date started, darlin'?" Clay asked her with a flirty smile as he started the engine.

"Um, yeah. Where did you say we were going?" Her nervousness was already causing her to forget what he'd said.

"I didn't, but I have a good feelin' you'll like the destination." He winked at her as he rested his arm on top of the seat cushion behind her.

Feeling the butterflies return, all Tricia could do was look out the passenger side window. Even though she and Clay had already kissed plenty of times, she still felt the nervousness a first date brought.

"Enjoyin' the view?" he asked, watching her keep her head turned toward the window.

"Yeah, it's nice." She wondered if he could tell how nervous she was. "Hey, do you mind if I turn on the radio?"

"No, be my guest."

"Great." she answered, tuning it until she found a country station.

"Ya good now?" he asked.

The only way she could make the date better for him was if she slid over and sat next to him.

"Pretty much."

Clay found himself glancing over at Tricia's legs. *Damn, the inside of my truck has never looked so good,* he thought as he stared at her long, bare legs. *But I'd better pay attention to the road, otherwise, I'm gonna wind up gettin' us into an accident!* He mentally forced himself not to stare at her legs. He could just imagine the look on Bryan's face if he ended up totaling his truck because her long, gorgeous legs had distracted him.

Tricia enjoyed getting to ride in a classic truck. She found it surreal that the scene in her mind was now a reality. This day was almost how she had pictured it. From her ideal guy driving them to their location, in the truck of her dreams, no less, to enjoying the sound of country music coming out of the radio. All she needed was the road covered in autumn foliage. If that came into view, then the day would be absolutely perfect. She couldn't believe how everything seemed to be coming together for her. It was like God was finally answering her prayers by her meeting Clay and him taking her out on their first date.

"We're almost there, darlin'," she heard Clay's voice.

But just as she was about to acknowledge him, there it was: the two-lane road with the myriad of colorful leaves awaiting them.

"Oh, Clay, this is so beautiful!" she exclaimed as her nervousness evaporated.

In seconds, she was returning to her previous position right beside him so she could experience the moment just how she'd imagined it. Feeling his arm find its home around her, Tricia took in the intimate drive.

"Clay, thank you for this." She kissed his cheek as their destination came into view.

"You're very welcome, darlin'." He smiled, thanking God that he was the man in the truck with her.

CHAPTER
- TWENTY-FIVE -

Parking on a dirt road underneath a tree's covering, Clay turned off the engine. "Okay, darlin', we're here."

Looking around, Tricia could see a large grassy area with a willow tree nearby and a pond in the distance. "You did a good job, Clay."

"Glad ya think so."

"How did you find this place?"

"I did my research," he answered before getting out of the truck and heading for the tailgate.

He did his research?

Clay was continuing to surprise her as his actions showed his genuine desire for her. He was the most unexpected man Tricia had ever met, and yet here he was, proving his ability to sweep her off her feet.

"Hey darlin', ya ever gonna get out and join me?" she heard Clay yell out.

Watching him close the tailgate, she saw that he had already unloaded his truck. On the grass by the willow tree now lay a blanket while he carried over the picnic basket.

"Oh, yeah. Sorry, I'm coming."

"Glad ya finally decided to join me."

Taking a seat on the blanket, Tricia watched him unpack what he had prepared for them.

"I figured we'd eat first and then go for a swim in that pond. Sound good?"

"Yeah, that sounds fine."

As Tricia watched him set everything up, she was blown away by his effort. He had everything from sandwiches to potato salad. "You really know how to spoil a girl, don't you?"

"What can I say? When I wanna impress a girl, I go all out."

Clay couldn't thank God enough that they were finally on their official first date. Just knowing that it was only the two of them out here made him even more thankful that he wouldn't have to share her attention with anyone else.

"I . . . uh, don't know what to say."

"Why say anythin', why not just dig in?" He saw how hard she was trying to hide her blushing.

"Um, okay."

Soon, Tricia was settling into their date as she filled up her plate.

"Oh, before I forget." He took out two bottles of Diet Coke from the basket. "I wasn't quite sure 'bout what ya liked to drink, so I figured I'd just stay safe and get ya what ya ordered at the restaurant."

"Thanks, I guess. You remembered what I'd ordered?"

"Tricia, I took in everythin' that ya did. But don't worry, I like a girl with an appetite."

"Wow, I had no idea that you did that."

"Yep, and I enjoyed every minute of it. Tricia, ya have no idea what ya do to me."

As the two enjoyed their picnic, Clay found himself getting stuck on Tricia's eyes. Her beautiful hazels captivated him in a way no other woman's had. There was just something about them that made him never want to look away.

"You really do like to be straightforward, don't you?" she asked, fixing her eyes on his gorgeous baby blues.

"I just tell it like it is, is all."

"You certainly do. Not that I mind it. I like your directness. I'm just not used to all the flattery."

"I can tone it down if ya want," he offered.

"No, Clay, it's fine. It's like I said, I'm just not used to it."

"Good. Ya enjoyin' the food I made for us?" he asked after seeing her empty plate.

"Yeah, I am. You really have a talent, Clay," she answered with an embarrassed smile.

"Ah, it's just somethin' I enjoy doin', especially if I have someone to do it for," he brushed her compliment off with a wink.

Feeling the butterflies, Tricia smiled as she hoped to God that nothing was on her face after eating her last bite. It seemed with every facial gesture of his, Clay had no problem reminding her of the chemistry they shared.

"So ya think you'll be ready to go swimmin' soon?" he asked anxiously.

"Yeah." She was curious to see what he looked like in just his board shorts. "But what'll we do until then?"

"I know, why don't ya show me that bikini you're wearin' underneath?" he asked with a devilish grin.

"Tell you what, Clay, I'll show you my top, but you'll have to wait a little while for the bottoms, okay?"

"If that's all I can get for now, then I guess it'll have to do." He nodded.

"It is." She began to slide off the overshirt.

One more piece to go and then I get to see her bikini top.

Clay was like a little kid anxious to open his Christmas presents as he waited for her to remove her tank top.

"Actually, I just got a better idea."

"Hey, wait a minute, what'd ya do that for?"

"Just hold on, Clay. I think you'll enjoy what I have in mind."

"Okay, go 'head." He was curious to see what she was talking about.

"Instead of me just stripping for you, I want to turn this into a game."

"Oh?"

"Yep. Instead of this being a one-person show, we're both going to strip."

"How do ya mean?"

"Well, we're each going to take turns asking the other questions until we're both down to our swimwear."

"Ah."

"Yep, so who would you like to go first, me or you?"

"Ladies first."

"Okay, then. Here are the rules before I ask you your first question. First, the person being asked the question is the one to take off a piece of clothing. Second, we only ask the number of questions it takes to get down to the swimwear. Third, if either one of us doesn't want to answer a question, we don't have to. Agreed?"

"Agreed." He enjoyed her creativity.

"Okay, so my first question for you is where is that sexy southern drawl of yours from, anyhow?"

"That'd be Stockton, North Carolina, darlin'." He grinned and took off his plaid overshirt to reveal his white undershirt.

"Very nice. Now it's your turn."

"Okay, what did ya first think when I had asked ya if Kate's seat was taken?"

"How insanely surreal it was to see my perfect type asking me to sit down at my table and that I'd never seen a man with such gorgeous blue eyes before."

"I see ya've got a bit of charm in ya too, darlin'."

"As you like to say, Clay, it's the truth."

"Well, regardless, I appreciate it nonetheless." He watched her take off her overshirt.

"My turn again. Are you and your parents close?"

"My mama, yes. My father, no. My father walked out on my mama and me when I was four years old for some floozy he met at a bar. She told him that he could be somethin' if he would just run away with her. So it's been my mama and me ever since." He thought about the bastard and his gold-digging, homewrecker of a mistress who had probably just used him for a ride out of town.

"Wow, Clay, I'm so sorry," she apologized. She could see the pain and anger he'd kept for the man lingering in his eyes.

"It's not a big deal anymore." He shrugged before taking off his hat.

Damn, his hair looks good with the sweat mixed in. His sex appeal lit up her face.

"Ya enjoy me hatless, huh?" he asked with a smile.

"Yeah, I do." She wanted to mess up his hair with her fingers.

"Have ya always lived in California?"

137

"Yes, born and raised." She took off her tank top. "If you ever had the chance to see your father again, would you?"

"Honestly, Tricia, I really don't know. He hurt my mama and me real bad...so I really don't know." He took off his T-shirt to uncover his muscular upper body.

Damn! She couldn't help but stare at his lightly tanned skin and well-toned muscles. His upper body was just the way she liked it. His abs had just the right amount of definition, which was a little less than a fully chiseled six-pack, and his biceps gave her a good visual of how strong he really was. He even had no chest hair. Clay Gibson definitely had the kind of upper body she enjoyed seeing on a man.

"I take it ya like that too?" he asked with a sexy grin after watching her well-satisfied expression spread across her face.

"Well, it does look like you do a really good job of taking care of it, Clay." Tricia was unable to remove her eyes from his chest. Just the size of his biceps made her wish that she could see them being put to use.

"Glad to know I've given ya some eye candy, darlin'," he replied with a smile. Her pleased expression made him feel proud of his physique.

"You definitely have, Clay," she assured him with a shy smile.

Now that she had seen him shirtless, Tricia felt a strong desire to move a little closer to him. Urgently, she moved their picnic's leftovers out of her way and crawled over to his side. She folded her legs up against his and felt their intimacy return.

"Tired of your seat, darlin'?" he asked with an ever-knowing grin.

"I just love that you have plenty of hair for me to run my fingers through." She remembered how it'd felt while she kissed him in her parents' den.

"Glad you're enjoyin' it, darlin', but I do believe I've still got one more question to ask ya," he reminded her with an inward excitement, knowing that he would soon be seeing her bikini bottoms.

"Okay."

"When ya grabbed my underwear, were ya really curious 'bout the kind I wear? Or were ya just tryin' to get me sidetracked in order to get your underwear back?" He was curious but also wondered what her reaction to the question would be.

"What do you think?" She repeated her action from that night.

"I think ya oughta just answer the question, darlin'."

"Well, to answer your question, it was both. Though I'm definitely still curious to know what style of underwear you wear," she teased with a not-so-innocent smile of her own. Then as if Christmas had finally come, she removed her fingers from his pants and slipped off her shorts.

"Glad to hear it, darlin'. Now it's your turn," he replied as he heard their conversation take on a different tone.

"What was going through your mind each time I got bumped into you on the dance floor?"

"That I was damn glad ya had, and I was hopin' ya were too." He answered with a smile as he thought back to that night and the knowledge that he was now getting to see her in just a bikini.

"Oh, so then each time I apologized . . ."

"There was really no need 'cause I was happy it happened."

"Oh."

"Tricia, I was happy it happened 'cause that meant I got to feel your body against mine and stare back into those beautiful hazel eyes of yours each time ya felt the need to apologize," he finally explained when he could see in her eyes that she had been looking for a more captivating response from him.

"Oh, that's so sweet, Clay." *Jackpot!*

"It's the truth, darlin', every word." He realized that his ability to pay attention to her facial reactions was going to come in very handy for him in the future.

"I guess that means I get to go again, although, I think that answer deserves a kiss." She brought a hand up to his face and pulled him into a kiss.

"Anytime, darlin', and especially when I know I'm gonna get a kiss from ya as a reward," he replied, gladly welcoming her lips against his.

CHAPTER

- TWENTY-SIX -

As Clay enjoyed her kiss, he found himself hungry for more. As he tasted the deliciousness of her chapstick-covered lips, he moved his mouth to the side of her neck.

Hearing her moan out in pleasure as he aroused her senses, Clay kept with his lips against her skin. Concentrating on the sensuousness of each kiss, he added his tongue. As he lightly licked her skin, he could hear more moans of delight as he briefly glanced at her face to see that her eyes were closed and she had taken on an expression of sweet serenity.

"I believe I've found your weakness, darlin'," he informed her as his mouth traced her neck and jawline.

"Uh huh," was all Tricia could respond. Clay's ability to arouse her made her want to return her fingers to his hair.

Enjoying Tricia's body was Clay's main goal. He removed the black elastic from her hair and gradually brought her down to the blanket where he returned his lips to hers. No matter how many times he kissed her, he could never get enough of her lips. It was like she had found the secret ingredient to keeping him coming back for more. As he kept the passion going with his lips, he began caressing her soft skin. With his hands free to roam all but her most feminine areas, he eagerly explored her body.

"Uh, Clay . . . even though I'm enjoying the way you're making me feel right now, I uh, think we need to stop."

"Why? Is somethin' wrong?"

"No, it's just . . . I want to wait for marriage."

"Do ya now?" he asked after sliding off her and propping his left arm up to support his head.

"Yes. Are you okay with that?"

"Of course, what makes ya think I wouldn't be?" he asked. He moved a few strands of hair from her face.

"Well, I just figured . . ." she began, thinking an incredibly hot guy like him must've slept with his share of women already.

"What? That with all the women after me, I must already have plenty of experience in the bedroom? Is that it?" He raised his eyebrows.

"Well, it's not like you're the ugliest man on the planet, Clay. So, it stands to reason that you would have at least some experience under your belt."

"Well, Tricia, I'm sorry to disappoint ya, but I'm actually waitin' for marriage myself." His fingers softly caressed her cheek and jawline.

"So you mean you haven't slept with a single woman?"

"Nope. So, I, like you, have absolutely no experience in the bedroom."

Clay's words were an aphrodisiac to her ears, and Tricia returned her lips to his. As their making out welcomed her to another new experience with a guy, she felt Clay lick her lips a little. Realizing that meant he wanted more, she gave in. Instead of just kissing him with her lips, they were now french kissing.

As his mouth kept hers busy, she remembered the enjoyment of her fingers through his hair. As their kissing kept their heat on high, she began to feel the urge to be even closer to him. Just the feeling of his body against hers as his kiss fueled her desire made her realize that they needed to stop.

"Clay." He moved his mouth back to her neck. "I think we need to stop."

"Okay, darlin', no problem. Damn, had I known ya'd react like that to my waitin' for marriage, I would've told ya a long time ago!"

"Funny. This is something new for me, Clay. I'm not used to having these feelings running through my body. So, when you're making me feel so damn good and I don't want you to stop, it's hard for me not to just be curious to see where it'll lead."

"Tricia, it'll lead to sex."

"Does it have to, though? Can't I just push it to the edge and then stop?"

"Darlin', that's what we just did. Either you or I would get to a point where we would just be too aroused."

"Oh."

"Yep, so stoppin' is fine since neither one of us is ready for that next step." He had never made out with a woman who'd made him want her so badly like Tricia did when they kissed. "Now what do ya say we go get in that pond? After all, that is why I had ya wear that bikini as well as why we played that strip game." He stood up and took off the remainder of his outer clothes to reveal the board shorts he had on underneath.

"Okay," she agreed.

Taking in his new look, Tricia took off her Converse to join him.

"I'll race ya to the water, darlin'," he yelled out.

When he looked back to see that she hadn't chased after him, he immediately stopped in his tracks with a better idea.

The next thing Tricia knew, he was running back to her and picking her up. "Clay, please tell me you're not planning on throwing me in?" she asked as he carried her over to the water.

"Okay, I won't. I'll show ya instead," he teased.

"No Clay, please don't!" she cried out, doing her best to wriggle out of his grasp but with no luck.

"Sorry, darlin', but you're goin' in."

"No Clay . . . ahh!" Tricia felt the cold water make contact with her body as she was submerged.

Clay stood waiting. To his delight, she gracefully emerged from the water. He had never seen anything so beautiful as the way she looked with the water pouring down her body as she stood to face him.

"Clay, I can't believe you just did that!" she exclaimed with her hands on her hips.

"What can I say, darlin', ya weren't movin' fast enough." He brought her to him.

"So you had to drop me in?"

"I could've thrown ya over my shoulder and then dropped ya in."

"Well, now that I'm all wet, it's your turn." She pushed him into the water.

"Oh, gettin' rough with me now?" he teased after wiping the water from his face.

"I'm only making things fair, Clay." She was unable to get over how incredibly hot he looked as the water dripped down his body.

"Uh huh. You just wanted to get back at me for droppin' ya in."

Or maybe I just wanted to see that hot body of yours all soaking wet. This wet look of his spurred on another fantasy. "So does this pond have any place for some real privacy, Clay?"

"Tricia, ya do realize that there ain't no one else 'round here, right? So there's no one out here to see us doin' anythin' anyway."

"I know, but I want complete privacy with you, Clay." She slipped her arms around his neck, giving him a kiss.

"Oh, well, in that case, follow me." He removed her arms from his neck and dove into the water.

CHAPTER
- TWENTY-SEVEN -

Following Clay's lead, Tricia swam with him to the other side of a waterfall.

"Wow, Clay, this is so beautiful!" she exclaimed after seeing the water wall on one side of her and the rock wall on the other.

"I thought ya'd like it."

"Oh, I definitely do!"

"And as ya requested, it gives us complete privacy. So, we can do whatever it is ya wanted us to have all this privacy for," he reminded her with a smile.

"That's very good to know because what I wanted us to have complete privacy for was this." She wrapped her arms around his neck and tasted his mouth. "You know, with all this kissing we're doing, I'm going to end up becoming an expert at it."

"Is that what you're after, Miss Perkins?"

"Well actually, Mr. Gibson, what I'm after I've already told you that I'm not yet ready for." She moved a hand to his chest.

"Darlin', don't tempt me 'cause even though I told ya I'm waitin' for marriage, too, seein' your hot body in that wet bikini is makin' it damn hard for me to keep resistin' ya."

"Sorry about that, Clay. Just the sight of you dripping water and with your hair all messy like this is making me want you just the same." All of a sudden, she felt her bikini top loosen.

"Uh, darlin', what's wrong? Why ya actin' so shy all of a

sudden?" he asked after watching her randomly cover her chest with her arms.

"Um, this is rather embarrassing, but the strings of my top just loosened . . . it's an old bikini."

"Oh, well, come here then," he instructed as if her problem was no big deal.

"Why, what are you going to do?" she asked.

"Tie the strings back together, of course."

"Oh, okay."

"Now ya can either come a bit closer or turn 'round. Take your pick."

"I think I can handle coming closer." She closed the gap between them. As she pressed her body up against his, she decided to rest her head on his shoulder making sure to keep her hair out of his way.

"Almost done," he informed her as his hands went from retying one pair of strings to the next, all the while enjoying every second that her body was so close to his. "Ya know, this seems a little backward given it's usually the guy takin' off the bikini, not the other way 'round."

"I guess you can just add it to the list of everything else we've done backwards in our relationship."

"Guess so. Well, I'm done."

"Thank you."

"No problem, although ya know I could always untie 'em for ya and we could go skinny dippin' instead?" he grinned.

"Clay, I don't know you well enough for that," she declared with a quick shake of her head. "Besides, the only man I want to see me like that is the man I marry."

"I know, I was just jokin' with ya, Tricia. If it makes ya too uncomfortable to do that, then we don't have to. Although, if I were to keep my head 'bove water the whole time then ya wouldn't have to worry 'bout me seein' anythin' anyway."

"True, but suppose you wanted to kiss me or hold me in your arms? You may not be able to see my body, but you would definitely be able to feel it."

"Tricia, are ya 'fraid it's gonna lead us to havin' sex?" he asked point-blank, "'cause ya don't always have to worry 'bout that happenin'.'"

"No, at least, I wasn't before you mentioned it."

"Then what is it? What's the problem, if not that?"

"Clay, other than you, I've never been this close to a guy before, much less naked in front of one. So, I would feel extremely vulnerable and uncomfortable if I were to be that close to you with nothing on. Especially since I know we'd both want to show our affection for each other, probably even more so," she explained. "I'm not used to being that open with my body, Clay, and knowing that you'd be completely naked in front of me . . ." She paused to glance at his trail of black hair that came to a stop at the waistband of his shorts before looking back up at him. "Well, I'm just not ready for that yet." She hoped that he got the picture and that her issue wasn't always just about having sex.

"Okay, I get it." He realized that her reason made her a lot more conservative than most women her age.

"But who knows, Clay? If you're fortunate enough, you might be that lucky man I finally show my body to." Hooking her hand around the back of his neck, she brought her other hand up to his chest. Then with a teasing smile, she gave him a quick kiss before swimming back to the shore.

"Damn, that woman sure knows how to keep me hooked!" he exclaimed after she had put in his head the possibility of seeing her naked.

CHAPTER
- TWENTY-EIGHT -

Back on shore, Clay and Tricia walked to his truck to grab the towels. As the warmth from the sunlight disappeared, Clay took two towels from the bed of his truck. He handed her one so they could both dry themselves off before the coolness of the night had a chance to chill their wet skin.

"Clay, given the fact that I've already told you about my boyfriendless past, you've never once mentioned your dating history. What about you, how many girlfriends have you had?"

"Just one," he said as they walked back over to the picnic for dessert.

"Really, was it serious?"

"Yeah. I thought I was gonna marry her."

"Oh, so then you must've had some really strong feelings for her if that was the case." She couldn't help but wonder if she should be worried about competing feelings. Her feelings for him, and his for his ex.

"Yeah, at one point, I did. We were together not long after I first got into racin' durin' high school."

"What happened?"

"The day after I'd bought her ring, she told me that she'd been cheatin' on me and was leavin' me for the other guy."

"Wow, Clay, I'm so sorry." Tricia could see the discomfort in Clay's body language as he talked about it.

"Ah, it's over and done with."

"And you don't have any residual feelings for her that I need to be worried about?"

Not after my last conversation with her, he thought. "Tricia, if I did, I wouldn't be here with you."

"You may think that, but I don't want to be opening up my heart to you if you still have a longing for your ex. After all your hard work in fighting for us to be together, I don't want to finally give in to you only to find that a part of you still wants to be with her."

"Tricia, it's not that way at all. Yes, I wanted to marry her, but I've also realized that the woman I thought I wanted to marry was completely wrong for me."

"So you're telling me that I don't have to worry about you eventually wanting her back? Because if I do, tell me now so that I don't naïvely give you my heart."

"Darlin', Nikki was my past. You're my present and, hopefully, my future," he assured her truthfully.

"So her name's Nikki, huh?"

"Yep, Nikki Reids. We were childhood friends."

"Well, I guess her loss is my gain." They returned to the blanket.

"I'm glad ya think so. Now how 'bout we enjoy some dessert?"

As she savored the decadent treat, Tricia began to wonder if cooking was another one of Clay's qualities. If it was, Clay was the man of her dreams come to life.

"I just have one question for you."

"And what's that, darlin'?"

"Did you make this, or did you buy it?"

"And not end this date with a Clay Gibson creation? Of course I made it. The rest is back in my motorhome."

After she had slowly eaten the last bite, Tricia stated contentedly, "I'm going to love being in a relationship with you!"

"Speakin' of, what do ya say we end this date with ya bein' my girlfriend?"

"I, um . . . wow! I thought we would've at least gone on a few more dates before I would hear you asking about calling me that."

"Why? Is callin' me your boyfriend at the end of our first date a bit too soon for ya?" he teased.

"I just wasn't expecting to hear it so soon." She was still shellshocked by it.

"Well, considerin' the fact that we've already gotten pretty physical with each other, I think it's safe to say that it makes sense."

"You do have a point."

"Besides, ya don't think I'd go to all that trouble of gettin' ya to date me if I didn't wanna further our relationship at some point, did ya?"

"No."

"So then, what do ya say to us endin' this date with you callin' yourself my girlfriend and me your boyfriend? 'Cause ya damn well know that even after the next few dates, I'm still gonna want the same thing with ya."

"I guess that means I've accomplished another first," she smiled.

"Glad to help ya check that off your list, darlin'."

"Me too, because I honestly don't think I would've ever been able to get you out of my head if I ever wanted to date someone else."

"Yeah, I could see how gettin' someone as hot as me out of your head might 'come a problem."

"Clay!"

"What? I was just jokin'."

"Way to ruin another defining moment for us."

"Aw, darlin', ya know that I'm damn glad to be your first boyfriend. Hell, this is all I wanted ever since ya first told me 'bout your never havin' a boyfriend 'fore."

"I certainly put up quite a fight, didn't I?" She felt proud that she hadn't given in to his smooth southern charm.

"Yes, ya did. But honestly, Tricia, 'fore you, I'd never met a woman who made me wanna work so damn hard to win her heart over. Ya've no idea how much I thank God for Bryan noticin' you and Kate."

"Ah Clay, this is exactly why I said you were too dangerous for me. You know just how to hit the spot with your charm."

"Tricia, I ain't tryin' to charm ya right now. I'm tellin' ya the God's honest truth 'bout the way I feel 'bout ya. I know ya've had your worries 'bout me, but my desire for ya has turned me into a man who would do whatever it takes for you."

"And I appreciate that so much, Clay. I was very glad to hear that you're waiting for marriage too."

"Oh, and why's that?"

"It means that you respect the woman you're going to marry enough to wait for her."

"Is that right?"

"Yes, especially if you want that girl to think that she's completely worth your wait." She was happy to know that none of his previous girlfriends had ever been that intimate with him.

"Tricia, are ya tryin' to tell me somethin'? Do ya think you're 'the one' for me?" he asked with flirty eyebrows.

"I'll let you wonder that for yourself."

"Damn, ya can be so sexy sometimes!" he exclaimed with a hand over hers. Smiling back, Tricia watched his hand play with hers.

"Is that so?" She seductively removed her towel from her body to expose her dried bikini to him.

"Yep, and you're definitely makin' me wanna experience more of ya."

"Really?" she asked, keeping the façade going.

"Uh huh," he answered, wanting to make her his right there.

"Well, it's too bad that I'm not actually that way," she laughed as she broke out of her character.

"Damn, I wish ya would've kept goin' with it. I was really gettin' into that side of ya."

"I know, I could tell. Though, to lessen your disappointment, I suppose I can change seats," she offered. She moved their dessert plates out of the way so she could sit between his legs and relax her body up against his.

"This definitely works for me." With Tricia in his arms, they enjoyed the night's cool air and the moon's glow.

"I thought it would. But honestly, Clay, that side of me is just for fun. I'm really not that girl, and even if I was, we aren't in the right place."

"Oh, and where would this right place be for ya?"

"I've always had a fantasy of being with a cowboy in a hayloft.

The guy would be shirtless but wearing the hat, jeans with the belt buckle, and boots."

"I think I can picture that."

"Really, Clay."

"No, not the fantasy, darlin', the location. Yeah, ya may be from the city, but the country's more to your likin'."

"Yep, I definitely prefer the country to the city."

"I was a cowboy for a few summers in high school, and my style does contain the required articles of clothin' on your list, so I do believe I qualify for your fantasy," he surmised with an entirely too-sexy grin. "In fact, I even know of a barn that has that desired hayloft you're lookin' for." He winked as the image of the barn next to his childhood home came to mind.

"You'd have to put a ring on my finger first, Clay."

"Ooh, just a second ago I 'came your first boyfriend, and now ya wanna be my fiancée? Ya sure like to move things fast, don't ya, darlin'?" he teased.

"Now you know that is not what I meant!" she began. But as soon as she saw the teasing grin on his face, she realized what he was doing. "Oh you!" she exclaimed. She turned around and pushed him down to the blanket.

"Ooh, is this ya takin' charge of me, city girl?" he asked as she lay on top of him.

"What do you think?"

"I think ya need to quit talkin' and kiss me!" he answered as he pulled her lips down to his.

CHAPTER
- TWENTY-NINE -

"Mm, Bryan, that restaurant was a good decision!" Kate exclaimed.

Entering his hotel room after a night out at a fancy restaurant, Kate found herself a little tipsy.

"You're just saying that because you've had too much to drink." He clumsily took off his tie after closing the door to the hallway.

"True, but I'm also saying that because the food was great!"

As she watched him struggle, Kate grabbed the tie to stop him.

"If having small enough portions to make you want to order room service later is your definition of great, then yeah, their food was great."

"Bryan, right now I'm too drunk to care." She forced his lips to hers with a quick pull of his tie.

"Babe, are you sure you want to do this?"

"Definitely!"

Pushing him onto the bed, she took off her heels and straddled him.

"Okay, then."

They tumbled around on the bed and hurriedly stripped each other of their clothes. "Ooh, I forgot the condom!" she blurted out once he'd gotten her down to her lacy, black underwear. Pausing the action, she headed for her purse. Bryan had some bad news for Kate once he had taken the condom and attempted to put it on. "What's wrong?" she asked when she saw the look on his face.

"It's this condom, babe," he began but ended with a smile, "I'm too big."

As if he had just pushed her turn on button, her eyes lit up and a big smile spread across her face. "Ooh, lucky me!"

"Babe, you have no idea!" He got up from the bed to grab a condom from his wallet. "Crap!"

"What's wrong now?" she asked, using the sheet to keep her covered.

"The condom. I forgot to replace the expired one I'd thrown out."

"Oh, well, I still want you."

"Kate, are you sure? If we have sex, there's a good possibility I could get you pregnant."

"Bryan, I know. I'm not that drunk."

"Okay, I just wanted to make sure."

"I appreciate that."

Getting up from the bed, Kate slipped her dress back on. She walked over and put her arms around his neck. "Bryan, even though I am admittedly a little tipsy, I love you. I love you, and I want to be with you."

"I love you, too, Kate Bransin," he returned with a kiss. "I want us to do this right. No rushing. Just enjoying each other in the moment for as long as that moment lasts." Picking her up, he brought her back to the bed.

With that teeny bit of romantic foreplay, Kate unleashed all the passion she'd felt for him ever since the night she'd showed him her car. Bryan Walker was everything to her. He possessed a listening ear for her parents' crap, knew how to treat her right, and could match her sophisticated ways. She had fallen head over heels in love with him.

"Oh my God, Bryan . . . that was amazing!" she exclaimed as her sweaty body fell off his. "You were right, I had no idea!"

"I'm glad you enjoyed that, Kate."

"Oh God, yeah . . . you were just . . . wow!" she continued as her breathing returned to normal.

"Good. I'm glad. Now I have a question I want to ask you." He turned onto his side so he could look into her eyes. "Now mind you, I would've asked you this, sex or no sex. It just so happens that I'm asking you after our first time together."

"Yes?"

"Will you marry me?"

For her answer, she slid back onto him and gave him another round of mindblowing, incredible sex.

"Bryan, you were serious about asking me to marry you, right?" she asked once they'd exhausted themselves for the night.

"Yes, Kate." He held her, thanking God that she had caught his eye at the club.

"So you weren't just asking me because I gave you drunk sex?"

"No, Kate, I want to marry you. I would've asked you regardless."

"Good, because I want to marry you too. In fact, I've wanted that for quite some time now."

"Me too. Even though I made a joke about it to Clay right before I went and introduced myself to you, you've made me fall in love with you. Babe, you wouldn't believe how much I look forward to hearing your voice at the end of every day. Or how it soothes me whenever Clay and I have had a busy day at the speedway. I love to call you just to say hi and see how you're doing."

"Oh, I'm pretty sure I have a good idea about that."

"Right. Well, I want to make us permanent. And since neither of us are traditional like Clay and Tricia, what do you say to moving in with me as the first step toward us getting married?"

"I say I can't wait! The sooner I'm out of my house and away from my parents, the better."

"Speaking of, did you want me to ask your father for his blessing?"

"No. I'd rather us just elope."

"I suppose we can do that, but don't you want your parents to be there? I know you guys don't have the greatest relationship, but don't you think your parents would want to see their only daughter get married?"

"Bryan, calling my relationship with my parents 'not the greatest' is an understatement. Besides, I bet you that my mom would intentionally take on another shift at the hospital just because she'd be too damn jealous that I've actually found a man who will love me for the rest of my life while she still has to deal with my dad."

"Okay, but let's not put that on the save-the-date card if you change your mind."

"Funny."

"Kate, I only asked because most women appreciate that. Being from the South, that's sort of the protocol down there."

"Then isn't it a good thing you don't follow Southern protocol too strictly?"

"Yes, but then again, you also aren't a Southern belle, or from the South, so my asking your father for his blessing isn't necessarily expected."

"And aren't you lucky for that? We can skip the steps of asking my father for his blessing and waiting until marriage, and go straight to the sex." She jabbed her finger at him.

"Yep, we sure can." He caressed her skin.

As Bryan held Kate in his arms, he found himself more content than ever. Just the feel of her skin against his made him damn glad that he'd taken advantage of getting her number.

CHAPTER
- THIRTY -

"Bryan proposed to you?" Tricia asked as she drove Kate back to the airport.

"Yeah, last night, after dinner. I'll admit that it wasn't as romantic as you would've preferred. But it was definitely heartfelt."

"Wow, that's huge. So how did he do it?"

"See, that's the thing, Trish. He didn't really do it any creative way. He just asked me right after our first time together."

"Oh. Are you sure it wasn't just his south-of-the-border head asking you because that's how he felt in the moment?"

"Yes, he made it clear to me afterward that he wanted to marry me and that his timing just happened to be when we had sex."

"Huh."

"Trish, before we slept together, I told him that I loved him, and he told me that he feels the same way. God, I've never met a man like him before. Hell, he even made sure I was okay with not using a condom."

"So you had unprotected sex with him?" Tricia exclaimed with wide eyes.

"Yes. If I get pregnant, then I get pregnant."

"But you barely know the man, Kate. You've only known him for the same length of time that I've known Clay, which has only been a few months!"

"I may not have known him for very long, but I definitely know him well."

"I don't doubt that. You've certainly spent enough time on the cellphone with him."

"Hey, it's not my fault I was the one who chose to take advantage of getting to know my boyfriend sooner rather than later. You were the one who chose to keep battling it out with Clay instead of just giving in to your desire for him right from the start."

"Kate, now that's not fair."

"Yet you attacking my relationship with Bryan is?"

"Kate, I never attacked your relationship with Bryan. I simply questioned his genuineness when it came to the timing of his question since a man asking a woman to marry him right after they've had sex doesn't exactly sound very genuine to me."

"Trish, just because he didn't use some damn creative way to ask me like you require, doesn't mean he wasn't genuine!" she shot back.

"Kate, you've really got to stop dealing out these low-blows that throw my point of view back in my face."

"Okay, I'm sorry for pulling out the extra punches, but your opinion of his proposal hurt me."

"And I'm sorry about that, but that's just how I feel about it. Don't get me wrong, it's great that he asked you. It's just the timing that gets me. I want him to be serious about it."

"I appreciate your concern for how he treats my heart, Trish. I suppose it's your version of the speech I gave Clay right before you guys went out on your date."

"Wait a minute . . . you talked to Clay before we left?"

"Yep, and I told him that even though he's persuaded you into being with him, he's not off the hook with me."

"Kate, you had no business telling him that."

"You mean like how you had no business telling me your opinion on Bryan's proposal?"

"That's not the same thing, and you know it."

"Sure it is. Your opinion of Bryan's proposal is your way of watching my back so I don't get burned. I made it clear to Clay that he better not mess with you or he'll have me to deal with, which is my way of protecting you from getting hurt."

"Kate, mine was an opinion about a proposal. Yours was launching an attack before the war had even begun."

"So I gave Clay a preemptive warning for how he should treat you. You should feel lucky to have a best friend who'll do that for you." Tricia pulled into the airport.

"I suppose you're right. It is nice to know that my best friend's got my back," Tricia agreed, pulling up to departures.

"Always."

"I'm glad to hear it." Tricia parked her car and unloaded Kate's suitcase from her trunk.

"Well, bye . . . and don't forget to call me when you get home."

"Why, so you know I got there safely?"

"No, so I know if you forgot anything."

"I appreciate how much you care."

"Of course I do, now hurry up before you miss your flight."

"You know, I think that should be the other way around. I think it should wait for me."

"Just go." The girls hugged.

Kate headed into the airport, and Tricia drove back to her dorm.

CHAPTER
- THIRTY-ONE -

Pulling into the parking lot, Tricia wondered if her new roommate had arrived yet. They shared a white cinderblock room with one medium-sized window that gave the room its only sunlight.

"Oh, hey, you must be Tricia Perkins," a girl with long, black hair and dark-green eyes said. "I'm Claire Blackburne."

"That'd be me. Glad to finally meet you." She took in the girl's indie band T-shirt, distressed jeans, and black Converse.

Claire was arranging her side of the room. She had a zebra print bedspread with hot pink sheets and matching pillows, a lime-green, multifunctioning desk lamp stocked with essentials, and a matching lime-green trashcan. Photos were strategically displayed on a fabric-covered board with ribbons crisscrossing it.

"Are you heading up to the student union soon for tonight's raffle?" Claire asked.

"Actually, I had completely forgotten about it."

"No big, but from what I've heard, they've got a lot of cool prizes and the school will be serving pizza and soda. I think it's SKSC's way of welcoming everyone to the new school year."

"Yeah, I read that on a flyer. So out of the thirty-two-inch Samsung flat screen, NASCAR tickets, and Kinect, which would you want?"

"As much as I'd love to jam with the Kinect, I think I'd have to go with the NASCAR tickets. I would really love to watch Clay Gibson do his thing in person."

"You know, if you really want to watch him race, you don't actually have to participate in the raffle," Tricia began excitedly, anxious to tell someone that he was now her boyfriend.

"And why not? Unless you actually know him somehow."

"Well, that's the thing. I kind of do."

"You do? How? Like one of those 'friend of a friend' type things?"

"Actually, no. Clay Gibson's my boyfriend."

"Really, are you serious?"

"Yeah, I am. So, if you want to watch him race, I can ask him for a couple of tickets. Heck, he probably wouldn't even mind setting up a personal tour of the pits for you either." Tricia couldn't help but flash back to her conversation with him about it at the restaurant.

"That would be so cool, except I already bought a raffle ticket."

"That's okay, it's not a big deal. If you win, cool. If not, then I can get Clay to get you a pair."

"Either way, I think I'm damn glad that you're my roommate!"

"You're welcome. I'm glad my NASCAR connection can come in handy for you," Tricia chuckled.

"Oh man, me too. I just think that Clay Gibson's the best driver in the whole circuit. He is so awesomely aggressive that he's the only reason I watch the damn sport in the first place. Otherwise, it's just a bunch of fast cars making one left turn after another. Without him, the races are always so freaking boring. I don't have the patience to just sit there forever until a driver messes up."

"I definitely know what you mean. I remember going to the AAA 500 with my dad and a couple of his friends only to end up resting my head against his shoulder and taking a nap because the race was so damn boring."

"Man, you don't know how many times I've wanted to head back to my car to do just that," Claire agreed.

"Tell me about it. Do you remember what time the raffle is supposed to start? I think the flyer said seven or seven thirty, but I'm not entirely sure."

"Nope, but since it is a quarter to seven already, we might as well head up there now. We don't want to end up missing out on all the free pizza once the football guys get there and have to deal with it already being cold," Claire suggested.

"Yeah, I suppose you do have a point there."

Making the short walk to the student union, Tricia and Claire added themselves to the already crowded event.

"Damn, I guess we were right to leave when we did!" Tricia exclaimed. She watched the students empty the pizza boxes and grab a beverage from one of two ice chests. The feeding frenzy turned into smaller groups.

"I think I'm going to grab a couple of slices before I'm left with just the grease stains on the box," Claire informed her. The smell of hot pepperoni and sausage were calling to her taste buds.

"I guess I'd better join you," Tricia agreed as she watched someone walk by with a plate of her favorite pizza.

As Tricia waited to get her pizza, she turned her head just in time to see Clay walk into the building wearing his fire suit. Thinking it had to be an illusion brought on by hunger, she closed her eyes and looked again. Sure enough, there he was, walking across the student union. *Damn, he even looks hot in a fire suit!*

"Oh my God, Tricia . . . can you believe it? Clay's here! He's actually here! Clay Gibson's in our student union!" Claire exclaimed.

"I see that," Tricia replied. *Though I wonder why he is here?*

"Why don't you go say hi? Better yet, introduce me to him," Claire pushed as she grabbed the last two slices of pizza.

"I suppose I can," Tricia agreed, grabbing a Diet Coke.

"Sweet! You are such an awesome roommate!" Claire couldn't believe she was actually going to meet the driver she'd seen race on TV and at the speedways.

"Clay!" Tricia tried calling out.

Hearing his name, Clay immediately looked around. To his delight, he saw Tricia waving at him with one hand while her other held a soda balancing a plate of pizza on top of it. He waved back and began to head in her direction. That was until he was suddenly ambushed by several college students wanting his autograph.

"I um, guess we'll just have to wait," said Tricia. *God, why does he have to be so damned hot and effortlessly charming?* She watched the ladies continue to adore him even after he'd given each his autograph and showed his well-mannered thanks for their support.

Just as Clay was about to excuse himself from the crowd and say hello to Tricia, a student body government member escorted Clay to where the raffle drawing would be held.

"Well, so much for that opportunity." Tricia focused her attention on her food.

"Ah, it's not a big deal. Maybe you'll get a chance to introduce me to him after the drawing?" Claire suggested.

As Tricia and Claire finished eating, the drawing was announced. Soon the dining hall was filled with students and staff.

As each prize was awarded, Tricia kept wondering why Clay was making a professional appearance at her school. On their date, he hadn't told her that he was going to be here. Yet here he was, sitting on one of the tables, dangling his legs off the side as he waited his turn for whatever it was he was here to do.

Damn, that man sure knows how to be secretive! The crowd continued to wait for the three major prizes to be awarded.

"Ladies and gentleman, as you all know, the three main prizes for tonight's raffle drawing are a thirty-two-inch Samsung flat screen TV from Big Al's TVs, two tickets to the next NASCAR race with additional passes for the speedway's FanWalk, and finally, an Xbox 360 Kinect," the student body president began, only to be interrupted by excited howls from some of the guys. "And I'm sure many of you are wondering why NASCAR driver Clay Gibson is here," he continued but with a brief pause to keep the suspense going. "Well, the driver of the Evergreen Tools number-zero-six car is here to personally hand out those two tickets and the FanWalk passes to the lucky winner," he concluded amid catcalls from the ladies.

"So that's why he's here . . . to hand out the tickets!" Tricia told herself.

CHAPTER
- THIRTY-TWO -

"And the TV goes to Ticket Number 0-3-8-5-2-0-3," the student body president announced.

"Yes, that's me!" a guy called out.

"And now, we have the NASCAR tickets." Clay got off the table and prepared to hand out the tickets to the lucky winner.

With one quick shuffle of the bag, the vice president pulled out another blue ticket. "And the lucky winner of two tickets to the next major NASCAR race and two FanWalk passes is Ticket Number 0-2-3-8-7-5-4."

"Hot damn, that's me!" a girl shouted out.

"Congratulations." Clay hugged her after handing her the tickets.

"Thank you," she returned with a smile.

"And now, for our final prize of the night, an Xbox 360 Kinect!" the president announced, bringing on another onset of howling male voices. "The winner of the Kinect is Ticket Number 0-2-2-9-8-4-5!"

Knowing that she hadn't put a ticket in, Tricia didn't have to worry about it being hers. Claire looked at her own ticket and saw that the numbers matched. "Sweet, I won."

"Congrats." Tricia realized that her roommate was now going to get her chance to see Clay up close.

"Thanks, be right back."

Claire made her way through the obstacle course of tables,

students, and staff to claim the last prize. Her ticket was confirmed and the drawing was brought to a close.

"Thank you all for coming out to tonight's raffle drawing and for supporting Southwestern Kansas State College. Go Hillbuilders!"

As Claire began to head back to Tricia, she realized she had a chance to meet her favorite driver. Turning to Clay, she nervously blurted out, "My roommate's your girlfriend."

"She is?" Clay asked after he'd returned to sitting on the table.

"Yep, she told me about you two before we came over."

"Ah, and you are?"

"Claire Blackburne. I'm a big fan."

Smiling appreciatively, Clay said, "Thank ya . . . though if you'll excuse me, I've gotta go finish up."

After shaking the student body president's hand and signing the final autograph, Clay concluded the promotional duties for himself and Walker Motorsports.

"I apologize for that, Claire. Ya said ya came with Tricia?"

"Yep, we were sitting in the back."

Glancing in that direction, he saw Tricia sitting at the table waiting for them.

"Then let's not keep her waitin'," he replied, gesturing for Claire to lead the way. "Hey darlin', I'm very glad I get to see you again."

Pulling her into his arms, he gave her a brief hello kiss, forgetting about Claire and not even thinking about Tricia's possible discomfort.

"Clay, why didn't you mention that you were going to be making another appearance here?" Tricia asked. She wanted to be more affectionate, but with Claire as an audience, limited it to hand-holding.

"'Cause I wanted it to be a surprise."

"Then you were successful. I see you met my roommate in the process."

"Yep, right after she'd claimed her prize."

"Sorry you didn't win the tickets, Claire," Tricia added as she looked at the game box.

"Ya were hopin' for the NASCAR tickets?" Clay asked Claire.

"Yep, that's what I'd originally put my raffle ticket in for."

"Oh, well, in that case, I'll have a couple at Will Call for ya both."

"Are you serious?" Claire asked in amazement.

"Yeah, and if ya'd like, I can even throw in a couple of pit passes."

"Really, Clay?" Claire continued.

"Sure. I'd be glad to show ya both 'round the speedway."

"Wow, this is going to be so cool! My favorite driver giving me a personal tour of all the behind-the-scenes stuff."

"You're very welcome, Claire. I'm happy to show my gratitude to such a devoted fan."

"Yeah, Clay, thanks. This is really nice of you," Tricia added, but with a kiss on his cheek.

"You're welcome, darlin'," he replied. He slipped an arm around her waist and hooked a thumb through her belt loop.

"Clay, you are so awesome, and you definitely never have to ever worry about me not being a fan of yours! Now, if you two will excuse me, I've got some friends I got to go brag to!"

"Glad to hear it." He watched her hurriedly disappear from sight.

"Well, you certainly made her day, Clay," Tricia commented.

Now that they were alone again, they took their time walking back to her dorm room.

"Yeah, I definitely did, and I'm hopin' that you'll make mine after I give ya your tour."

"You've been hoping for this since the restaurant, haven't you?"

"Well, it ain't a bad idea, darlin'."

"How do you plan on keeping Claire busy long enough for me to really show you my appreciation?"

"I know a couple of other drivers who'll gladly step in to take my place," he answered, unaware of how true his statement really was.

CHAPTER
- THIRTY-THREE -

"Are you ready to go, Tricia?" Claire asked. Pulling her black hair into a ponytail and then slipping on a hat with Clay's car and number on it, she realized that all she was missing was his autograph on the hat.

"Yeah, almost," Tricia answered as she mirrored her roommate's hairstyle.

"Man, this is just so freaking exciting! It's so awesome that Clay's your boyfriend, Tricia!"

"Wanting to reap the benefits, huh?"

"I'm so sorry . . . that must've sounded really superficial."

"Hey, I'm glad he is too. He's got a lot of great qualities that make me damn glad he is."

"I don't want it to seem like I'm abusing your connection to him because that's not my intent at all."

"It's fine, Claire. Heck, he left a ticket for me, too, and it isn't like I'm refusing it."

"Are you sure? I'd really hate for you to think that I'm just using him, or you, for the perks."

"Yes. Besides, I'm sure your taking advantage of his generosity is the last thing on his mind."

"I hope so. Are we ready to head to the speedway?" Claire asked with her purse hanging from her shoulder.

"Yeah, I believe so."

"Great, then, let's go."

As Claire drove them to the speedway in her lime-green Toyota Matrix, they listened to the pre-race show. As the announcers rambled on about each driver's statistics and what to expect from their racing teams, they heard some of the attention go to Clay and his driving stats.

"Wow, his stats do sound pretty impressive," Tricia commented.

Clay had been the official pole leader more often than any other racer, led the most laps in each race, and his number zero-six car had landed him in the winner's circle more times than most.

"Well, he is number one in the standings, so his stats don't really shock me," Claire pointed out.

"How long have you been following him?" Tricia asked.

"Since he first appeared on the scene. His looks sort of helped me get interested, but it was his skillful racing that kept me hooked. Had it not been for Clay, I would've left NASCAR a long time ago."

"According to the announcers, he sounds like one of the best."

"Yeah, he's definitely got that Earnhardt aspect going for him. He likes to be a bit more aggressive behind the wheel than all of the other drivers."

"Ah," Tricia responded.

"Yep. A lot of drivers don't like that attitude too much."

"Yeah, I could see it pissing some of them off, but it's not like he does anything illegal, right?"

"No, he doesn't. His driving just tends to push some of the other drivers over the edge, and their fans too."

"Oh."

"So I take it that even though your boyfriend's in NASCAR, you don't follow the circuit all that often?"

"Actually, no. I love watching NASCAR. In fact, my dad was the one who got me into it. I guess I'm just not current with it."

"Well then, you got into it at a good time. Clay sure knows how to make each race very entertaining. He wasn't as famous a few years ago. I guess NASCAR is just now starting to take notice of how his talent is bringing more viewers to the sport."

"Damn, you know a whole lot more about his career than I do, and I'm his girlfriend!"

"True, but you know a whole lot more about his personal life than I do, and I'm a devoted fan."

After arriving at the speedway, the girls headed for Will Call. Tricia let Bryan know they had arrived. "Clay's in a drivers' meeting, so I'll be there in a few to pick you up."

Watching the multitude of other race fans make their way to the concession area and grandstands, they saw Bryan maneuver a motorized cart around the crowds of people walking.

"Nice. Do they provide you with one at every speedway?" Tricia asked as he zoomed them over to Clay's motorhome.

"Yeah, but Clay wants to buy one for himself so he can supercharge it."

"Sounds like a man after my own heart," Tricia replied.

"Ha, the man's a damn speed demon if you ask me," he retorted.

After hearing the cart stop outside his motorhome, Clay opened the door and watched the girls disembark.

"Hey, aren't you supposed to be at that drivers' meeting? Just because you're kicking all of the other drivers' asses out on the speedway doesn't mean you can go rogue," Bryan said.

"It just got finished . . . and I ain't goin' rogue, Bryan."

"Uh huh, that's not what I hear at the owners' meetings. All their drivers think you're a loose cannon."

"Please. I just wanted to make sure that I was here to greet the girls when they arrived. That's all."

"Right. Just remember that you've got an hour until you've got to be in your car, Clay

"Yes, boss." Clay saluted.

"Clay, thank you again for doing this. It really is nice of you."

"It's my pleasure, Claire. Now let's get this tour started. I hope ya girls don't mind walkin', 'cause Bryan's the only one with a cart." He stepped down the door's retractable steps to join them.

"No, walking's fine," Tricia answered.

"Good. Well, as ya can see, this is my motorhome." He gestured at the metal home on wheels as if it were on display.

"Oh, it's so beautiful, Clay. I couldn't imagine you living anywhere else," Tricia teased.

"Thanks, darlin', your compliment means so much." He placed a fist to his heart.

"Touché."

"That's what I thought."

Clay led them in the direction of their next stop as Logan pulled his cart up next to them. Nikki was in the passenger seat and Reese and Tyler were in the back. Immediately feeling his playful mood leave him, Clay wondered how this was going to play out. Especially since his ex-girlfriend was now seeing his new girlfriend.

"Hey, Clay, who are these two lovely ladies with you?" Logan asked as he eyed each one.

"This is Tricia Perkins, and that's her roommate, Claire Blackburne," Clay answered.

"Nice to meet you both. I'm . . ." Logan began only to be cut off by Claire.

"Logan Austen. You drive the number thirteen car, right?"

"That's right, and the one behind me is Tyler Woods. He drives the number twelve car."

"Wow, I can't believe I'm actually getting to meet two more NASCAR drivers in one day. This is so incredible!"

"Make that three. Reese McKibbon drives the number eight car."

"Wow, this is so crazy!" was all Claire could think to say.

"So, Clay, whatcha doing with these two ladies, anyhow?" Tyler asked, taking a special interest in Claire.

"I'm givin' them a private tour of the pits," Clay answered.

"I'd ask if you want to join us since I'm sure you'd rather ride than walk, but all I can offer is my lap for Claire," Tyler offered.

"Wow, I um," Claire responded.

"Actually, I can make this my stop, so you and Tricia can have this seat if Tricia's comfortable on your lap," Reese added.

Hearing the offer, Nikki immediately turned around. *How dare he even suggest that!* She waited to see how Clay would answer.

Grabbing Tricia's hand, Clay remembered the threatening voicemail and felt the need to protect her. "While we appreciate the offer, we're good. Claire, if ya wanna go with 'em, that's fine."

Feeling slightly uncomfortable after watching Clay slip a hand into Tricia's, Claire realized that she might as well go with the others. Even though she had come to get a private tour from her favorite driver, getting to sit on another driver's lap was a bonus.

"So whatcha say, Claire, you want to join us?" Tyler asked.

Reese took his cue to leave, and Claire realized that Tyler's lap was now no longer her only option.

"Sure, why not?"

With a glance back at Tricia and Clay, it was clear to her that she would now be the third wheel to their romance. Climbing onto the cart, Claire settled in next to Tyler who was already putting his arm on the backrest behind her.

"Have fun," Tricia added before Logan hit the gas. "Clay, who was the girl sitting next to Logan?"

"Nikki."

CHAPTER
- THIRTY-FOUR -

"I can see why you didn't want us to go with them," Tricia stated as the cart became immersed in the crowd of people.

"Yeah, sharin' a cart with my ex and her new boyfriend while my new girlfriend is sittin' on my lap . . . not exactly my ideal situation."

"I guess it wouldn't be mine, either, if I had an ex."

Clay responded with a smile. "Darlin', that is hopefully one thing ya will never have."

"I guess that means we can never break up, then."

"Tricia, I don't even wanna think 'bout ya possibly bein' with another man."

"Clay, I was only joking, but if we're going there, then you should know that I'm a date-to-marry kind of girl."

"So it's either break up or marry ya?"

"Exactly."

"Then since I don't wanna imagine ya movin' on from me, marriage will have to be down the line."

"Clay, you're not asking me to marry you right now, are you?" she asked worriedly. Their conversation sounding eerily like he was nearing a proposal.

"Of course not, darlin', but given the fact that I never wanna be referred to as your ex, that's my only choice."

"Ah, you make marrying me sound so romantic."

"Tricia, considerin' I don't ever wanna think 'bout ya kissin' another man or holdin' another man's hand, it is my only choice."

Tricia returned his heartfelt sentiment with a kiss.

"So what do ya say we continue with this tour since it's now just you and me?" he asked.

"I say I'm glad it's just you and me." She squeezed his hand and rested her head on his shoulder.

Feeling at peace, Clay walked with Tricia to the pits where he pointed out his team's garage, introduced her to his crew members, and gave her an up-close view of his car. Introducing her to other drivers they passed along the way, he led her back to his motorhome so she could properly thank him for her private tour.

"Wow, Clay, that was really cool!"

"I thought ya'd enjoy it. Especially with me as your tour guide."

"Your presence certainly did add to my enjoyment," she agreed as he handed her a bottle of cold water from the fridge. "So you think Claire will end today with a date with Tyler?" she asked, twisting off the cap and taking a swig.

"Considerin' how Tyler was eyein' her, I wouldn't doubt it," he answered, backing her up against the kitchen counter.

"I take it you're ready to receive my appreciation?"

Clay trapped her against the counter with a hand on each side of her. "Somethin' to that effect." Clay watched her take another sip of water only to have some of it drip onto her chin.

"Oops." Tricia was ready to wipe it off with the back of her hand. As she lifted her hand to her chin, Clay stopped her.

"No, let me." He licked the droplets off of her skin, arousing her a little.

"Clay, are you trying to seduce me?"

"Maybe I am, maybe I'm not, but if that ends up bein' the case, I certainly won't complain."

He took his water and dripped some of its contents onto the skin right above her shirt's rim.

"Clay, isn't foreplay reserved for sex?" she asked, sliding her fingers into his hair.

"It can be, but that doesn't mean I can't also be a little creative when it comes to my kissin' ya."

Moaning at the feel of his mouth against her skin, Tricia wished they could take it so much further. Taking in every sensation he was giving her, she closed her eyes and felt his lips against hers. She kissed him back as soon as she felt the familiarity of his tongue in her mouth. She felt him pick her up and set her on the counter.

"We don't . . . need to . . . worry about . . . Bryan interrupting us, do we?" she asked in between the kisses.

"Nope. He leaves me to myself 'fore the race starts. It's sorta my way of preparin' for it. So you're all mine for the next fifteen minutes."

"Glad to hear it." She wrapped her legs around his waist.

"Ooh, wanna get close to me, huh?" he asked with a sexy grin. He cupped her butt and pulled her to him, forcing her body right up against his.

As he continued to kiss her, Tricia returned the favor with the partial removal of his fire suit. Clay grabbed the back of her belt and forced himself to stop. Leaning in he whispered, "Tricia, I wanna be so much closer to ya."

"Clay." She felt her breathing get heavy. Feeling his body that close to hers and his low baritone whisper adding to her seduction, Tricia ached for him to pick her up and carry her into his bedroom. The only thing she could think to do was clutch at his shirt as she took in the fact that he'd just told her he wanted to have sex with her.

Feeling his heart beating against hers, Tricia found herself unsure of what to do. She wanted to kiss him back and tear off his shirt, but then she also knew she wasn't ready until she had a wedding ring on her finger.

"But we're both waiting," she whispered back.

"I know."

Returning his lips to her neck, Clay realized he just couldn't take it anymore. Hearing Tricia moan out in pleasure, he finally picked her up and carried her into his bedroom. He was playing with fire as he laid her down, bringing them closer and closer to the edge. He removed the elastic from her hair and slipped it into one of her back pockets and could feel her hip pressed into him. He knew that it wouldn't be long until he was ready for sex. He began to remove her shirt when he heard his cellphone buzz. He paused briefly to decide whether or not he should check it.

Looking down at Tricia, Clay knew that he didn't want to rob her of her virginity before her wedding night. "Darlin', we might as well stop." He put his shirt back on.

"Okay."

Turning his attention to his cellphone, Clay read the text message. "Shit!"

CHAPTER
- THIRTY-FIVE -

"Clay, what's wrong?" Tricia asked. Sitting up, she pulled the elastic out of her pocket and put it back into her hair.

"I . . . uh . . . it's nothin', Tricia. Sorry I yelled that."

He wasn't about to fill her in on the threats and that Nikki had stalked them.

"Then why were you staring at your cellphone?"

"I already told ya, darlin', it's nothin'." He hoped she would just drop it.

"Bullshit."

"What did ya just say?"

"The one word I needed to in order to find out the truth for myself." She grabbed the cellphone out of his hand. "Clay, what the hell does this mean?"

"Tricia, that's why I yelled."

"So somebody's threatening you?"

"Not just somebody. Nikki."

"Wait a minute, your ex sent you this message?"

"That, I don't know. But she did leave a message on Bryan's machine that involved you."

"She did? But I haven't actually met her."

"Yeah, she was warnin' me that if I wasn't careful, I'd end up havin' ya watch my career go up in flames."

"And did you tell the authorities?"

"No, at least, not yet."

"Why not, Clay?" She thought that should've been the obvious next move. "Your ex is clearly threatening your livelihood. I would think that would merit a visit to the police station."

"'Cause I didn't know it was her 'til Bryan told me the day you and I reconnected."

"Does Nikki know that you know?"

"I highly doubt it."

"Then you still have the edge on her, Clay."

"Yeah, I do, but that still leaves this and the other text messages I've received unanswered."

"Wait a minute . . . this isn't the first one you've received?"

"Nope. I've received a few of 'em since the day we met."

"And you never said a damn thing to me? What the hell is wrong with you, Clay? I'm your girlfriend for crying out loud!" she exclaimed as her hurt and anger mixed into one emotion. "I have a right to know when someone's threatening my boyfriend!"

"I'm sorry, but even if I'd told ya, there was still nothin' ya could do 'bout it."

"Clay, you don't know that."

"Tricia, unless you're some kinda technical genius that can trace a number from a blocked text, there is absolutely nothin' ya can do."

"Then don't race."

"What?"

"Clay, if somebody's out to destroy your career like this text says, and apparently all of the other ones you've received, if you don't listen to it and stop racing . . . then don't do it. Don't race."

"Tricia, no matter what this text says or the warnin' on Bryan's answerin' machine, I ain't gonna let any of it stop me from racin'."

"But why not, when giving in to whoever's behind the text messages could save your life?"

"'Cause Tricia, racin' is my passion, and I ain't willin' to give that up just 'cause somebody wants to send me threats to mess with my head."

"But what about me, Clay? Don't you care that if you don't follow what this text message says, I could lose you?" She held up his cellphone in her hand. "Clay, I care way too much about you to see that happen!"

She wanted to say I love you but knew she just wasn't ready yet.

"Tricia, I'm sorry. I just didn't wanna worry ya 'bout any of it."

"Well, damn it, you should've!" Her anger spilled out of her eyes and onto him. Had they been bullets, he would've been dead.

"I know, and I'm sorry I didn't. I just care way too much 'bout ya to get ya involved in somethin' that won't do ya any good to worry 'bout."

"But Clay, isn't that my choice to make?"

"Not when it's you bein' used as a ploy to get to me."

"How does Nikki know anything about me, anyway?"

Getting comfortable on the bed, Clay stretched his legs out as she curled up next to him. He put his arm around her. "My guess is she's been stalkin' me. She watched me kiss ya goodnight the night after I surprised ya at your house."

"You don't think she watched us on our date, do you?"

"No, we were alone that day."

With a big sigh of relief, Tricia waited for the rest of what he had to say.

"Darlin', ya can trust that I will always do my damnedest to keep ya protected. 'Cause as I said 'fore, I care way too damn much 'bout ya to ever let anyone take ya away from me. In fact, I can honestly say that I love you." After moving his other arm to rest on her legs he locked eyes with her. "Now I know that I already told ya 'bout my lovin' Nikki to the point of wantin' to ask her to marry me, but what I never told ya was that I was never in love with her. And I know that now 'cause I never felt for her what I feel for you. Tricia, I'm in love with you," he confessed.

"You are?"

"Yes, and I think you're the most beautiful girl—woman—I've ever met. Ya have one hell of a sexy side that can get me so turned on whether you're meanin' to show it or not. Your damn hardheadedness challenges me to the point of lovin' it and hatin' it all at the same time. Ya have one hell of a sense of humor that I just can't get enough of and are one of the most passionate people I know. So if my feelin' all that 'bout ya means I'm in love with ya, then yes, I'm in love with you. And to tell ya the truth, Tricia, I've never felt this way 'bout any other woman 'fore in my life." He looked into her hazel eyes that he adored so much. "God am I glad I convinced ya to give me, and us, a chance!"

"Sure you're not just saying all of that because you've got me in your arms and on your bed?" she asked, slipping a hand over his and intertwining their fingers.

"No, Tricia. I mean every word of it."

"Wow, Clay! I don't know what to say." She kept her eyes on his and took in everything he said. "I had no idea you felt so strongly about me."

"Well, I do, and don't worry, I'm not expectin' ya to say anythin' in return. I just wanted to tell ya so ya could understand why I held back all those threatenin' texts from ya."

"And I appreciate your wanting to protect me, Clay, because I've never had a guy feel so strongly about me to want to take on that job."

"Darlin', it ain't a job . . . and I'm very glad to do it."

"I honestly don't know if I feel the same way about you," she began as she let his heartfelt words continue to slowly digest in her head before settling into her heart.

"That's all right, Tricia. As I said 'fore, ya don't have to return my words."

"I know, but I think it's important that I share how I feel about you."

"Okay, then, have at it." Clay removed his hand from hers and intertwined his hands behind his head.

"You comfortable enough, Clay?"

"Darlin', the clock's tickin', so I only have so much time till I gotta go get in my car," he reminded her.

"Oh, right. Well, to start off, I think you're a very incredible guy. You have all of the qualities I want in a man. Honestly, Clay, I couldn't believe a man like you showed up the night we met. Just to hear you ask me if her seat was taken in that southern drawl of yours and then to see you wearing the kind of look I find so incredibly hot on a guy . . . well, I thought God had tipped the universe for me that night."

"Can't get enough of my look, huh?" he asked with a sexy grin.

"Damn you and your sexy smile. But, no, that damn look of yours has been haunting my dreams and fantasies ever since."

"So you're fantasizin' 'bout me too, huh?" he asked with flirty eyebrows.

"That's another conversation in and of itself, Clay."

"Okay, so besides these erotic fantasies, what else drives your heart wild 'bout me, darlin'?"

"Well, I love that you want to protect me and how charming a woman is second nature to you. Heck, I even love the fact that you like to cook. I could marry you for that alone."

"I certainly won't mind cookin' for ya, darlin', especially breakfast in bed." He looked down her body.

"Clay, you'll only get to enjoy what's underneath these clothes if we get married."

"I can't wait!"

"You sound rather confident about our future."

"I just know what I want, is all."

"Well, anyway, your interest in cooking will make it so that if we ever do get married, we wouldn't have to hire a chef since you already know that I'd rather watch sports than be in the kitchen."

"And there's that sense of humor I love so much."

"No, Clay, that's the truth."

"Ya crack me up, beautiful."

"Glad to hear it. Now, I do believe it's time for you to go kick some ass in your race car."

"Glad to, darlin'. I'm also glad to hear that you're thinkin' 'bout me turnin' ya on," he teased as they made their way off his bed.

"You're never going to let me forget that I told you that, are you?" she asked as they stood up.

"Not as long as I have the chance to make it happen."

Pulling her to him by a front belt loop, he sensuously slid his hand across her jeans' back pocket, cupping her butt. Seeing her surprised look, he just smiled. With his hand maintaining its firm grip, he thrust her up against him and gave her an arousing kiss where he slipped his tongue into her mouth and stroked her tongue with his. Bringing his other hand to the base of her head, he slowly applied even more pressure. "Now if that doesn't get your fantasies revvin' for me, then we got a problem."

Dazed by the force of his sexual prowess, Tricia stood in shock as he gave her a quick, and much less forceful, kiss before heading off to his car.

CHAPTER
- THIRTY-SIX -

"Ladies and gentlemen, boys and girls, let's all say those four famous words together!" the announcer's voice rang out over the PA system, "Gentlemen . . . start . . . your . . . engines!"

From that moment on, the only noise heard was the sweet rumbling that came from each stock car. Tricia watched intently from behind the safety gate in front of Clay's motorhome as each driver swerved their car up and down the track, preparing their tires for the wear and tear of the race. Two by jagged two, the decalled cars followed the pace car around the track until it was time for each one to venture off on its own.

Once the green flag had been waved, Tricia fixed her eyes on Clay's number zero-six car so she wouldn't miss a single second of his racing skills. Her gaze also captured other drivers' attempts at taking the lead. First, one driver would show his strength by moving to the front, then remain there for a few laps until another driver bested him. Despite each driver's fight to be number one, she continued watching Clay as all of the cars zoomed past her. Watching him smoothly weave around each car that obstructed his ability to get to the front, she understood Claire's comparison of him to Earnhardt.

"Damn, he really *is* good at this!" she exclaimed. Watching his car finally take the lead position, Tricia realized that his talent wasn't just a bunch of hype. She continued watching him repeatedly zoom by and found it ironic that she used to wish that one of the drivers would do something exciting during the race. But now that she was Clay's girlfriend, that was the last thing she wanted to see happen.

"So how'd your private tour go?" Bryan asked, pulling up to her in the cart.

"Fine, but shouldn't you be where you've got a good view of the whole race?"

"I'll get back to it. I was just coming to get you so you could get that view as well."

"Oh. Do you know where Claire is? Logan and Tyler never brought her back to Clay's motorhome after they finished her tour."

"Ah, Claire's fine. They brought her up to the Sky Box a little while ago."

"Well, I hope she didn't mind having them as her tour guides considering the whole point of Clay being her tour guide was because she's a big fan of his."

"From the way Logan was taking on the role and how Tyler kept his attention on her, I'd say she was pretty smitten by it all and probably didn't care who her tour guides were just as long as they were drivers."

"Sounds like she and Tyler made a connection, then."

"You can definitely say that. Now hurry up and get in so I can take you over there."

"Oh, right. Sorry."

Bryan quickly switched his foot to the gas so he and Tricia could head back to the air-conditioned Sky Box.

"Bryan, Clay told me that he's in love with me." Just hearing herself say the words made her heart race.

"Oh. Did you say anything in return?"

"I didn't tell him that I'm in love with him, too, if that's what you mean."

Damn, I hope he's okay, Bryan thought to himself as he pictured Clay reeling over a second woman with unrequited feelings for him.

"No Bryan, it wasn't like that." She stopped after seeing his facial expression. "I guess I just don't know what I feel for him. I've never been in love with a guy before, so how would I really know?"

"Tricia, are you sure you don't want to talk to Kate about this?

I think she might be able to help you figure this out better than I can. She knows you a whole lot better than I do." He wished the Sky Box wasn't so far away.

"Bryan, I'm telling you this because Clay is your best friend and maybe you could give me some advice on how to handle the situation."

"Well, in that case, I can tell you one thing for certain. The man's crazy about you. He has been ever since he first decided he had to win you over. Tricia, Clay's not the type to admit something like that unless it's the truth. He's not one to play with a woman's heart or his own. If he told you that he's in love with you, then that means something."

"Thank you, Bryan . . . that helps."

"You're welcome. Now, how about we go upstairs and watch the rest of the race?"

With a nod of agreement, Tricia followed him up to the Sky Box where she saw Claire taking advantage of the free snacks and beverages. "Hey, so how was your private tour with Logan and Tyler?"

"It was nice. After they brought me up here, Tyler gave me his number."

"That's great. He did seem pretty interested in you."

"I know. Soon, I could be dating a NASCAR driver too!"

As Tricia returned her attention to Clay's car, a wreck reminded her of the threat he'd been dealing with. Just watching one car slam into another nearly gave her a heart attack. Fortunately for her, his car was well ahead of the wreck.

"I'm gonna win this race for ya, darlin'," Clay said to himself as he kept his lead. He couldn't have been more elated that he'd told Tricia that he'd fallen in love with her. Yeah, not hearing her say it back had stung a little. But he also knew that she needed time and then he would eventually hear those beautiful words returned.

As he began to round the next turn, his crew chief, Rich Wilkes, got his attention.

"Hey, be careful . . . you've got number thirteen edging on your right bumper."

"Thanks."

Doing his best to stay ahead of Logan, Clay attempted to

adjust his position. Despite his slight turn of the wheel, Logan managed to stay right on him.

"Clay, you'd better figure something out or Logan's going to get you," Rich warned.

"I know, and I'm tryin'." Clay attempted one more move, but Logan was eager to finally prove himself and he bumped Clay, sending him fishtailing into the wall.

"Clay!" Tricia screamed out in total panic. Tricia glued her eyes to the scene hoping that Clay would climb out of the mangled metal and walk off the track without a single injury, but he didn't. Instead, an official waved the red flag, stopping all action on the speedway. As she heard the disheartening sound of each car's engine turning off, a deafening silence took its place as everyone anxiously waited for Clay to get out of his car.

"Come on, Clay . . . show me you're okay!" she pleaded. To her horror, she watched the engine catch fire as flames spewed out from under its hood. "Clay, just get out of the damn car already!" she screamed again. She was forced to watch an ambulance drive to Clay's totaled car while EMTs blasted the burning metal with a fire extinguisher.

"I'm sure he'll be okay," she barely heard Claire say.

Despite the reality, Tricia kept praying to God that Clay would miraculously unbuckle himself from the car and slowly climb out to show everyone that the crash hadn't killed him. But after the EMTs had put out the fire, she was forced to watch him be carefully pulled out and onto an awaiting gurney. As her eyes stayed magnetized to the scene, she felt like her heart was going to beat right out of her chest. Just seeing his unresponsive body caused the thudding of her heart to drown out the world around her.

"Oh God, please let him be okay!" she quietly prayed as she watched him being loaded into the ambulance. Knowing that she couldn't be there to hold his hand made her feel so damn helpless and broke her heart. "I've got to get to him!" she stated to no one in particular as she watched the ambulance rush him off the track. "Does anyone know where they're taking him?" she asked. She finally tuned in to what was going on around her.

"Mercy Medical Center," Bryan answered.

Following Bryan down to his cart, Tricia and Claire were driven to the hospital. Tricia restlessly waited for Bryan to pull up to the hospital's entrance and wondered what injuries Clay might have sustained. She hated knowing that right that very second the EMTs could be giving him CPR. The thought of him taking his last breath on that gurney and her not being able to give him one last kiss before he did, practically killed her. She couldn't and didn't ever want to, imagine living in a world without Clay Gibson.

CHAPTER
- THIRTY-SEVEN -

Within seconds of Bryan bringing his white Dodge Ram to a stop at the hospital's entrance, Tricia pushed open the back passenger door just in time to see the ambulance pull up. She rushed over as the EMTs carefully brought Clay out. Seeing that he was unconscious, she watched his labored breathing into his oxygen mask. He lay with his eyes closed, his fire suit unzipped, and his T-shirt cut open. "Clay!" she exclaimed when she realized what that meant.

Slipping her hand into his, she leaned down and whispered into his ear. "Clay, stay with me. I . . . I need you in my life." Her tears moistened his skin as she kissed him on the cheek.

"Ma'am, you'd better hurry up," an EMT warned her as he watched the doctors heading toward them.

Nodding her head, Tricia squeezed Clay's hand. As she was about to put it back down, she felt his thumb barely twitch against hers.

"Ma'am, here they come," the other EMT informed her.

With another nod, Tricia gave Clay's hand a quick kiss before laying it back down next to his side, transferring him to the doctors' care. She heard Clay's stats being given to the doctors and she watched them take him inside. She went to find Bryan and Claire now that she'd had a chance to see Clay postcrash.

"So . . . how'd he look?" Bryan asked Tricia the moment she'd found them waiting by his truck.

"He was unconscious, and they had to administer CPR," she answered, choosing to keep his thumb's twitching to herself.

"Damn!" Bryan replied.

"You don't think it was a threat, do you?" Tricia asked.

"Clay told you?" Bryan asked.

"Yeah, right before the race," she answered. "I told him not to. But of course, he didn't listen."

"But wasn't it just an accident?" Claire asked.

"I hope, for his sake," Tricia answered. She wasn't about to fill Claire in on all the drama Clay had unloaded onto her just minutes before he'd jumped into his race car.

Heading into the hospital, Tricia anxiously waited for a doctor to tell her Clay's status. Even though he had labored breath, she didn't know if he could be on the verge of death again.

As she waited, she thought about telling a nurse at the nurses' station that she was Clay's wife. She contemplated the story she would give to the heavyset woman wearing pink scrubs and wondered if the woman would even believe her. The woman looked at a computer screen wearing a pair of multi-colored reading glasses attached to a string of beads around her neck. Tricia knew she couldn't pull it off.

Sure she could say, "I was cleaning the house when I got the call about his accident, and after I rushed here, I realized I'd forgotten to put my wedding ring back on in the chaos." But the truth was, no matter how much fake information she gave in order to know Clay's injuries, it was still a lie, and she just couldn't live with that. She had an innate need to be honest.

Tricia imagined what it would be like to be known as Mrs. Gibson: to have Clay's last name attached to hers and actually be known as a NASCAR driver's wife. As she imagined Clay as her husband, she saw a couple of NASCAR officials enter the hospital. Making a brief stop at the nurses' station, they were given the access to Clay's room that Tricia had to keep waiting for. She wondered if Nikki's threat was about to become public knowledge.

What seemed like hours later, but probably wasn't nearly that long, Tricia watched the same two officials leave the hospital. She was curious about what they had learned. It kept her mind occupied, and the waiting became insignificant.

"Bryan Walker?" a doctor called out as he entered the waiting room.

"That's me," Bryan quickly answered.

They shook hands. "I'm Dr. Roberts. Clay put you as his emergency contact."

"How's he doing?"

"He's currently unconscious, and unfortunately, the EMTs had to give him CPR on the way here."

"But he'll wake up, right?"

"Hopefully. The good news is that he's breathing on his own, though it is very labored due to the smoke inhalation."

"When can we see him?" Tricia jumped in.

"Now, if you'd like. He's in Room 308. Third floor, down the hall, and to your left."

"Thank you," Tricia replied, immediately heading for Clay's room.

"You're welcome . . . and I'm sorry I couldn't give you better news," Dr. Roberts added.

"We understand . . . she's his girlfriend," Bryan explained. Dr. Roberts headed to the nurses' station with Clay's chart.

Peeking her head inside Clay's room, Tricia took in the unwelcome sight of him lying in a hospital bed practically lifeless. Had it not been for her barely able to see his chest rising up and down, she wouldn't have known if he was actually breathing.

"Clay."

Going over to his bed, she carefully sat down next to him. She took his hand and intertwined their fingers. Looking at him laboring for breath as his eyes remained closed, she flashed back to the crash. Her tears easily made their way down her face as she prayed to God that He would work a miracle.

"Please wake up, Clay," she softly cried as the love she felt for him became more and more evident to her. "I . . . I."

Watching his eyes slowly open, Clay responded slowly, "Ya . . . what . . . dar . . . lin'?"

"Clay!" she answered. "I love you."

"And . . . it took . . . a car . . . wreck . . . for . . . me to . . . hear . . . it."

Patricia L. Powell

"Clay, I'm sorry . . . I just . . ." she tried to speak as more tears streamed down her face.

She wanted to tell him how much her heart had ached for him to be all right and how she didn't want to live without him. But all she could do was wrap her arms around his neck and thank God that Clay was not only alive but able to talk to her.

CHAPTER
- THIRTY-EIGHT -

"Clay, I've never been so terrified in my life! I had no idea whether you were going to live or die! Just seeing you motionless like that was the worst experience I've ever gone through!"

Clay responded with ragged breath after slowly pressing the button to sit up. "Tricia . . . it takes . . . more than . . . a car . . . wreck . . . to kill . . . me."

"But that's the problem, Clay. Your life was in danger, and there wasn't a damn thing I could do!"

"Aw . . . darlin' . . . I'm . . . sorry."

"Clay, I don't want to be forced to have to identify your body because you've ended up on a cold metal table in the morgue!"

Clay continued to respond slowly. "And it's . . . highly . . . unlikely . . . that ya . . . ever . . . will. Tricia . . . in all . . . my racin' . . . career . . . that crash . . . has been . . . the only . . . serious one . . . I've ever . . . been in . . . so . . . ya really . . . have nothin' . . . to worry 'bout."

"Clay, you weren't there seeing what I was seeing. Facing the possibility of never seeing you alive again. I felt like my heart was going to explode right out of my chest. I prayed for you to just walk away from that damn crash completely unscathed!"

"Darlin' . . . I . . . am truly . . . sorry . . . that ya . . . had to . . . go . . . through . . . all . . . that."

Tears flooded Tricia's face. "Clay, I know that this sport is your career, but I just can't deal with seeing that happen to you again."

He clasped her hand in his. "Tricia, I hate . . . that . . . my crash . . . caused ya . . . so much . . . pain."

Tricia wrapped her arms around his neck as her tears flowed nonstop.

"Aw . . . darlin, I love . . . you . . . and I . . . always . . . will."

"Clay, after I was given the chance to imagine my life without you, I now know what it means and feels like to not only love a man but to be in love with him."

"I'm glad . . . to finally . . . hear it, darlin'. It certainly . . . makes . . . my crashin' . . . my car . . . and endin' up . . . in this . . . hospital bed . . . worth it."

They sealed their feelings for each other with a kiss.

"What can I say, I told you I'd make you work for my heart, didn't I?"

"Ya . . . sure . . . did. Though . . . after this . . . ordeal . . . I think I . . . deserve some . . . vacation days."

"I suppose I wouldn't mind becoming your nurse temporarily," Tricia laughed.

"Can I . . . get ya . . . to wear . . . one of . . . those . . . sexy . . . nurse . . . outfits . . . for me, then?" he asked with a teasing grin. "I bet ya'd . . . look real . . . hot . . . in one of . . . 'em."

"I'm sure I would . . . but no."

"Is . . . Bryan . . . here?"

"Don't tell me you're already tired of talking to your girlfriend?"

"Of course . . . not, darlin'. I . . . just got . . . somethin' . . . I need . . . to . . . talk to him . . . 'bout, that's . . . all."

"Well, then, yes, he is. He and my roommate are probably right outside."

"Probably?"

"The second the doctor told us which room you were in, I came right up. I didn't wait for them."

"Ah."

"Clay, you don't think Nikki was behind all of this somehow, do you?"

"Tricia, I . . . honestly . . . have . . . no . . . idea."

"In that case, I should let Bryan have his turn with you while I go call Kate and tell her what happened."

"Tell . . . her . . . I said . . . hi."

"Of course, since she is the reason we're together."

Smiling, Clay tried to give Tricia another kiss.

"Clay, you should be careful. You're recovering, so you need to take it easy."

"I appreciate . . . the concern . . . darlin', but . . . sometimes . . . a man's . . . just gotta . . . kiss . . . his woman."

His woman. Hmm, that definitely doesn't have a bad ring to it. She was acclimating herself to the new label.

"Hey, buddy, how you holding up?" Bryan asked him.

"I've . . . been . . . better."

"So what the hell happened out there?" Bryan asked.

"Logan . . . hit me . . . just right." Clay thought about Tricia's reaction.

"So your car wasn't messed with?"

"Not . . . that I'm . . . aware . . . of."

"I wonder if that means Nikki's threats were just that."

"Couldn't . . . tell . . . ya."

"Well, once the officials inspect the car, we'll know for sure."

"Bryan, . . . I don't think . . . she's got . . . any . . . leverage . . . with anyone . . . to do . . . that."

"Not unless she persuaded Logan to do her dirty work."

"I . . . highly . . . doubt . . . that."

"Either way, now that you're awake, you can let the officials in on all the threats."

"Were they . . . here?"

"They were earlier. So I'll give Rich a call to let them know you're awake and talking. Then you can give them a statement regarding Nikki and watch her be hauled off in handcuffs."

"Sounds . . . good. But . . . 'fore ya . . . go, I . . . wanted . . . to let . . .ya know . . . somethin'."

"And what's that?"

"I . . . plan on . . . proposin' . . . to . . . Tricia."

"You do? That's great!"

"Yeah . . . so I'm . . . gonna . . . need . . . your help . . . with it."

"Anything, Clay. I know how much she means to you."

191

"Yeah . . . she . . . told me . . . she's . . . in love . . . with me."

"Glad to hear it. It's about time that sentiment was returned for you."

"Tell . . . me . . . 'bout it, and . . . by . . . the right . . . woman . . . too."

"That's the only part of it that matters, Clay."

"Knock, knock," Clay heard Tricia's voice.

"Come on . . . in, darlin'," he answered.

"Bryan took Claire back to the speedway, so it's back to just you and me."

"More . . . alone time . . . with . . . ya."

"Yep."

"Then . . . why don't . . . ya . . . join me . . . on this . . . bed?" he asked, scooting over a little and patting the empty space.

Smiling, Tricia climbed onto the bed and curled up against his side. With his arm around her, she watched him grab the remote and turn the TV on to the race.

"I'm sorry you're not still in the race, Clay, but I definitely enjoy you more, right here, like this."

"I'd say . . . the same . . . but . . . ya've got . . . your clothes . . . on."

CHAPTER
- THIRTY-NINE -

One Month Later

"Trish, how's Clay doing?" Kate asked her over the cellphone while making a sandwich.

"A lot better."

"Did you ever figure out who was sending him the texts?"

"No," she answered, packing a small bag for her weekend getaway with him. "Fortunately, it appears that the person's given up since Clay hasn't received another one since the day of his crash."

"Maybe, but that could also mean that they're just biding their time for something else."

"True, but I highly doubt it. He's only just been released to drive again."

"Well, I hope you're right, for Clay's sake."

"Me too. His not being able to race this whole month has really affected him."

"How so?"

"He's just been really tense. Though I suppose that would make sense for anyone who couldn't live out their passion because of a serious injury."

"And speaking of passion, are you ready for your weekend away with the man?"

"Yes, in fact, I just finished packing," she answered, zipping up her bag.

"And what will you guys be doing about the sleeping arrangements?"

"We have one stop before we get to his childhood home. We'll figure it out," she answered. She thought back to the night she had shared his hospital bed.

"Right. Well, maybe you should stick to motel rooms with double beds."

"Kate, we'll be fine."

"Okay, but just don't be sneaking into his room once you get there."

"Kate!"

"What? I was joking. Besides, I know you. You're going to stick to your 'no premarital sex' rule no matter what."

"Damn, you make me sound like such a prude."

"Trish, I'm just being realistic. I mean, just imagine how it'll be for the both of you when it's time for bed. If you're in the same room, you'll get to see what each other wears. Then, as you're both trying to go to sleep, you'll be tossing and turning as you imagine him caressing your body and kissing your lips. Yet, because of your rule, you'll have to fight your mind on craving his touch and giving you a preview of what sex with him would really be like."

"Kate, as long as we're not sharing the same bed, we'll both be fine," Tricia forced herself to say. The image Kate had described made her question her ability to abstain from sex.

"Trish, you may tell yourself that, but I think that when it comes down to it, resisting the desire will be a lot harder than you think, especially now that you're in love with him."

"So you don't think I could sleep in the same bed with him and still be a virgin?"

"No, what I'm saying is that the temptation is going to put a lot more pressure against your want to stay that way."

"Oh."

"Trish, there's nothing wrong with you wanting to wait until marriage. You just shouldn't put yourself in situations where that value is challenged."

"And you think that's what I'm about to do with Clay? Kate, should I just cancel this weekend?"

Knowing that Clay was planning on proposing to Tricia once they had reached his childhood home, Kate realized that if she wasn't careful she would ruin the whole surprise.

"No, Trish, I definitely don't. I just wanted to warn you because, guess what?"

"What?"

"I'm pregnant."

"You're what?"

"I said, I'm pregnant. Remember that first night Bryan and I slept together?"

"Yes?"

"Well, that did it," Kate answered, feeling like she had just dodged a bullet. After she had, she felt bad for not telling Tricia in a more thoughtful way.

"Wow! Um, congratulations," Tricia replied, just in time to hear Clay's fist against the door. "I've got to go, Clay just got here."

"Okay, enjoy your weekend." Kate hung up the cellphone and let out a big sigh of relief for not accidentally blowing Clay's planned weekend.

Tricia grabbed her bag and opened the door.

"So ya ready for our weekend together, darlin'?"

"Yeah, I am."

"Well, great, then let's get goin'."

"Okay."

"Oh, hey, let me carry that for ya."

"Sure, if you want to." She handed him her bag. As she did, their hands collided, causing them both to stop in the moment.

"Ya know, I thought I had forgotten somethin'," he replied, bringing her to him for a missed 'hello' kiss.

"This is now the norm for us, isn't it?" Tricia asked as she wrapped her other arm around his neck.

"It's not a bad norm, if ya ask me."

"No, it's definitely not."

"So ya excited for our trip, darlin'?" he asked as they walked out to his truck.

"Yes, I am," she smiled.

"I hope you're ready, 'cause this weekend's gonna be one that you'll never forget." He opened her door before heading for his side.

"Why do you say that, Clay? What's happening?"

Turning on the engine, Clay responded, "You'll just have to wait and see, darlin'."

"Okay, if you want to keep it a surprise."

"Trust me, Tricia. You'll like this one. Hell, I imagine you'll even love it." He slipped his hand into hers, slightly caressing it.

"Clay, do you think we'll be fine sleeping in separate beds in the same motel room?"

"Why wouldn't we, darlin'? After all, ya shared my hospital bed with me and nothin' happened."

"Kate just brought up a good point about it."

"Ah, and what'd she say that's got ya questionin' the idea?"

"Oh, just that it might test our willpower once we see each other going to bed."

"Would ya prefer I get us two rooms instead?"

"To be honest, no, but what if she's right?"

"Tricia, if we can lay in a twin-sized hospital bed together and have absolutely nothin' happen . . . with me in just that gown and boxers, mind ya . . . I think we'll both be fine."

"So you're a boxers man?" she asked, remembering their conversation as she glanced at his jeans.

"Yep, and just to forewarn ya, that's all I wear to bed," he answered with a grin.

"Huh," she replied, picturing him that way. "Well, then, I guess it's a good thing I sleep in a T-shirt and pajama bottoms."

"Why, ya 'fraid anythin' less will get me desirin' ya?"

"Clay, this is all new to me, so I don't know what the reality will end up being."

"Tricia, it ain't like I've ever shared a motel room with a woman 'fore."

"True, but you still have more experience in this area than I do."

"Darlin', the extent of my experience is makin' out till I needed to end it 'fore the desire 'came too much."

"Then I suppose as long as we have a room with two beds, or at least, a couple of options for sleeping, we should be good."

"I think you're worryin' 'bout it too much."

"Then how about we put this to the test?"

"How so?"

"Well, you don't think it'll be a big deal, and I do, so why don't we try it and find out?"

"Ya wanna turn this into a competition?"

"Sort of. I want to see if sharing the same bed will be harder to deal with than what you think."

"Okay."

"Clay, I'm sure it'll be a real eye-opener for both of us."

CHAPTER

- FORTY -

C lay pulled into the Four Seasons Hotel and parked his truck. Before he could get out, Tricia straddled him. Within seconds, she was giving him a deeply sensuous kiss and grabbing his jeans and boxers with both hands so she could slide her fingers down his skin.

"Okay, let's start tonight." She released his mouth to the air and got out of his truck while he remained shellshocked.

"Damn!"

Her kiss had been so damn erotic that he was surprised his member had only risen a little underneath her.

"Well, are you coming, Clay?"

Aw shit! He realized she might be right about their sleeping situation.

"Yeah, darlin', I am." He still felt a little dazed as he joined her by the tailgate after grabbing their bags. They walked hand in hand into the lobby where magnificent gold-trimmed furniture and marble flooring awaited them.

Stopping at the front desk, Tricia waited as Clay paid for the room.

With their room key now in hand, they headed up to where their challenge would take place.

Opening the door to the king-sized bed with a couch adjacent to it, Tricia wondered if the challenge would make a difference in the end. Even if she found herself too aroused by him, she didn't want him sleeping as far away as the couch.

"Ya hungry, darlin'?" Clay asked as he dropped their bags. "I can order us some room service."

"Yeah, that sounds fine."

"Then just let me know what ya want," he replied, handing her the menu.

"Mm, a cheeseburger and fries sound good."

With a nod, he picked up the cellphone and placed their order, adding her favorite soda.

After tipping room service, he and Tricia ate as they mentally prepared to see how far they could push temptation.

Tricia was finishing her last fry when she began to rethink what they were about to do. "Clay, maybe we should wait until you've at least proposed to me."

"So ya think you're gonna be gettin' a proposal from me at some point in our future?"

"Clay, I'd better, considering how serious we are about each other. Don't you think that should come at some point down the road?"

"Probably."

"Probably? Clay, I'm about to be more intimate with you than I've ever been. So if I'm not going to be getting a ring from you at some point in our future, then we might as well forget the challenge and tomorrow you can take me back to my dorm room. If you never plan on proposing to me, there's no point for any of this."

"Okay, then, what's your preference? In the winner's circle right after I've won a big race? Or as your consolation prize after I've won our challenge?"

"Neither," she answered, purposely ignoring the second option. "I want it to be something so creative that I'll be blown away. I also want it to be something special that just the two of us get to share. I don't want it during a champagne shower or with applauding fans cheering you on as you're dropping to one knee and asking me the question."

"Any more requirements, darlin'?"

"Just that you make it memorable. I want my only proposal to capture everything I've ever dreamt up when it comes to how we feel about each other."

"I think I can handle that."

"I hope so," she answered, finishing her Diet Coke.

"Darlin', 'fore we get to this challenge, I'm gonna go brush my teeth."

"What, you don't think I'll like your mouth tasting like your dinner?"

"Don't know, but after a while, ya may not."

Watching Clay come out of the bathroom, Tricia decided to do the same as her nervousness began to take hold. She watched him take a seat on the bed and take his boots off and realized that she didn't want him stripping down any further, just yet.

With her mouth now refreshed, she headed over to him. Slipping off her shoes, she straddled him once again.

"Ya sure like this position on me, don't ya?"

"I just thought it would be the easiest way to start."

"It definitely works for me," he replied, putting his hands on her sides.

Taking his hat off, she tossed it onto the couch. Wrapping her arms around his neck, she kissed him.

Clay took his time kissing her back. He slipped his hands under her shirt and began gliding them up and down her soft skin.

Feeling her relax, he took it a step further with his kiss. Letting her know he wanted more, he opened his mouth so she could feel his tongue against hers. As their kissing increased, so did his desire to run his hands over more of her body. Lifting up her shirt, he easily helped her get rid of it.

"Clay, can we really do this and not be too tempted?" Tricia asked now that only her bra covered her chest.

"Tricia, I'm gonna feel the temptation whether ya got your shirt on or not, but ya can sure as hell believe I ain't 'bout to ask ya to put it back on."

With a shy smile, she returned her lips to his, removing his two shirts in the process.

Their lips heated up their desire for each other. Clay removed the elastic from her hair and flipped Tricia onto her back. Relentlessly kissing her skin, she moaned out her pleasure. Smiling at his ability to turn her on, Clay brought his mouth back to hers. The taste of his tongue kept hers busy as his hands roamed around the confines of her bra.

Hearing her enjoy his every action, Clay found himself wanting to unhook her bra. But as it lay securely against her skin, he knew that he couldn't. Despite her cleavage beckoning a taste from his mouth, Clay knew that this was one area that had to remain off-limits to him. At least for now.

Aroused by his touch, Tricia wondered if she needed to start worrying. Despite his hands feeling so good against her skin and her mouth craving more of his, she knew that she'd eventually reach her limit. The question was when would that be? As she continued to feel his skin against hers, she felt him slide a hand up to her butt. The feel of his hand heightened her sensitivity and made her want to keep her body close to his.

Forgetting about the challenge, Clay found himself lost in arousing her. The way her mouth welcomed his kept his brain sidetracked. It wasn't until Tricia straddled him again that he was reminded.

Feeling his erection, Tricia stopped. "I . . . uh, Clay . . . um . . . wow!"

"Ya wondered what would happen, darlin' . . . well, this is it."

"I um . . . do you want me to get off of you?"

"Well, you'll eventually have to."

"Clay, maybe we shouldn't have tempted each other like that."

"Tricia, my erection is 'cause ya've turned me on so damn much."

"Oh."

"Yep, and if we weren't waitin' for sex, I have a feelin' you wouldn't be too far behind."

Giving him an understanding kiss, Tricia got off of his lap so he could use the bathroom. "When you're finished, I want you to join me in the bed, Clay."

"Are ya sure, darlin'? 'Cause I really don't mind turnin' the couch into a makeshift bed."

"Yes, I am. I want to feel your warm body against mine as your arms keep me close to you."

"Okay, then."

After grabbing her nightshirt and pajama bottoms, Tricia changed in the bathroom before getting into bed. Clay crawled in next to her and gladly welcomed her into his arms. Snuggling up against his warm body, Tricia found herself more content than ever.

"This is certainly much more cozy than ya sleepin' in this big ole bed by yourself, or me alone on that couch, for that matter."

"I know, and it's definitely something I wouldn't mind getting used to," she added with a kiss goodnight.

As Clay lay there with Tricia so comfortably positioned against him, he knew that he'd found the right woman for him. There was no doubt in his mind that just holding her against him was enough. The feel of her sleeping in his arms where he could easily breathe in her scent and feel her every movement against him made him thank God that He had brought her into his life.

CHAPTER
- FORTY-ONE -

"Morning, Clay," Tricia greeted with a smile as she opened her eyes to him.

"Mornin', darlin'."

Feeling a kind of contentment he had never known before, Clay took in her beauty. He looked into her eyes and couldn't believe how in love with her he was. The way her brown hair lay messily on the pillow and how her adoring eyes gazed into his was enough for him to wish this moment of theirs would last forever. He wanted to take her into his arms and make passionate love to her.

Looking back into her beautiful hazel eyes, Clay knew that proposing to her was the right thing to do. Tricia Perkins was everything he'd ever wanted in a woman, and then some. She had a fight in her that he couldn't help but find so damn irresistible and she exuded passion like no one else he'd ever met. Sure, at one point he thought he had wanted to marry Nikki, but after being subjected to Tricia's intensity when it came to her affection for him, his true feelings for each couldn't have been more different. Tricia affected him like no other woman ever had. Even though at times she could drive him absolutely crazy, it only made him love her more. Tricia Perkins was truly the love of his life.

"So how do ya like wakin' up to me?"

"I absolutely love it, Clay. It feels so surreal to me because I've fallen so deeply in love with you that it gets me every time I think about how I put up such a fight against you . . . and us." She stroked his facial hair lightly with her fingers.

As Tricia took in the intimacy of sleeping in the same bed, she stared into his eyes and found that she had never felt more comfortable with a man than as she did just lying next to him.

Clasping his hand over hers, Clay looked at her with eyes that shone with more love than he had ever known before. He then removed their hands from his cheek and kissed her fingers. "Tricia, I can guarantee ya that this . . . you and me . . . is definitely one hundred percent real. Hell, I'd ask ya to marry me right now if I didn't already know that ya wanna be romanced into the question."

"You're *that* in love with me, Clay?"

"Tricia, I have honestly never felt for another woman what I feel for you, and if I didn't believe in waitin' until vowin' my love to ya 'fore God, I would make ya mine right now!"

"Well, you're definitely right about asking me since I really don't want the same kind of proposal Bryan gave Kate. Though, Clay, rest assured, that when you do ask me to marry you, I will definitely say yes. Because you're the man I've always dreamt about meeting and falling in love with. You've swept me off my feet with your charm and love for me, and marrying you would mean everything to me."

"Glad to hear it, darlin'," he said with a smile.

Removing his hand from hers, he slid it down the side of her body and up to the crook of her knee before giving her a quick kiss that let her know it was time for them to get up.

"Ya ready to go, darlin'?"

"Yep," she announced with her bag in hand.

Clay drove them to his next surprise.

Several hours later, with Tricia sitting comfortably against him, he took a turn onto a dirt road. Tricia could see fields of wheat swaying in the wind bordered by a weathered, gray wooden fence.

"Ya see that old one-story house up 'head and the barn right next to it?" he asked.

Gesturing with his arm, Clay pointed at what looked like a

very decrepit and condemned house with a faded red barn that looked to be at least one hundred years old.

"Yes, is that where we're going?" Tricia asked. The house resembled Jenny's home in *Forrest Gump*.

"Yep, that's where I grew up." Clay parked in front of it. "I know it's not much, but at one time, it was my home." He turned off the engine, leaving the remnants of a whirlwind of dust briefly circulating in its path.

"Wow, it looks so . . . shabby." Tricia quickly covered her mouth. "I'm so sorry, Clay, I shouldn't've said that." She mentally wished her Asperger's would've given her a better filter so she wouldn't be so blunt all of the time.

"Don't worry 'bout it, darlin', I know how it looks."

Scanning the deplorable living conditions, Clay realized it wasn't much better than when he was a kid.

"I really don't know how you both managed to survive it."

"That'd be God's grace, darlin', and it looks like it hasn't changed much." He watched a piece of wooden siding fall to the ground with a dusty crash.

"Clay, you really had to grow up in that?" she asked, grasping his arm for security.

"Yep. Now I know it's no house in Newport Bay, but this is where everythin' started for me. Oh, and down the road a bit is Bryan's old home. He used to spend practically every night here 'cause his dad would always be bringin' women back from the bar."

"Wow. That must've been so hard for him."

"Yeah, but that was only 'cause my mama once told me that his mama had died durin' childbirth and his dad knew of no other way to deal with it. So Mr. Walker would go to the bar, get drunk, and bring a woman home. Bryan had to deal with a revolvin' door of women comin' in and out of his house. Hell, I'm surprised he even knows how to have a healthy, and monogamous, relationship with Kate."

"Damn, the four of us grew up so differently."

"Yep, we sure did, but there's somethin' to be said 'bout a homegrown country boy and an irresistible city girl findin' their way to each other." He winked, only to receive a shy smile in return. "So what do ya think, darlin'?"

"Please just tell me that your mama doesn't still live here."

"No, she lives in a nice condo in West Cliff now. I have absolutely no idea where my father lives, and to tell ya the truth, I really don't care."

"Clay, I feel so bad for you. It sucks that you and your mama had to deal with that."

"I appreciate the thought, darlin', but don't worry 'bout it. It's all been over and done with for many years. So ya ready for the royal tour, Tricia?" He unbuckled his seatbelt and got out.

He wants us to go inside. He's got to be freaking crazy! Tricia looked at the ominous farmhouse. *If something happens to me in there, God's going to tell me that I brought it on myself!* She shook her head at Clay's craziness.

"Tricia, come on. You'll be fine. Besides, ya've got me to protect ya."

"Not if the roof falls in on us, then we'll both be screwed!" She reluctantly got out of his truck.

"What, ya don't think my fast reflexes can whisk ya out of harm's way if the ceilin' comes crashin' down on us?" he teased after taking her hand and leading her into his past.

"Not unless you've been hiding your real identity as a superhero from me. But speaking of death by ceiling, weren't you and your mama ever afraid of that happening?"

"Yeah, but we just thanked God every day that we even had a roof over our heads. We didn't have to 'come beggars on the street, holdin' up a sign for food or money."

Reminiscing about his childhood, Clay remembered how they'd always used a pot or pan to collect water from their leaky roof.

"Right."

"Hey, what can ya do when ya've got a deadbeat dad who could care less 'bout the family he left behind and a mama who has to catch rodents and somehow scrape the money together to keep her son and herself in clothes?"

There was such a huge difference between Clay's childhood and him becoming an adult. Instead of being known as the poor kid whose mama could barely afford thrift store clothes, he was now one of NASCAR's most promising drivers of 2012. He had made so much money from all of his sponsorship deals and races that he never knew what to do with it all.

"I guess you do have a point there. Though it does make me really sad to see the conditions you were forced to live in as a kid. I hate that you had to suffer because your father couldn't be man enough to own up to his responsibilities by sticking around to take care of you and your mama." She gave Clay a sympathetic hug.

"I knew there was a reason why I love ya so much!"

"So you mean it isn't because of how I look with my shirt off?"

"Well actually . . ."

"Clay!" she exclaimed with a playful push to his chest.

"Well, ya do have a hot body, darlin'."

"So what's next now that you've given me the official tour of NASCAR driver Clay Gibson's childhood home?"

"That depends. Are ya hungry?"

"If it means me finally being able to remove myself from my potential gravesite, then yes, I'm hungry."

"Funny."

"Aw, Clay, you know I'm just teasing you. I love that you want to show me where you grew up. It's a side of you I've never seen before," she softly explained, hugging his side.

"Well, with an apology like that, I suppose I have no choice but to forgive ya." He put his arm around her back.

As they were about to head out of the house, a family of rats decided to make their way out first. With a scream, Tricia jumped into Clay's arms.

"Don't tell me you're 'fraid of a little family of rats?"

"No, it was just the combination of their noise and my not expecting them that scared me."

"Hey, it works for me. Besides, enterin' the barn like this might actually be a lot more romantic for ya, anyhow."

"There's a romantic way to enter a barn?"

"Darlin', it ain't 'bout how ya enter it, it's 'bout what ya see when ya do." He thought about how Bryan and her father had helped him rid the barn of its cobwebs and years of dust to prepare for his proposal.

Clay carried Tricia to the barn. "Now if you'll do me the honor of openin' one of the doors, I'll take care of the rest."

Letting go of him, Tricia pulled on the black, metal handle. "Oh wow, Clay, it's absolutely, beautiful!"

"I was hopin' ya'd like it," he replied, setting her down.

Closing the door behind them, he watched Tricia take in the barn's interior. Instead of years of unuse, it had been transformed into an enchanting candlelit dinner for two on one side, while the other contained an equally captivating area for dancing.

Looking at everything, Tricia found herself completely speechless. The table consisted of four white-cloth-covered hay bales. Two bales were used for seats and two were stacked with fine china filled with their three-course meal, silver flatware, crystal wine glasses, and a lid covering each plate. As she continued to gaze at the extravagant table setting, she noticed little silhouettes of celestial string lights as their shapes made imprints on the table's décor.

When her eyes had followed their shine, it brought her attention to a nearby path of red, white, and pink rose petals. As her eyes made their way down to its end, she became awestruck when she saw the connecting circle of lit white candles. The petals' path led to the entranceway into the enchanted circle.

"Oh Clay, it's all so absolutely breathtaking!"

"I had a feelin' ya'd enjoy it." He was proud and happy to give her the romantic evening she'd always dreamt of.

"You did all of this for me?"

"Yep, I want this to be a night you'll always remember." He thought about getting down on one knee later.

"Wow, I don't know what to say."

"You're welcome, darlin'. It's my pleasure. Now, what do ya say ya quit standin' there and starin' at everythin' and come enjoy the dinner with me?"

"I say I'd be honored, Clay." She answered with a smile, waiting for him to join her so he could walk her over to her hay bale.

With her napkin in her lap, Tricia started on her first course, the salad. When she had eaten the last bite, she lifted the lid off the plate to see her favorite dish, lasagna. "Wow, Clay. This tastes amazing, better than any restaurant's I've ever had." She couldn't help but savor the juicy meat, melted cheese, and layers of noodles.

"Actually, my mama made it. In fact, she made everythin' we're eatin'."

"Wow! And to know that she passed that skill onto you. It makes me glad that you're my boyfriend."

And I'm hopin' I'll be more than that to ya once dessert's over! He was anxious to get her one step closer to becoming his wife.

As Tricia finished her main course, she couldn't help but look at Clay through the candlelight and thank God that she'd met a man who had no problem with showing her his romantic side. She was a hopeless romantic, and knowing that Clay had absolutely no problem with romancing her made her feel like the luckiest woman in the world.

"Ya ready for dessert, darlin'?" he asked, moving their empty plates aside and sliding a single plate of chocolate mousse pie between them.

"Yes. So where's your plate?" she teased, pulling the plate in front of her.

"Ha. I thought we'd share it," he informed her, leaning in and holding up his fork.

"Then how about I decrease the distance between us?" she offered, getting up from her seat and sitting down on his lap.

"Don't like your seat anymore, darlin'?" He wrapped an arm around her, securing it with his thumb through her belt loop.

"Not as much as I like this one." She pulled their dessert back over to his side so they could take turns eating it. They finished the chocolatey treat down to its last crumbs, feeding each other a bite every so often.

"Darlin', for what we're 'bout to do next, I'm gonna need ya to get up."

Doing as requested, Tricia returned to her hay bale and waited for whatever Clay had planned next. She watched him lean over and heard the intro to Sara Evans' song *I Could Not Ask for More.*

"Clay, this is my first dance song. I love this song!"

"I know. Now may I have this dance?" He stood up and offered her his hand.

"Absolutely." He led her down the path of rose petals and into the candlelit circle. "Wow, Clay! This is all so romantic!" He took her into his arms and they slow danced to the music's lyrics. Tricia was mesmerized.

"Darlin', I want this night to be as romantic as I can possibly make it for ya."

"Well, I don't know how much more romantic you can make it. I think you've pretty much outdone yourself."

"Not quite, I've still got a couple more surprises left for ya."

"You do?"

"Yep, and after this song's over, I'll be glad to show ya what they are." Clay knew that when the song came to an end, he would be asking her a question that would change their lives forever.

"Hey, should I be worried about our belt buckles clinking again?" Tricia asked.

With a smile at her reminder, Clay assured her, "If they do, it'll definitely be one scratch I won't mind rememberin'."

Taking in the warmth of Clay's body against hers and the candlelight romance he courted her with, Tricia found it so natural to return her head to his shoulder as the music continued the ambiance he had created for them. Closing her eyes, she let him direct their night. But as she heard Sara Evans' voice fade, she found herself hesitant to let their dancing come to an end as a part of their night's ambiance drifted away. Sensing the change in the mood now that they no longer had the sweet sound of the lyrics continuing their slow-paced movement, she opened her eyes back to his.

"Darlin', for my next surprise, I'm gonna need ya to wait right here while I go turn off the CD player."

Clay momentarily left her to stand in the middle of the glowing candles as Tricia watched him turn off the CD player. She wondered what was going on as she anxiously waited for him to rejoin her amidst the candles.

"Tricia, I have a very important question I need to ask ya, and I'm prayin' that what ya'd told me earlier was the truth."

Covering the black ring box with his fingers, he kept his surprise hidden from her sight.

"I guess that depends on what you're talking about, Clay."

"Tricia, from the moment ya began resistin' my want to be

with ya, I knew that even though it was gonna be a challenge to win your heart over, it was gonna be well worth it in the end."

"I'm glad you thought that, Clay. But what is this question you need to ask me?"

"Darlin', I'm gettin' to it, but I don't wanna rush into it. So, if you'll just let me finish with tellin' ya what's in my heart, I'll ask ya it when I'm done, okay?" With Tricia's nod of acceptance, he continued. "Now as ya already know, Tricia, ya've captured my heart with yours. Your bein' in my life has not only shown me how crazy in love with you I am but that you're the woman God made me for. Darlin', I wanna spend the rest of my life with you, and I'm prayin' to God that your answer regardin' that earlier, is as ya'd said. 'Cause I've never been more in love with a woman, or wanted one, as much as I want you."

"Oh my gosh!" she exclaimed, bringing her hands to her mouth. "Clay, are you about to ask me to marry you?" Tears of joy streamed down her cheeks. Hearing how much he loved her made her feel more overwhelmed with emotion than she'd ever felt in her entire life.

"Yes, Tricia, I am. And I hope to God that ya will give me a yes like ya said ya would when we were talkin' 'bout it in bed this mornin'." He brought his hand up to her face before giving her a brief kiss.

"Oh wow! I can't believe this is actually happening!"

She watched him bend one knee in front of her.

Clay's romantic setup had been the foreplay to his question. Everything had been done to set the stage for the most important question he would ever ask her.

"Tricia, now I know that my doin' this feels completely surreal to ya, but trust me when I say that the love we feel for each other is as real as my kneelin' on the ground in front of ya."

"I know it is, Clay, and I meant what I said about my answer earlier."

"Then, Tricia Lane Perkins, will you marry me?" he finally asked, offering up the treasure he had been hiding in his hand.

Opening the box, he revealed a white-gold band with a heart-shaped diamond set in the center. Its simplicity matched her personality perfectly.

Staring down at it, Tricia was awestruck. Despite his proposal being real, she remembered when she'd thought this day would only stay a dream in her mind.

"So darlin', presumin' that my heartfelt words were able to convey to ya what's truly in my heart, will ya do me the honor of becomin' my wife?" he asked. "Will ya marry me and take on my last name?" Still kneeling, he waited for her answer.

"Oh Clay! I love you so much, and I'll be thanking God for Him bringing you into my life for the rest of my life. So as I told you this morning . . . yes, I'll marry you!"

"Darlin', ya've just made me the happiest country boy in the whole world!" he declared as he slid the ring onto her finger.

Now that they were symbolically connected, Tricia jumped into his arms the second he stood up. Giving him a blissful kiss, he spun her around in celebration. As they looked into each other's eyes as a newly engaged couple, Tricia and Clay took in the deeper understanding of what this defining moment meant for each of them.

For Tricia, it meant never having to worry about not ever finding Mr. Right. Clay was the man she could claim as her soulmate. He would be her lifelong companion who would provide her emotions with a listening ear and fulfill her every want and desire for affection. As for Clay, it meant that he now had a lover who would always choose him over any other man. Tricia was the woman who he could fully give himself to and know that, when he did, he would be her everything. She was also the woman he would create a family with to carry on his family's last name.

"Well, darlin', now that ya've accepted my heart in return for yours, I've got one last surprise for ya!" he informed her once he'd set her back down on the ground.

"You do? So my ring wasn't it?"

"Well, that was my main one . . . but no, ya've still got one last surprise waitin' for ya."

"Wow! So this is why you decorated the barn so extravagantly for me and why you wanted to show me where you grew up? To set up the scene for your proposal?"

"Yes, darlin', though, I did have a little help in decoratin' it."

"You did? Who?"

"Go open that barn door and you'll see."

Tricia pushed open the wooden door and she saw their family and friends waiting to congratulate her. With familiarity for all but one of them, she welcomed his last surprise.

"So, did he do it? Did he ask you?" Kate excitedly asked. She was eager to know if her best friend was now engaged to the man she'd put up a fight against when it came to giving him her heart.

"Show us your hand!" she continued as Bryan waited for the reveal by her side.

"Yes, he did. We're engaged!" Tricia exclaimed, holding out her left hand to show off the shiny new ring Clay had just placed on her ring finger.

"Oh, it's so beautiful, honey!" his mother complimented.

Tricia heard congratulations explode into her ears as the ring continued to be scrutinized.

"So mama, how'd I do?" Clay asked, showing up at Tricia's side.

"You did excellent, Clay."

"Wait a minute, Clay, how long had you been planning on asking me to marry you?" Tricia asked.

"'Bout a few months now," he answered with a smile.

"A few months? We haven't even been dating a few months!"

"Well darlin', when ya know ya've found the one, it really doesn't matter how long it's been," he replied with an arm around her.

"So you already knew you were going to ask me before your car crash?"

"Well, yeah. Ya didn't think I was gonna let myself die without askin' ya to marry me first, did ya?"

"I guess not, but I had no idea you were already thinking about this step until our conversation this morning."

"That was the point, darlin'. I didn't want ya to know that I was plannin' all this till I was absolutely sure ya were the one for me and ya were gonna say yes."

"So that means . . ." she began when she realized that it meant he had to get her father's permission first.

"Yep. Whenever Bryan went to see Kate, I would tag along to stop by your house and pay your folks a visit. On my last visit there, I sat down with your father and told him that not only was I in love with his daughter but that I wanted to marry her and spend the rest of my life with her. As ya can see, he gave me his blessin'."

"Oh, was he cleaning his shotgun while you were asking?"

"Your father owns a shotgun?" he asked with slight alarm.

"Only for when his daughter finds the man she wants to spend the rest of her life with."

"Then he must've been cleanin' it especially for me."

"Ah, Clay," she replied, pulling him into a kiss that caused an uproar from their celebrators.

"However, he did tell me that in exchange for your hand, I'd have to get him access to all the major races in NASCAR even if I wasn't in 'em," he added with a laugh.

"Smart man."

"I'd have to say so since we are now engaged," he agreed, giving her a kiss on the cheek.

CHAPTER
- FORTY-TWO -

"So you're the woman my son can't stop talking to me about," Dana Gibson said with a smile as she ushered Tricia into Clay's motorhome.

"Yep, that would be me," Tricia replied, taking a seat at the kitchenette where freshly baked chocolate-chip cookies and sweet tea awaited her.

"Well, I'm glad to finally meet you, Tricia. I've never heard my son so excited about one woman before."

"Oh, well, thanks."

"Since it won't be long until you're officially a part of the family, I think it's time I introduced you to Clay as a little boy." She brought out their photo albums and laid them on the table. Tricia got to hear the stories accompanied by pictures of Clay's early years. Giving Dana a hug, Tricia thanked her for the trip down memory lane before rejoining Clay as he talked to Bryan and Kate.

"So how was spendin' some quality time with my mama, darlin'?" Clay whispered to her.

"It was fine. Your mama showed me pictures of you as a baby, then growing up, and shared the stories that went with them. You were a very cute kid, Clay. But you're an even better-looking man." She hugged his side.

"Ya were a cute little girl yourself, darlin', and I definitely like how you've grown up." Tricia's mother had shown photos to Clay as well.

"Glad you think so," she replied, feeling him sensuously slip his hand into her back pocket.

"Feeling up your fiancée already, Clay?"

"Just takin' advantage of my ability to show ya my affection."

Smiling, she let him keep it there as they listened to Bryan talk.

"She also told me that you talked about me nonstop."

"That sorta comes with the territory of bein' in love, darlin'."

"Which is why she said that she was happy to finally meet me."

"Glad to hear it, considerin', I barely got to know your father 'fore I asked him for his blessin'."

"I'm glad you did. It's one of the things I love about you being a true southern gentleman."

"I was happy to do it, darlin'. Nervous, but happy just the same."

As Kate stood there listening to Bryan go on and on about something concerning Clay's race car, she was motivated to bring an end to her status as an unwed pregnant woman. With Tricia's engagement in the forefront of her mind, she made an announcement that put an end to whatever he was talking about.

"Bryan, I want us to get married right now! I don't want to wait to elope. I'd rather just find a small wedding chapel so we can officially become husband and wife," she proclaimed.

"Are you sure?" Bryan asked.

"Yes. I'm tired of being known as just your fiancée. I want our baby to start hearing us refer to each other as husband and wife while he or she is growing inside me."

"Okay, then, I guess tonight will be the last night for that. Now all we have to do is find a church."

"That shouldn't be a problem, Bryan. There's a little white church on the edge of town, and the minister lives in the cottage right next to it. Ya know, the one right as ya get onto the dirt road to come here," Clay said as he pointed out the direction.

"I think I know where you're talking about. Isn't that where Mason Landry and Carly Shultz got married a few years back?" he asked.

"Yeah, although I don't know if the minister would still be up at this time of night."

"Well, I guess we're about to find out," Kate responded. She grabbed Bryan's hand and led him to their rental car.

"Well, Clay, I suppose that means our celebration is over," Tricia pointed out. She watched everyone make their way back to their cars after receiving a 'goodbye and thanks for coming' from them.

"So what do ya say we go watch a couple of friends get hitched?" Clay asked, bringing her into a kiss.

"I'd say that if we don't, they won't have witnesses." They walked to his truck holding hands and followed Bryan and Kate over to the church.

It was already ten o' clock by the time they reached the small white church. After driving into the unmaintained parking lot, Bryan and Clay parked in the dirt next to each other. They could see how poorly lit the surrounding area was. Whoever had provided the artificial light for nighttime visitors had lacked the ability to put up proper lighting. Instead, they had strung lights that were connected by outer poles that also outlined where the church's boundary lay.

Bryan looked at the dark cottage. "Damn, it doesn't look like the minister's up!"

"That doesn't mean he's not home," Kate pointed out.

"True, but . . ." he began, only to watch her head straight for the cottage.

Tricia thought it best to stay by Clay's truck as she watched her best friend's quest to wake the minister. She rubbed her arms after feeling a sudden breeze chill her skin. "Oh, wow, it's cold."

"I think I can help with that." Clay came up behind her and started warming her arms with his hands.

She could feel his body's heat resonating through his clothes. "Mm, you certainly can." Leaning into him, she found a sense of contentedness that she had waited her whole life to feel.

"You're welcome, darlin'. I'm glad to be of service," he smiled before giving her neck a kiss.

"Me too, your hot body's definitely getting the job done." She brought his hands to intertwine with hers as they rested against her waist.

"Speakin' of, now that we're engaged, ya do realize that I'm one step closer to seein' your hot body with nothin' on it, right?" he reminded her with another kiss on her neck.

"Um, yeah," she answered, realizing he would actually be that man. "But you'll have to wait for our wedding night for that."

"Oh, I know. I'm just sayin' that I can't wait to see your naked body ready for my affection."

"Um, me neither, Clay."

"Tricia, I know you're nervous 'bout that, but I promise ya, I'll ease ya into it."

Feeling his warm breath against her skin as his baritone voice lit her senses on fire, Tricia let go of his hands and grabbed his belt. "Um, Clay, what if we got married now too?"

"Are ya sure?"

"Possibly. I just know that being that close to you is a big step, and with the way you're making me feel just having your body pressed up against mine right now . . . well, I don't know if I want to wait several months before we finally have sex."

"I've got no problem with that if that's what ya really want."

"Clay, I just know that resisting being that close to you is getting harder and harder for me. I'm constantly fantasizing about us being together. My dreams won't let me forget that desire either."

"Tricia, if ya want us to have one of the shortest engagements in history, I'm completely fine with that."

"And then we can go back to your family's barn . . ." she added, whispering the rest into his ear.

"That definitely sounds good to me. I'm ready to finally make ya mine. Though this'll be for our knowledge only, Tricia. To everyone else, we'll still be considered engaged up till we say 'I do' in front of 'em all."

"I know. I won't say anything. I'm just happy I'll finally get to be with you tonight," Tricia agreed as they watched the cottage's lights come on.

"Me too, darlin'."

CHAPTER

- FORTY-THREE -

Opening the front door of his cottage, the minister found Kate immediately informing him of her desire to be Bryan's wife. With a complying attitude to perform their late-night nuptials, he graciously instructed them to meet him in front of the church. But as they headed back over to the little house of worship, Tricia surprised Kate with her own desire for a quickie ceremony.

"Tired of waiting to get into his pants?" Kate teased Tricia.

"Kate, keep it down. I don't want him hearing us talking about it," she pleaded. Glancing in Clay's direction, she found that he was too immersed in his own conversation with Bryan to have been paying any attention to what she and Kate were talking about.

"What's the big deal, Trish? It's just sex."

"But that's the thing, Kate. It isn't 'just sex' to me. It's me finally giving my complete self to him, and him doing the same."

"Okay, so you like to romanticize it a little more than I do, but it is still just sex."

"Maybe that's how it was with you and Bryan, but for me and Clay, it will be making love. It's our two bodies coming together to become one. Giving him my virginity, and vice versa, is going to be about us showing each other how passionately in love we are. So, it's definitely not going to be just sex."

"Hey, just because I didn't wait for Bryan and we didn't wait

219

until marriage to have sex, doesn't mean that we didn't feel just as passionately in love with each other as you and Clay do."

"True, but I also consider sex to be a sacred act that should only be shared between a husband and his wife."

"Yeah, yeah. That part sort of got lost in translation for me around the time I started liking the opposite sex."

Tricia was about to make another comment when the minister opened the church door.

"So are you ready to do this, Trish? Are you ready to walk into that church a single woman and walk out as Clay's wife?" Kate asked her.

As Tricia was about to answer her, she watched Bryan break away from his conversation with Clay to hurry to Kate's side. They hastily followed the minister inside so he could officiate their ceremony and be that much closer to getting back to bed. She took a last glimpse of her best friend as a single woman and couldn't help but let Kate's last question soak in. She felt a sudden nervousness for what she and Clay were about to do. Despite being the one who had suggested their quickie nuptials so they could finally have sex, she now worried that maybe she was just rushing her want to be with him.

"Darlin', are ya sure ya wanna do this now?" Clay asked her.

"Of course, what makes you think otherwise?"

"'Cause I can see the anxiety in your eyes."

"It's just pre-wedding jitters, that's all."

"Tricia, we don't have to get married right now if ya don't wanna. I'm fine with holdin' off till we have the weddin' of your dreams."

You may be, but I don't know if I am. "Clay, I want to be close to you like you desired in your motorhome," she replied with tears streaming down.

"Tricia, I know ya do. But I also don't want ya makin' a rash decision 'cause of that," he said, wiping her tears away. "Gettin' married is a big step. So unless you're actually ready to 'come my wife, sex will have to wait."

Looking into his eyes, Tricia realized that she was. Even though they'd only just gotten engaged, by his words, she knew she could take that next step with him with complete assurance.

Slipping her hands into his she replied, "I think we need to let the minister know that he's got two ceremonies to officiate now."

"Are ya sure 'bout this, Tricia?"

"Yes, Clay. I've never been more sure of anything in my life. I love you, and I'm ready to be your wife."

"Okay, let's head inside, then."

Heading through the doors and into the main chapel, they saw that they were just in time to witness Kate and Bryan's 'I do's'. After taking a seat in the first row of pews, Tricia and Clay watched the minister begin their impromptu ceremony with the familiar, traditionalized vows they were to repeat. Once Bryan had taken his cue to kiss his bride, Kate smiled with delight for finally being able to be called Mrs. Bryan Walker.

With a tired smile and equally sleepy congratulations, the minister directed them to their marriage license so he could go back to bed once they'd signed it. As he waited for the blessed moment when he could finally return his head to his pillow, Tricia informed him of her and Clay's wish for their own last-minute nuptials. Giving her a sleepy nod of agreement and an added yawn to not so subtly emphasize his wish to be back in his bed, he officiated their vows.

"Now will you two be exchanging rings, or just accepting my announcing you as husband and wife like the other couple?" the minister asked.

"He will; I won't," Tricia answered, slipping off her engagement ring and handing it back to Clay.

"Tricia, are ya sure 'bout this?" Clay asked again.

"Yes, Clay. I want your ring to always remind me of this night. Whenever I look at it, I want it to be a lasting memory of the night I first became your wife."

"Okay. I guess it'll be your engagement-weddin' ring, then."

"Talk about two for the price of one . . . told you I was low maintenance, Clay."

"Darlin', ya have no idea how much this ring cost me. Hell, for the price, I would love for it to be both!"

"True, but you know you'd spend the money again in a heartbeat, right?"

"There's no doubt 'bout that. Now let's finish this part up so the minister can get back to his warm bed," he suggested.

"Thank you. Now please repeat after me . . ." the minister quickly began.

"With this ring, I thee wed," Clay repeated. He looked into Tricia's eyes and felt a deep love for her that couldn't be matched by another woman. He then slid the ring back onto her finger so he could soon hear the words that he'd been longing to hear ever since he knew he wanted to marry her.

"As the minister of this church, and by the great state of North Carolina, I now pronounce you husband and wife. You may now kiss your bride, son," the minister declared.

With a nod, Clay took Tricia into his arms. Dipping her back, he gave her first kiss as his wife.

"Now since I only came prepared with the other couple's marriage license, you'll have to follow me back to my office so I can get another one," the minister informed them.

"Oh, there's no need for that. We don't need a marriage license," Tricia quickly responded.

"But don't you want your marriage to be considered legal by the state?" the minister asked.

"No, we don't need that. We just wanted to be officially married in God's eyes," she answered.

"Oh, I see. Never mind, then, and bless your heart for allowing an old man to return to his bed that much sooner."

"You're welcome and thank you for fulfilling our late-night requests."

After receiving a gracious welcome in return, Clay, Bryan, and Kate followed with their own thanks for his late-night services. Then once it became even more blatantly evident that the old man needed to get back into his bed, the couples gladly vacated the small country church and headed back to their vehicles. They watched the church lights go out and the minister relock its doors before finally heading back to his cottage.

"Now what do you guys want to do?" Tricia asked.

"Actually, I think the minister's got the right idea. I'm ready for bed too," Kate answered with a big yawn.

"Why don't we head back to the hotel, Kate?" Bryan suggested.

"Sounds good to me," she answered.

"Good, then let's get going before a rooster crows."

After exchanging congratulations and goodbyes with Tricia and Clay, Kate and Bryan got into their rental car and headed back to their hotel. Tricia and Clay lingered in the parking lot, taking in the cool night air.

"And now that it's just us, what would you like to do, Clay?" Tricia asked.

"Well, I do believe there's a barn callin' our name, darlin'."

He placed his hands on both sides of her making her captive against his truck.

"Ready for that now?" she asked, wrapping her arms around his neck.

"Yep, Tricia, I'm ready to give ya a night ya will always remember." He leaned in and gave her a kiss.

"Clay, I think I'll remember it, regardless, since it will be my first time."

"True, but ya could always end up with a bad memory of it, and bein' that it's my first time too, I definitely don't want that!"

"So then, what's your plan?"

"I'm gonna get ya so damn turned on that ya at least won't have to worry 'bout not bein' wet enough when it comes time for us to finally be together."

"You will?"

"Tricia, ya remember how aroused ya were at the hotel?"

"Yes."

"Well, just imagine that . . . but more so."

"Oh!"

"Tricia, last night was just a preview of what I'll do to get ya turned on for sex." He gave a sexy grin and another brief kiss. "Now get your hot body in my truck, Mrs. Gibson."

Mrs. Gibson, Mrs. Tricia Lane Gibson. She joined him in the cab enjoying her new name. Glancing down at her engagement ring now turned temporary wedding ring, she thought about officially being his wife. Even though they hadn't actually legalized it with their signatures on a marriage certificate, that didn't matter to her. Just the fact that they had made a covenant to love each other for the rest of their lives in front of God and the minister was all that was important to her. She could now give her body to Clay with the peace of mind knowing that it would no longer be a sin in God's eyes.

CHAPTER
- FORTY-FOUR -

"So ya ready to make that fantasy of you and a cowboy rollin' 'round in the hay a reality, darlin'?" Clay asked once he'd brought his truck to a stop in front of the barn.

"You've been wanting to play that out ever since I told you about it, haven't you?"

"Well, it is a very doable fantasy, darlin', especially since we do have access to a barn."

"Then I just have one question for you."

"Yes?"

"Will we have to worry about anyone accidentally interrupting us?"

"Doubt it, but I can lock the doors like I was plannin' to do, anyway." He added with a sexy grin, "Ya could always just consider the interruption as an adrenaline rush . . . ya know, somethin' to keep ya turned on."

"Clay, if your mama were to walk into that barn at the wrong time and see us in the middle of sex, she'd wonder why we jumped the gun, especially since she knows that we're both waiting for marriage."

"Ya do have a point there, darlin', but I highly doubt my mama'll be comin' back out of my motorhome after headin' inside."

"How about you bring that picnic blanket you've got in the truck? That way, not only will we have something to keep us covered if someone does come in but it will make the sex more comfortable too. Even though making out in the hay is a fantasy of mine, getting poked by the stuff and having it stick to me isn't."

"No problem, ya just wait here while I go lock the barn doors," he agreed with a chuckle.

He began to get out of his truck until she stopped him.

"But Clay, if you lock the doors, how will we get in?"

"There's a door in the back, darlin'."

After watching Clay make double sure that the doors were securely locked, he got back into his truck and drove them around to the back. Once there, he made sure to grab the picnic blanket and unlatched the door so they could re-enter the barn.

They walked back into the old wooden building and saw that everything but the lights, their makeshift table and chairs, and two tapered candles had been cleaned up and removed. There was also a second plate of chocolate dessert, but this time, with only a single fork.

"Ah, your mama cleaned up after us!" Tricia announced.

She took a seat on the haystack table while Clay found an area of the barn with enough scattered hay to spread the picnic blanket over.

"Yep," he said. He walked over to her and put his hands in her back pockets.

"Are you trying to cop a feel on your wife, Mr. Gibson?" she asked, taking in his closeness. The knowledge that they were going to actually have sex before the night was over made her nervous.

"Maybe, Mrs. Gibson." He caressed the edges of her pockets with his thumbs.

"Clay, are you hungry for some dessert? The first slice was really good."

Sensing her nervousness, Clay responded, "Sure, darlin'. Why don't ya feed it to me."

Nodding, Tricia picked up the fork and scooped up a bite. She wanted to cry for how nervous she felt, but with a deep breath, she fed it to him.

"Do you want another bite?"

"No. I'd rather give ya a taste of it myself."

Tricia watched Clay take off his hat and set it on the haystack before kissing her. Easily dropping the fork to wrap her arms around his neck, Tricia let herself succumb to his seduction. As she tasted his kiss, his tongue turned it erotic. Running her fingers through his hair, she quickly found his mouth. It made her hot. As he kissed her neck she yearned to be closer to him. Removing her fingers from his hair, she slipped off his overshirt before scrambling to do the same with his T-shirt.

As the intensity of his lips made their impression on her body, Clay smoothly slipped his hands underneath Tricia's shirt and began feeling her up. As if her skin were made of satin, he sensuously glided his hands between the barriers of her bra and jeans making sure to leave her breasts alone as his hands teased her.

Clay watched Tricia hurriedly take off her shirt. With a smile, he took some of the chocolate syrup that had been used to decorate the plate and dabbed it down her cleavage and licked it off. Her body was driven wild as she touched his hair.

Returning his mouth to hers, he slipped his hands down the back of her jeans, cupped her butt, and thrust her body up against his. The aggression kept her turned on. Tricia wrapped her legs tightly around his waist. Clay picked her up and carried her over to the blanket, gently laying her down on it.

Taking out her hair tie and slipping it into a back pocket, Tricia kicked off her shoes before caressing his legs with hers. She couldn't believe how good his lips felt as they drenched her skin with his affection. They were so intoxicating to her senses that she couldn't help but feel an addictive want for more. As his hands slid over the unobstructed parts of her skin, she found herself wishing her clothes were already off.

Clay's lips kept her senses alive and his tongue teased her skin with its wet and tingly sensations. He slowly and sensuously moved his mouth down her body. Reaching her jeans, he was forced to stop.

"I think it's 'bout time I got to see your underwear now." He slowly unbuckled her belt before moving to her jeans. After unbuttoning and unzipping the opening, he gradually pulled the jeans back to expose them. "Nice, matchin' underwear . . . very sexy!"

"It's the same kind you saw in the package."

"Bikini-style, I remember," he continued, slipping off her jeans.

He lowered his head to her body, sensually kissing her skin. She could feel him heightening her arousal. With each sensation his affection brought her body, she found it surreal that she was actually about to make love to the man of her dreams. She thought about everything Clay had done to seduce her heart into loving him. She was astounded that, within moments, they would soon be having sex for the first time.

"Tricia, since I wasn't hopin' we'd be havin' sex tonight, I didn't bring any protection," he informed her as he took off his boots.

"It's okay, Clay. Even if you did, I wouldn't want to use it."

"But aren't ya worried?"

"Nope."

Hearing that, he added all but his boxers to the rest of the clothes scattered on the barn's floor.

With a passionate embrace, he continued to show her body his unending love. His touch worked its magic in getting her ready for making love. Clay moved Tricia onto his lap, letting her feel his hardened member. He remembered how he had turned her on by kissing her neck and returned his mouth to her neck's soft skin. After hearing her moans of delight and seeing her outstretched neck, he added the tingling sensation of his tongue. Tricia moaned in ecstasy. She never wanted the sensations to end.

"Darlin', as much as I love turnin' ya on by tastin' your neck, I love kissin' ya more!" he whispered to her.

With his mouth keeping hers busy, he brought a hand to the base of her head and slowly dripped sensuous kisses down the center of her neck. As he did, he used his other hand to ever so gently slip off her bra straps, leaving her skin without a barrier guarding her from his touch. However, he could feel the bra still clinging tightly to her skin by its clasp.

"Tricia, I love you, and I want to express that to ya on every inch of your body," he whispered again as he wrapped his fingers around the clasp.

"I love you too, Clay." She felt pleasure from his mere touch as well as the presence of his member underneath her. She slipped her hands through his hair and grasped onto his black locks as her desire for him spread throughout her body. Clay unclasped her bra, one step closer to finally making love to her.

Moaning out in pleasure, she felt his mouth on her bare breasts. As he kissed her most sensitive areas, she could feel herself becoming more and more aroused. It was a feeling that she had only felt a glimpse of before but nothing as intense as the way he was making her feel right now. "I'm ready for you now, cowboy," she softly whispered into his ear as her body told her that she needed him now!

"Then darlin', your wait for makin' love to me is finally over!" he whispered back.

"Clay, I have never been more ready for you to make me yours!"

Looking into his gorgeous blue eyes, she understood the overwhelming love he felt for her.

"Well, darlin', all I've got to say to that is that I'm damn glad we both waited for each other!"

Smiling, he returned his lips to the sweet taste of hers. As they took in each other's flavor, Clay slipped a hand down her lower back and effortlessly removed the last piece of clothing from her body. With the last barrier gone, he realized he could now slide his hands over every part of her.

After Tricia felt him slip off her underwear, she returned the favor. With each now ready for the other, Clay took control and finally took her virginity. She returned his passion as they finally became one, and he fulfilled her every craving for him as they made love for the first time. Every touch of his was pure dynamite. He released his deep desire for her with every sensuous kiss and caressing touch his lips and hands brought to her body.

CHAPTER

- FORTY-FIVE -

Feeling exhausted after experiencing her first climax, Tricia found herself at home wrapped in Clay's strong arms. She could feel his bare skin against her and was reminded of the love they had just shared. It was sobering to feel his naked flesh without the intoxicating taste of his lips. She had never felt more comfortable in her life.

Waking up several hours later as bits of light shone through the barn's siding, Clay had kept them connected with his right arm across her torso. She moved her right arm to intertwine her fingers with his.

"Mornin', darlin'. How's it feel to no longer be a virgin?" he groggily asked with a kiss on her shoulder.

Letting go of his hand to turn her body to face him, Tricia responded. "A little sore . . . and a shower would be nice."

Clay smiled. "You'll get used to me. As for the shower, you'll have to wait till we get back to your dorm."

"Considering I haven't had anything bigger than a tampon in there, I would hope so."

"Thanks for the visual, darlin'."

"Well, it's the truth." She shrugged, reaching her hand out to play with the hair on the nape of his neck.

"Then, yeah, I'm definitely a lot bigger than a tampon," he replied, placing her leg over his.

Taking a deep breath at the knowledge of still being able to feel his bareness, Tricia did her best to keep her eyes on his instead of looking down his body.

"Tricia, what's wrong?"

"It's just . . . Clay, I'm not used to this." She forced herself to glance down his body.

"Ah. Well, then, it's another first for both of us."

"Then why are you so comfortable just like this?"

"'Cause I grew up goin' skinny dippin', so I'm used to bein' this open."

"Oh."

"Though I have no problem helpin' ya into it."

He then removed his hand from her leg and gave her a slight nudge so her body would be right up against his.

"Clay, did you really need to do that?" she asked, now feeling her chest against his.

"No, but I wanted to."

Shaking her head at him, she gave him a kiss before searching for her underwear. After finding them, she handed him his boxers.

"I take it this means you're ready to get up?" he asked, watching her keep her back to him as she slipped them back on.

"Right now, I'm just hungry, and I have to pee." She made her way back over to the haystack with her arms covering her chest.

Slipping back on his boxers, Clay joined her.

"I see ya don't mind wearin' my clothes," he pointed out after watching her stop to slip on his overshirt.

"It was quicker," she replied, buttoning a top button that kept her chest closed to his view.

"Tricia, we just had sex . . . and I had my mouth all over both of your breasts. There's nothin' to be 'shamed of."

"I remember," she answered, briefly cleaning off the fork before taking a bite of the dessert.

"Then why are ya so shy 'bout me seein' em?" he asked, standing in front of her with his arms crossed.

"I'm not, Clay. Like you said, you just saw them during sex."

"Tricia."

"What? Just because I show you my chest when we're intimate means that I have to be okay with showing it to you now?" Her eyes welled up.

"Darlin', ya've got a gorgeous body. Besides, I'm your husband now. So ya have no need to fear showin' 'em to me."

"Clay, it's not that simple."

"I know it's not."

"So then, why does it matter?"

"'Cause I love you, and I want ya to be comfortable with me."

"And I'll get there, Clay, you just have to give me time. It's one thing for me to show you my breasts when you've turned me on and we're actually about to have sex, but it's a whole other thing when it's just us talking."

"And that's fine, darlin'." He closed the gap between them and slipped his hands around her waist to come to a stop on her butt. "I just want ya to be honest with yourself . . . and me."

Giving him a smile for being so understanding, Tricia devoured the rest of the pie.

"Since you're going to have to go back on the road soon, do you mind if I keep your shirt?"

"Not at all, darlin'. I got plenty more."

"Thank you. Because when you're gone, I have a feeling it's going to become what I sleep in."

"Then, I guess it's a good thing ya look damn good in it."

"You're just saying that because you know I'm not wearing a bra."

"Tricia, I'm saying that 'cause ya do. Hell, a bra would probably be just as sexy, especially if I could see it."

"I'm sorry, Clay, that I'm not more confident in myself."

"Tricia, you'll get there. Ya just gotta give yourself time."

"Damn, you are an amazing husband."

"And I'll 'come even more amazin' when ya go put on the rest of your clothes so I can buy us both breakfast. 'Cause even though ya scarfed down that slice, I'm still hungry."

"Oh, right. Sorry I didn't offer you any."

"Darlin', it's quite all right. I'd rather ya get your fill first anyway."

"I love that you're such a gentleman."

Giving her a kiss, Clay added a slap on her butt after watching her grab her shirt.

So much for the gentleman part. She watched him slip his T-shirt back on.

"I'm so glad we finally got to do that last night!" Tricia exclaimed as they came back to her dorm room from breakfast.

"Tell me 'bout it. Me finally gettin' to see ya naked was definitely a nice surprise."

"I'm sure it was, Clay, but now what do you want to do?" she asked, dropping her weekend bag in her desk chair.

"Well, we could always spend some more time really gettin' to know each other again," he suggested, patting her bed.

"But what if Claire comes back? I don't want us accidentally getting interrupted in the middle of it."

"Darlin', ya can always put a sign on the door tellin' her that ya want some time alone with your fiancé."

"Clay, she doesn't know about that, and I also don't want our desire to be alone to make it so that she can't get back into the room if she needs to."

"Are ya sure 'bout that?" he asked, getting up from her bed.

"Yes, Clay. Besides, if I put a sign on the door, I think that'll end up sending her the wrong message," Tricia said, putting her stuff away.

"And what message would that be, darlin'? That ya wanna be intimate with your fiancé?"

Coming up behind her, he gave her neck a kiss. He slipped his hands underneath her shirt and smoothly brought them under her bra so he could once again feel her soft breasts. Hearing her moan, he swiftly turned her around to face him. He then pinned her up against the wall, slipping his hands into hers, and began sensuously kissing her neck.

As her desire was stirred up, Tricia felt his hands quickly undo her belt buckle and begin to unzip her jeans. She debated if they'd even have enough time for a quickie before her roommate got back from wherever she was. Tricia realized that it was too much of a risk.

"Clay, no, we need to wait."

"Fine."

"Hey, how about we watch a comedy to lighten the mood?"

"Whatever." He returned to her bed and stretched out.

"Good, because *She's the Man* is absolutely hilarious!"

After inserting the DVD into the player, she crawled onto the bed and curled up next to Clay. "Now, could you please take your boots off for me?"

"But why, when they ain't even on your bed?"

"Because of this, Clay." Tricia kicked off her shoes so she could join her sock-covered feet with his.

"Oh. I'm sorry, then."

Seeing that Tricia still wanted to be affectionate with him, but in a different way, Clay did as asked. He put an arm around her.

"It's okay, Clay. All is forgiven."

"Glad to hear it, darlin'." He placed a kiss on her forehead right as the feature presentation began. "Ooh, that reminds me, do ya have any candy to go with it? Say, a Musketeers maybe?"

"Ha! Now shut your mouth so we can watch the movie."

"I'll be glad to, darlin'," he agreed, giving her a kiss before turning his attention to the TV.

CHAPTER
- FORTY-SIX -

"Ladies, I'm sorry to tell you this, but according to rookie NASCAR driver Clay Gibson's rep, Bryan Walker, Clay Gibson is now slated to marry a woman named Tricia Perkins," the TV host announced, showing a picture of the newly engaged couple.

"Damn it! No!" Nikki yelled at the TV. "That woman is not supposed to be taking my place!"

Nikki couldn't believe it. Not only had she been replaced but Clay was in the process of making it permanent. Somehow, she had to convince Clay that a future with her was in his best interest. After all, there was no way this Tricia Perkins would ever look as good in a designer dress as she would.

The question was: what else could she do? She'd tried threats, but that only got her put in handcuffs. She'd tried seducing him, only to have him push her away. What else could she do that would get Clay to rethink this new woman in his life?

Nikki turned the TV off in the motel room. She had been forced to relocate after NASCAR officials had banned her from the speedway whenever Clay was there. Nikki had to figure out a way to convince him to forget about this new girl and give her another chance. After all, he wanted to have the right girl on his arm.

Hearing a knock on the door, Nikki realized that she would have to wait until later to devise her plan. "Nice job on putting Clay in the hospital, Logan. Glad to see you finally manned up."

Even though she wanted to be back on Clay's arm, she still had to keep Logan clueless to her scheme.

"Hey, I didn't mean to put him there . . . it just ended up that way."

"Either way, it got you to the winner's circle. You would've never come in first had you not knocked Clay out of the position."

"One of these days, it'll be for my own efforts."

"You must be talking in another lifetime, then. Logan, until you can beat Clay at his own game, your efforts will always come up short."

"Nikki, you don't know that."

"Well, you haven't done it yet. How long have you two been racing?"

"Okay, I get your point. The man is just better than I am. What the hell am I supposed to do about it?"

"Duh, get in his head and screw him up. Same thing I told you before."

"Nikki, it's pointless."

"Only if you quit trying."

Logan shook his head in frustration. He was in a no-win situation. Despite having Reese and Tyler's help, the text threats hadn't pushed Clay over the edge like he'd hoped. Then, as if to compound his inability to win just one race, his girlfriend was constantly demeaning him and his abilities.

"Nikki, I came to see if you wanted to get some dinner, but if you're just going to berate me, never mind." Heading for the door, Logan felt like he'd finally had it. Nikki couldn't possibly be worth dealing with her constant criticism.

"Aw, baby, did I hurt your feelings?" she began sweet talking him.

Using her sex appeal to keep him on her hook, she closed the gap between them and showed him enough affection that would make him rethink the possibility of walking out on her.

"Damn you, Nikki." Changing his mind, Logan moved her to the bed.

"See. This is why you'll never leave me," she reminded him as she seduced him.

I hate myself for this, he thought as he took her through the motions. Her orgasm made him cringe at his failure to leave her.

Minutes later, as both redressed, Logan knew something had to change. He couldn't keep living his life under Nikki's spell. No matter how good the sex was, he had long ago tired of her highlighting his shortcomings. The question was: when would he finally man up and tell her goodbye?

✿

"Tyler, did you destroy the burner cellphone?" Reese asked after hearing the news about Nikki.

"Yeah. After I sent the last text."

"Good, because now that Nikki's dumb ass got caught, I don't want either of ours to be next."

"Trust me, Reese, we'll be fine. The cellphone was paid for with cash so there's no way in hell it could've been traced back to us."

"Good, because it would be our asses if you messed up."

"Relax Reese, I know how to keep our asses out of trouble so we don't end up like Nikki."

"And that's exactly what we'll do as long as we continue to keep our mouths shut. Since there's still no questions about our involvement and we've being staying under the radar, no one will ever suspect us."

"They better not or my dad'll kill me if he hears something from somebody else," Reese reminded Tyler. It was never far from his mind that McKibbon Motorsports was one of the more prominent teams in NASCAR. Any wind of Reese's wrongdoing and the media would skewer his family's name.

"Relax, Reese, with only the two of us knowing what each other did, there is little room for accusation."

Reese forced himself to believe Tyler. Despite the minuscule uncertainty of a third party proving Tyler wrong, the worry refused to leave him.

CHAPTER
- FORTY-SEVEN -

Eight Months Later

"Only two more months 'fore we officially 'come husband and wife to everyone else, darlin'." Clay came into Tricia's bedroom with a freshly made sandwich in his hand.

"I can't believe fall's almost here."

As Tricia sat on her bed, going through a Ziploc bag full of wedding paraphernalia ideas she had collected over the years, it seemed unreal to her that she had actually gotten to use them.

"I know, the year's gone by fast," Clay agreed, stretching out on her bed. "What's all that?" he asked, seeing the scattered printouts.

"It's everything I used to plan our wedding day."

"Ah. I do remember ya jokin' to me 'bout all I had to do was just give ya my measurements and then just show up."

"Well, I did pretty much have it all covered."

"I know. It's the reason why I didn't want ya to rush the weddin' just for the sex."

"Honestly, Clay, it's crazy to me that we've even come so far. Just thinking about my first meeting you, and now we've had sex countless times."

"Yep, and that's 'cause ya didn't end up lettin' your fear rule your life."

"I guess it just astounds me because, even though I had always hoped this would be my reality one day, the fact that it actually is . . . I just have no words."

"Tricia, I'm just happy ya've learned to let your guard down with me."

"Me too. It sucked feeling so self-conscious just showing you my body."

"Well, when ya ain't used to it, it's understandable."

"Clay, you are so incredible. Your understanding alone is just amazing."

Putting his sandwich aside and pulling her to him, Clay said, "Darlin', that's just 'cause ya've opened my eyes to a different way of experiencin' the world. I love that your way of viewin' life makes me take a second look myself."

"It's just crazy that the night Kate and I went out in hopes of meeting our Mr. Rights, we actually did."

"God has His timin' for everythin', darlin'. Ya can't rush what He's already got planned."

Giving him a kiss, Tricia responded, "Yeah, only He could know that Kate would find a relationship with Bryan that her parents never had."

"Or get her pregnant their first time."

"Or that. Though, speaking of, I wonder if today's going to be that day."

"Don't know. But I'm sure glad you didn't wind up like that after our first time."

Tricia gave him another kiss. "The timing was off, though we've been together plenty of times since to give the timing another opportunity."

"Mm, we sure have . . . and in this bed." Clay took off his hat and put his sandwich down to return her kiss.

"Do you want another experience of that?"

"I wouldn't mind it," he answered, pulling his boots off as their kissing got hotter.

"Then I guess . . . it's a . . . good thing . . . my parents . . . aren't home," she replied in between kisses.

"Ya make it sound . . . like we're . . . back in high school, darlin'."

Smiling at his comment, Tricia easily slipped his shirts off as their time on her bed turned erotic. "You think we . . . can . . . have a . . . quickie . . . just in case . . . Kate . . . or Bryan . . . call?"

"Quickie or not . . . it's not . . . like . . . we have to . . . rush to . . . the . . . hospital . . . when they . . . call." But as Clay was taking off her shirt, his cellphone rang. "Damn, if that's them, they have miserable timin'." With their kissing at a stopping point, Tricia motioned for him to find out.

Clay saw Bryan's name displayed on his cellphone. "Hey, Bryan."

"It's time, Clay. Kate's just gone into labor."

"Thanks for the heads up. I'll let Tricia know."

"See you soon, buddy."

Ending the call, Clay relayed the message.

"Considering labor can take a while, do you want to continue?" Tricia asked.

"Darlin', ya make it too temptin' for me not to."

Returning his lips back to hers, he hurried off her shirt as sex became their priority.

"We should probably get dressed, Clay." Tricia took a few minutes to cuddle under the sheets.

"Yeah, we probably should," he agreed, getting out of bed and putting his clothes back on.

Since Tricia's comfort level had changed, she was now able to put her bra on without keeping her breasts covered from Clay's view. She grabbed his keys and tossed them to him.

Clay grabbed his sandwich and finished it on the way to his truck.

Clay parked at Newport Bay City Hospital twenty-five minutes later. After briefly stopping at the information desk for the maternity ward, they eventually found Bryan pacing in the waiting room.

"How far along is she?" Tricia asked.

"At this point, I don't know. I was just waiting for you guys to get here." He immediately returned to his wife's bedside.

"Great! Well, that means we got here with plenty of time to spare," Tricia replied.

"Yep, so now what would ya like to do, darlin'?"

"I don't know, sit here and wait, I guess."

"It's too bad we finished what we'd started in your room when we could've used one of the linen closets they got 'round here, instead," he teased, pulling her into his arms.

"Clay, no! That would not have happened."

"Darlin', I was just jokin', though it doesn't sound all that bad."

Tricia shook her head at Clay and gave him a humorless look. "I'm all for experiencing new things with you, but that is not ever going to be one of them." Tricia had her arms around his neck with her head comfortably on his shoulder. As the hours passed, they traded standing for chairs. Eventually, a doctor headed into the room.

"I guess that means it's time," Tricia commented. Moments later, the sound of Kate struggling through delivery confirmed her assumption. But as Tricia listened to her best friend deal with the pain, she couldn't help but imagine herself going through that with Clay providing her his support. Though, her old-fashioned-to-the-core way of thinking would mean a home birth.

"Guess so," Clay agreed. He was happy to not be in the same room. Kate's screaming made an imprint on his brain and so did the cry of her baby. Clay watched Bryan excitedly come out of the room as he announced their daughter's arrival.

Ushering them into the room, Kate and their new daughter received their first visitors.

"Oh wow, she's so beautiful, Kate!" Tricia exclaimed. She watched the newborn sleep as she lay tucked in a pink receiving blanket.

"I know. She's amazing, isn't she?" Kate replied.

Despite her daughter being the result of too much alcohol, when Kate looked down at her, she felt overwhelming love.

"Yes, she is, Kate. Ya did a good job, Bryan," Clay added.

"Thanks, buddy, I couldn't be happier!" Bryan said, kissing his wife's messy hair. He looked upon Kate cradling their daughter and captured the moment in his mind so he could remember it forever.

"Does your precious daughter have a precious name?" Tricia asked.

"Yes, Bryn Michelle Walker. Bryn for Bryan's name and Michelle for his mother's," Kate answered proudly.

"Well, Kate, that has got to be the best gift ya could've ever given Bryan, and I'm sure his mama would've been real proud that ya did that," Clay replied.

"Thank you, Clay," Kate returned.

"You're welcome," he accepted.

CHAPTER
- FORTY-EIGHT -

As Tricia looked down at Bryn, she couldn't help but think how adorable she was. She accidentally made a statement that would bring another change to her and Clay's life. "Oh, Clay, she's so cute! I can't wait until we have one of our own!"

"Great, Bryan, now look what ya've done."

"Oh, don't worry, Clay, you've got eight months to be ready for it," Tricia reassured him. Immediately, Tricia covered her mouth and widened her eyes after realizing that she'd just given her secret away.

"What did ya just say, Tricia?"

"I . . . uh . . . well, we . . ."

Stunned by her slip of the tongue, Clay quickly excused them from Kate's bedside. "Tricia, are you pregnant?"

"Well, I . . . um."

"You're pregnant, aren't ya? Answer me, damn it. Are we gonna have a baby or not?"

"I . . . um . . . well, yes. Yes, I am, Clay. So, yes, we are going to have a baby. I am going to be a mother, and you are going to be a father."

"Why didn't ya tell me this earlier?"

"Well, because I wanted to make sure first. I took a few home pregnancy tests and went to the doctor and found out I was pregnant. Plus, I wanted to wait and tell you in my own romantic way. I didn't mean to just blurt it out like that," she explained.

"Oh."

"I tell you that I'm going to have your baby and all you can say is 'oh?' There's no 'congratulations, darlin'? This is so incredible, ya've made all my dreams come true?' None of that, just 'oh?'"

"What can I say, Tricia? I'm still in shock. Besides, I thought ya had wanted to wait 'til after our official weddin' to have a baby."

"I thought so, too, until I kept forgetting to refill my birth control prescription."

"Ya mean . . . we've been . . . all this time?"

"Yes," she answered biting her lip.

"But how could ya forget somethin' so important like that? Don't ya normally take it every mornin'?"

"Well, it's not like I meant to, Clay. I would just get so damn sidetracked every time I remembered I still needed to refill it that it just never got done. Then, when you'd get me desiring you, I definitely wouldn't be thinking about it then," she explained.

"Huh. So, I'm gonna be a dad."

"Yes, Clay, you are." Smiling, she took his hand and put it on her belly.

"Well, darlin', I can't wait, and with this baby, ya will have certainly given me everythin' I ever wanted out of life."

"I'm very glad to hear you say that, Clay," Tricia replied with a contented smile. "Although you know what this means, right?"

"That we gotta keep this secret to ourselves."

"Yep, so even though Kate and Bryan now know, it needs to stay a secret to everyone else."

"How far along did ya say ya were?"

"Only about a month. Since the wedding isn't for a couple of months, we won't have to worry about me showing at that point."

"Who would've thought I'd get ya pregnant so fast?" Clay chuckled.

"Maybe it's just because we happened to have sex on one of the days I was ovulating," Tricia offered as her Asperger's supplied a more literal reason.

"Darlin', it's obviously that, too, but considerin' the fact that we're always goin' at it whenever we're alone in your dorm room or in my motorhome, I'm just surprised I didn't get ya pregnant sooner."

"Clay, you're forgetting your truck and my bedroom and bathroom."

"Darlin', I definitely ain't forgettin' 'bout us doin' it in any of those places . . . though bein' with ya in the shower was pretty hot!"

"No pun intended, I assume?"

"No, there was definitely a pun intended."

"Oh, you're such a funny man, Clay Gibson."

"For you, Tricia Perkins, always."

"So what are you thinking about now since that smile is refusing to go away?"

"Oh, I just like knowin' that it didn't take me long to get ya pregnant, is all."

"Clay, that's just because your manhood knows how to get the job done. And speaking of babies, we're going to need to start keeping this new secret of ours right now since everyone just got here."

"Ya bet your pregnant body it does," he agreed, bringing her into another brief kiss before they went to greet everyone.

Tricia stood contentedly in Clay's arms by the door to Kate's hospital room. "Can you believe that's going to be us in eight months, Clay?"

"Darlin', I honestly can't wait. Ya cradlin' our baby like that while our family and friends look on, well, ya'd make me one proud man."

Turning her head and giving him a kiss on the cheek, Tricia whispered, "I love you so much, Clay, and I can't wait to have that family with you."

"I love ya too, darlin'. Ya mean the world to me."

Snuggling her head against his neck, Tricia gave a happy sigh as she observed the joy that Bryn's birth had brought to everyone. Even though Kate's parents could barely be civil with each other, Tricia saw how their attitudes changed as they showed their adoration for their new granddaughter. She glanced over at her own parents' reaction and imagined how they would be when it was her turn to give birth to their grandchild.

Taking in the scene, Clay found it amazing how God worked things out. By the birth of a new generation, He provided a reason for faith.

Bryn remained the center of attention. Her eyes slowly opened, and she began reaching for her mama's breast.

"Okay, everyone, I think that means it's time to give my wife and daughter some privacy," Bryan announced.

As everyone headed back into the waiting room so Kate could breastfeed, Tricia and Clay decided to head back to her house. After giving both Kate and Bryan their congratulations, they said their goodbyes before heading for Clay's truck.

Clay drove them back into her parents' gated community. He saw Logan's Z83 Camaro sitting in front of a neighbor's house across the street.

Huh, I wonder why he's here? Clay slowly drove by the black muscle car with reddish yellow flames.

"Clay, whose car is that?"

"Logan's, but unless he knows one of your parents' neighbors, I don't know why his car is parked there."

CHAPTER
- FORTY-NINE -

"Clay, now that you know about my pregnancy, we only have eight more months of just the two of us," Tricia reminded him as they entered her house.

"Ya worried that it's not enough alone time for us?"

"Well, a baby is a big change."

"True. Though, Tricia, what would ya expect would happen when we never use protection?"

"I know. I guess each new change just takes me a while to get used to."

"Well, as ya told me 'fore, ya got eight months to be ready for this next one."

Heading up to her room, Tricia realized that she was actually pregnant, while Clay thought about actually becoming a dad. Both had hoped this would be their reality at some point in their lives, but as their dream became realized, it took them some time to get used to.

Tricia turned the doorknob to her room. She and Clay were surprised by Nikki and Logan waiting for them on the other side. Nikki had a gun in her hand while Logan stood by her side. Taking advantage of their shock, Nikki immediately strongarmed Tricia as her captive.

"Tricia!" Clay's eyes went wide. "Nikki, what the hell are ya doin'?"

It suddenly dawned on Clay why Logan's car was parked in front of a neighbor's house.

"Clay, she's not right for you," Nikki immediately began.

"What are ya talkin' 'bout?"

"Clay, you should be with me," she explained, gesturing with her gun.

"Nikki, you're with Logan. You chose to be with him. Why should my bein' with someone else matter to ya?"

"Because Clay, only I understand how to be in the spotlight. Your fiancée here doesn't have a clue."

"That's 'cause that's not what's important to her or me. The spotlight has always been your thing."

"Exactly, and since Logan has come to grips with the fact that you're just better than him, he's okay with me leaving him for you."

Watching how far Nikki was taking her obsession with the spotlight, Logan couldn't help but mentally shake his head. Had she not pulled her gun on him, forcing him to drive them to Tricia's parents' neighborhood, he would've finally been done with her.

"Nikki, you're delusional. I ain't gonna break up with my fiancée to take ya back."

Clay watched Nikki keep Tricia captive with her 9-millimeter as Logan stood by looking helpless. Yeah, the backstory of how Nikki and Logan got together stung, but in the end, it seemed like Logan should be more pitied than cussed out for doing Clay wrong.

"I'm not delusional, Clay, I just know that only I know how to be your better half, especially where your career is concerned."

"Nikki, I am in love with the woman you're pressin' a gun against. There is absolutely no second chance for us as I told ya 'fore."

"But you don't really mean that, Clay. After all, I grew up with you. Besides, I remember the whole reason why I started seeing Logan in the first place, and clearly, you changed your mind about that." Nikki glanced at the unmade bed with sheets that looked like they'd been used for more than sleeping.

"Nikki, what I do with my fiancée ain't any of your business."

"Fine. If you won't take me back, then there's only one other option for me."

Nikki released the safety as she snugly pressed the gun against Tricia's temple.

"Clay!" Tricia screamed.

"Nikki, ya don't have to do this."

"Clay, I can't have you with another woman." Seeing the fear in Tricia's eyes, Clay felt powerless. As his psycho ex threatened his fiancée's life, all he could do was watch the tears come down Tricia's face.

"Nikki, just think 'bout what you're doin'. You and Logan can leave here, and I promise ya, I won't press charges."

"No, Clay, that's not good enough."

"Then, what can I do that'll make ya let her go?"

"Marry me instead."

"I can't do that, Nikki. Tricia's the love of my life. There's no way I can turn my back on that."

"Then, you leave me with no choice," she replied, preparing to pull the trigger.

"Please, Nikki, I'm pregnant," Tricia sobbed through her tears.

"Prove it," Nikki returned as her emerald eyes turned cold. Another woman was going to have Clay Gibson's baby. How the hell could she ever deal with that?

"Go look in my bathroom. The stick's on the counter."

"Logan, do it," Nikki ordered.

Shaking his head at the ridiculous situation, Logan wondered if there was a way he could vindicate himself in Clay's eyes by disarming Nikki. Passing by Clay to get the proof, Logan came back with the stick in his hand, proving to Nikki that Tricia was telling the truth.

"How long?" Nikki asked.

"About a month," Tricia answered, hoping the stress alone wouldn't cause a miscarriage.

"Damn it, this won't work! You shouldn't have gotten her pregnant, Clay. This ruins everything." She pressed the gun harder against Tricia's temple. "Have you ever been unfaithful to him?"

"No."

"Damn it!"

Struggling to figure out what to do, Nikki felt like she was losing control. Clay was supposed to be hers alone, but now, he'd gone and changed the situation. She couldn't go back to him now that he was having a baby with another woman. No, that just wouldn't be right.

"Nikki, ya need to just give it up. Tricia has my heart, so I couldn't give it to ya even if there was the slightest chance I wanted to."

"She might have your heart."

"No. Nikki, my heart is gonna stay with her, and ya just need to deal with it. Ya need to get over this damn delusion of us gettin' back together 'cause it is just never gonna happen. I don't wanna be with ya anymore. That's all there is to it."

"No, Clay. I didn't push Logan to try to derail your career just to have you say no to me."

"So Logan had a hand in the threats?" Clay asked with alarm.

"After I'd sent you that first text threatening your career, I encouraged Logan to do the same so he could get you out of the winner's circle. I want my man to provide me with the spotlight. He can't, but you can. And I want that back."

"I knew ya attemptin' to seduce me seemed suspicious!"

"So? I tried to use my charm on you. Big deal. My sex appeal is what I've got to work with."

"Nikki, ya've got so much more potential than that. What happened?"

"Clay, I'm not going to give you some sob story about what you didn't know about my childhood. The truth is I just like the status you gave me, and I want it back."

Clay shook his head. "So ya got Logan to help ya with that?"

"Well, since I foolishly left you for him, I sure as hell wasn't going to look stupid for it. So yeah, I encouraged him, hoping he could man up and make me leaving you worth it. Sad thing is, he never did. Logan here just can't cut it. Not like you with your natural skill."

Logan felt like he'd just been punched in the gut. He wished to God he could take Nikki's gun and use it on her. He had reached his limit of her belittling him.

CHAPTER
- FIFTY -

"Clay, I'm sorry," Logan apologized. "I'd only wanted to prove myself to Nikki, but clearly, that didn't happen."

"Was anyone else involved?"

"I told them I wouldn't say."

"Logan, I ain't gonna press charges or get retribution. I just wanna know."

"Fine. Tyler and Reese."

"It figures. They've had it out for me ever since my first NASCAR race with 'em."

"And this is exactly why, Logan, you don't know how to be a man. Hell, you couldn't even threaten Clay without help," Nikki pointed out.

"Nikki, ya clearly don't even know what a real man is. The fact that Logan's ownin' up to what he did *makes* him a real man."

"Whatever. I just know that you being with Tricia isn't going to work for me."

"I don't care."

"Too bad. It's me or no one." She was about to pull the trigger.

Clay took Tricia's hand in his. "Tricia, just remember . . . I love you and always will."

Seeing how tender he was with Tricia, Nikki had reached her breaking point. Even if she pulled the trigger, Tricia still had Clay's heart. It was a no-win situation for her, leaving her with one thing left to do. Removing the gun from Tricia's temple, Nikki was about to take her own life when Logan saw his chance. Before Nikki could pull the trigger, Logan grabbed her gun. Surprised, Nikki fought for control.

Pushing Tricia behind him for fear the gun accidentally going off, Clay pulled out his cellphone and quickly dialed 911. Alerting the operator to the scene playing out in Tricia's bedroom, he and Tricia watched the battle continue until the trigger was finally pulled.

Completely in shock, Tricia stood frozen like a statue. She'd never witnessed a death before, much less one in her own bedroom. But in seconds, she was watching Nikki fall to the floor, her visible blood showing she had lost the fight.

Immediately releasing his hold on the gun, Logan watched it drop to the floor next to her.

"You shot me!" Nikki looked up at Logan.

Hearing the sirens, Nikki turned her eyes to Clay. The realization that she wasn't ever going to be with him again as he kept Tricia shielded became her last thought.

Shocked himself, Logan replied, "I did."

Ending his conversation with the operator, Clay held Tricia in his arms. He had been so scared for her life. It suddenly hit him just how damn much he and Tricia loved each other.

"Darlin', do I need to take ya to the doctor to make sure you're okay?" he asked with a glance at her belly.

"No, I'm pretty sure I'll be fine," Tricia answered. Tricia prayed that the stress she'd felt wouldn't cause any issues for the embryo.

Tricia and Clay headed downstairs to meet the police while Logan stayed with Nikki's body.

Directing the officers to her bedroom, they found Logan on the floor. His eyes now blinded by tears as he found himself finally free from Nikki's abuse.

An officer radioed dispatch for a coroner.

"Ma'am, do you have another place you can stay tonight?" an officer asked her.

"Yeah, I do," Tricia answered.

Looking at Clay, she realized that she was going to be spending another night with him in his motorhome.

Nodding, the officer turned to Logan for his statement.

"I'll also have to let my parents know that they'll need to stay in a hotel," Tricia realized. Tricia thought about them still at the hospital and it dawned on her that she would now have to tell them about the threats Clay had dealt with and how Clay's ex had turned her bedroom into a death scene.

"Well, it looks like I'll be sharing your bed tonight, Clay."

"Then why don't ya grab some stuff so we can head over there once we're given the okay?" he suggested.

Nodding, Tricia collected what she could from her room, doing her best to stay out of the way. She headed into the bathroom to grab some toiletries then rejoined Clay.

As the medical examiner arrived and pictures were taken for evidence, Tricia took a moment to call her parents and let them know what had happened before she and Clay headed for his motorhome.

"Whether it was Tyler or Reese tailing you, they must've told Logan and Nikki where I live," Tricia commented as Clay drove them past the gate.

"Yeah, I would have to say you're right since Nikki had left that voicemail 'bout ya. She must've let Logan know so I wouldn't be suspicious of her car."

"I just feel so bad for him, Clay. I know he's partially to blame for you and Nikki breaking up, but just how she treated him back there . . . I mean, man, that had to have taken a toll on him."

"It sounds like he'd been dealin' with the degradation for a long time."

"I'm just glad it's over. Were you serious about not pressing charges on Tyler or Reese?"

"Yeah, why? Do ya think I should?"

"Well, considering that they'd only stalked and tailed you and Nikki was the one behind it all, I don't think pressing charges would be worth it."

"True."

"Since Logan gave his statement to that cop, I highly doubt they'll get away with it without any consequences."

"Yeah, but it'll most likely be handed out by NASCAR since Logan never said who was doin' what."

"And to think, Tyler gave Claire his number. I wonder how that conversation's going to go."

"Tyler will probably end up single again."

"Clay, thank you for showing me what a real man is. I know that Nikki never recognized that gift, but I really thank God that He gave it to me with you."

"You're very welcome, darlin'. It's always my pleasure."

CHAPTER
- FIFTY-ONE -

A wedding, a new house, and about eight months later

"Oh, my sweet baby girl. Your daddy and I can't wait for you to finally come into this world," Tricia said, stroking her oversized belly.

Standing in her daughter's room, Tricia was amazed at how her life had changed since meeting Clay. She'd never thought that she'd actually become a NASCAR driver's wife, much less, be about to give birth to their daughter. The moment Clay had asked her if Kate's seat was taken, it was like her fate had been sealed that day. Just looking into his eyes had captivated her in a way she had never imagined. She couldn't thank God more that she had finally let go of her fear of the unknown.

"Hey, darlin', ya plannin' on comin' down to watch this movie with me sometime soon, or should I just go 'head and start it without ya?" Clay called out.

"I'll be right there," she called back.

"Is Kaylin's room all ready for her arrival?"

"Yes, and now we're just waiting for her to fill it," she answered, closing the door. She smiled at Clay's handiwork of pink bordered blocks spelling out Kaylin's name on her door. Making her way down the stairs, Tricia was reminded of how much she missed seeing her feet when she looked down to take the next step.

"Glad to hear it, now how much longer am I gonna have to be makin' conversation with ya while I wait for ya to be in the same room as me?"

"Clay, I'm almost there. Hold on."

"What should I hold on to?"

"I see you've been hanging around my dad way too much," she replied, recognizing the colloquialism.

"We do both enjoy NASCAR, darlin'."

"Yeah, I know. You two spend so much father-son-in-law time together that I think you've already replaced me as his racing buddy."

"Ya missin' your father-daughter time with him, darlin'?"

"Just a little. But I think that once our little one comes, it'll be a long time before I can return to spending that kind of quality time with him." She took a seat next to him. Resting her hands on her belly, Tricia did her best to get comfortable. Curling up by Clay's side, she found that regardless of how she adjusted her body, she would not be comfortable until she got her post-baby body back.

"Ya ready for our date night, Tricia?"

"Yeah, Clay, I am," she answered with a kiss.

"I'm kinda glad we don't use protection, darlin', otherwise, I wouldn't be gettin' to have my own father-daughter time to enjoy soon."

"Speaking of protection, Clay, do you think anybody questioned the timing of my being pregnant so soon after our wedding day?"

"Darlin', even though it's clear we had sex well 'fore we got married, nobody's gonna actually say somethin' 'bout it. That would be considered socially inappropriate."

"Oh."

"Besides, nowadays, a couple havin' sex 'fore their weddin' day isn't really a shocker."

"I know that. It's just that we made it clear to everyone that we were waiting for marriage, so when I started showing before it would be mathematically possible, I just think it looked odd."

"Tricia, the most anyone's going to think is that ya changed your mind. Since it was clear we were gettin' married, no one was gonna care either way."

"Damn, I just wish I'd realized this consequence that night."

"Are ya tellin' me that ya would've changed your mind 'cause of it?"

"I don't know, Clay. I just know that I don't like people thinking that I went back on my word to wait for marriage."

"Tricia, if ya'd like, ya can tell people we secretly got married the day we got engaged. I won't care, and I'm pretty sure that Bryan and Kate won't either."

"But I thought that was supposed to remain a secret between just the four of us?"

"It doesn't have to be if ya bein' pregnant right now is makin' ya regret that decision."

"Clay, I don't regret marrying you that night. You should know that. I also don't regret giving you my virginity because otherwise, I wouldn't be about to give birth."

"Glad to hear it."

"The only thing I regret is not realizing how the timing would look to others."

"But Tricia, it ain't like we did anythin' wrong. Even though we didn't legalize our vows, we did get married that night."

"I know. I guess at the time, I was just worried that my parents would feel hurt for not being there. So I figured that keeping it a secret was the best way to avoid that."

"Tricia, I have a feelin' they'd understand your urgency if ya told 'em 'bout it."

"Clay, I am not going to tell my parents I wanted to rush the ceremony just so I could finally have sex with you."

"Well, ya don't have to be so blunt 'bout it. But considerin' they'd already know 'bout your datin' history, I don't really think it'd surprise 'em."

"Maybe not but, no," she decided, determinedly shaking her head.

With a laugh, Clay responded, "Okay, then, don't."

"Don't laugh at me. Imagine telling your own mama that, Clay. Do you really want to have that conversation with her?"

Briefly thinking about it, Clay quickly agreed to keep that night a secret.

"Told you."

"And there's the first of many 'told yas' I'm gonna end up hearin' throughout our marriage."

"Hey, it's not my fault when logic prevails."

"Darlin', I don't know how ya do it, but somehow, ya make me fall in love with ya all over again every time that beautiful personality of yours shines through."

Giving him a kiss, Tricia decided to forgo the movie.

"Are ya hopin' to induce labor, darlin'? 'Cause I do remember what the baby books said 'bout us bringin' it on as a result of sex."

"Clay, maybe I just want to make out with my husband."

"Either way, it would be quite poetic if ya did. 'Cause bringin' our daughter into the world as a result of our bein' affectionate with each other would certainly bring it full circle."

"Maybe . . . but oh, I don't think that's going to matter anymore," she replied after feeling her water break.

"Ya okay, darlin'?"

"Clay, my water just broke."

"Guess that means it's time for me to go give the midwife a call." Getting off the couch to do just that, as well as let their family and friends know, Clay began to head upstairs for his cellphone until Tricia stopped him with her hand on his arm.

"Hold on. I need you first." She grabbed onto his forearm and squeezed as her first contraction sent pain soaring through her body. After the pain had subsided, she let go of his arm.

"Okay, I'll be right back to offer ya more pain management."

"Oh, and could you also let my parents and Kate and Bryan know what's going on? I'm sure they'll want to be here for Kaylin's arrival."

"No problem."

With the midwife and their family and friends alerted, Clay rejoined her on the couch as her pain manager. Feeling the strength of her hand grip his arm, he was given a sense of the pain's magnitude as it exploded throughout her body. With every shot of pain, he made sure to take notice of its timed intervals. He watched her scream out in agony and wondered if her decision to have a homebirth was worth not using the hospital's epidural.

"Ow, Clay, it hurts so much!" Tricia cried out.

"I know, darlin', but just think . . . at the end of this . . . we'll have a brand-new baby girl." He stroked her hair.

"Oh, ow! I can't wait for that!"

It wasn't long after a few pain-stricken contractions that the midwife arrived. After moving Tricia to the floor and changing Clay's job to support her back, the midwife took over keeping track of Tricia's contractions and regularly checking her dilation progress. After hours had gone by, and Tricia's painful contractions had ended, the midwife began coaching her through more hours of even more excruciating labor.

"Ahhh!" Tricia yelled out.

Keeping a firm grip on Clay's forearms, Tricia began pushing Kaylin through her birth canal.

"I know darlin', but you're doin' great!" Clay could feel her fingers digging into his skin.

"Damn it, why do I have to love having sex with you so damn much?"

Feeling embarrassed for her unexpected outburst, Clay just looked at the midwife with an awkward smile only to see that she was too concentrated on her job to have noticed. Reverting his attention back to Tricia, he felt her hand clench his forearms as she worked through another strenuous push. As he watched her, he couldn't help but inwardly smile as he mentally answered her question, *'Cause I know how to make your body feel so damn good!*

After several more hours of ardent labor and Clay encouraging Tricia, he felt like she was going to leave a permanent remnant of her fingers in his arms. Despite that, the midwife's announcement of each progression kept him anxious for his daughter's arrival.

"Okay, Tricia, your daughter's head is crowning, so I just need you to give me one more big push," the midwife informed her.

With a nod of acceptance, Tricia released her hands from Clay's forearms and slid them into his hands.

"Ya ready to give the midwife one last push, darlin'?"

"Yes, Clay, I am." With the last bit of strength she could muster, Tricia gave one final push that brought Kaylin into the world.

"Congratulations, Mom and Dad . . . you did it! Your daughter has arrived," the midwife announced.

Hearing the sound of Kaylin Lindly Gibson's first cry was proof that the delivery was over. Tricia relaxed slightly as the placenta was removed. The midwife handed Clay scissors so he could cut the umbilical cord. She then wrapped Kaylin in a blanket and handed her to her mother.

"Oh, Clay, look at her, our precious baby girl . . . she's so amazing!" Tricia now understood the love her parents held for her.

"She sure is, darlin', she sure is," Clay agreed with pride.

"Can you believe we created her, Clay? She is just so perfect, and she's got your gorgeous blue eyes!"

"Darlin', she is God's gift to us for Him blessin' me with you, so yes, I can," he answered with a smile.

"Oh, Clay, I love you so much!" she returned with a kiss.

"Darlin', I think I now know what your father felt when you were born." Staring down at his daughter, Clay realized that he'd give his own life for Kaylin.

"So does that mean you're going to start cleaning out your gun when the boys come around?"

"I may have to 'cause if she ends up lookin' like her mama, ya can bet that I'll be givin' a lesson on a daily basis."

"I suppose that is one of the perks of marrying a man from the south. Southern fathers do tend to be more influential when it comes to their daughters dating."

"Darlin', I say that only 'cause I remember how I first was when I started likin' the opposite sex."

"Oh, and how was that?"

"Well, I obviously had only one thing on my mind."

"Let me guess. Sex?"

"No, it was how I could best embarrass a girl so I could get her to show me how cute she looked when she blushed," he teased.

"Damn, to be so in love with a man that no matter what he says, I just have to learn to let it go. It definitely makes me understand my parents' relationship so much better," she replied, shaking her head.

"Welcome to married life with me, darlin'." He shrugged.

"And I wouldn't want it to be with anyone else."

"Always glad to hear that."

"And let me tell you something else, Clay. If our daughter follows in the same footsteps as her mama and finds a man like you, then she'll be lucky. I know I am. And I have her to prove it!" Holding Kaylin in her arms, Tricia realized that their daughter would keep them connected for the rest of their lives.

"I love you, too, darlin'." Clay took advantage of their bonding time together as they waited for their family and friends to arrive. He cuddled with Tricia while she cradled Kaylin and couldn't help but think that a boy would be the key to making their family complete. So with a quick prayer to God, he silently asked Him for a son to be His next gift to them. Little did he know, his prayer for his family's completeness would become the last thing on his mind.